Books in the Cardboard Cottage Mystery series  by Jane Elzey
Scorpius Carta Press
Available in in E-book, Paperback, and Hardcover


Dying for Dominoes  (2020)
Dice on a Deadly Sea (2021)
Poison Parcheesi and Wine (2023)
Killer Croquet on the Emerald Isle (2024)
Ouija and Haints in the Silent City (2025)


Join Jane Elzey's VIP Club for author gossip, special offers, autographed copies, and fun merch at JaneElzey.com. There's always room in the Killer Club for one more. #TheHusbandAlwaysDies

To schedule author signing and book club events,
contact Jane Elzey at CardboardCottageMystery.com

# KILLER

## CROQUET Or The EMERALD ISLE

### A Cardboard Cottage Mystery

## JANE ELZEY

Scorpius Carta Press

Arkansas

*For Doris*

*"Friendship never forgets. That is the wonderful thing about it."*
*— OSCAR WILDE*

# CHAPTER ONE

"Ireland is a country of lore and legends and flannel," the guide declaimed with a chuckle, her eyes wide and full of mischief. She stood with her legs rooted in the aisle, hands clasped on the steel poles on either side. Her body swayed slightly with the movement of the van when they met another tour coach on the impossibly narrow road. Amy held her breath, leaning involuntarily in her seat as if her weight could shift the van like a boat. Without even slowing, their Mercedes scuttled past with inches to spare, its wheels on what had to be the very edge of Earth itself.

"Flannel?" Amy echoed, when they were once again on the straight and narrow. "You mean as in plaid?"

"Flannel is me Gran's word for a tale. Some tales are tall ones. Some sound true even when they're not. And some, well, some are halfway in-between true and not." The woman's Irish brogue sounded like music. She laughed lightly, bringing out the impish dimples in her cheeks and then glanced out the window.

Amy followed her gaze, watching as the coach whipped around another curve. The van hugged the steep rolling hills on one side and a sheer cliff on the other. The sea shimmered on the horizon of a clear sky, and the waves crashed into the rocks with brute force in a cold, blue spray.

"A land of lore and lies is our Ireland," the woman added, nodding her head to make the point clear. "What land isn't full of such? There's always a fool who says he owns history. And even more is that fool who claims to own the past. History is written by the victorious, and mostly with a bias to make him look heroic."

Rian turned to Genna seated beside her in the coach. "There's our Winston Churchill," she said quietly. "He seems to show up everywhere we go."

The guide acknowledged Rian with a nod. "Churchill, indeed. But, as our own Oscar Fingal O'Flahertie Wills Wilde did say, 'the truth is rarely pure and never simple.'"

Amy nodded and hoped her confusion wasn't visible. She had been on the Emerald Isle for less than twenty-four hours, which, counting for lost time and jet lag, it was a wonder she could comprehend anything at all. Let alone a lesson in Irish literature and politics. Her brain felt like a fog as solid as the one that settled over Dublin shortly after they landed and taxied to the hotel. This day had dawned bright and sunny, but it had started way too early.

"I suppose flannel goes for the fairies and superstitions, too," Amy said. "I've read about your Irish superstitions."

"Have you now?" The guide brushed dark hair from her brow as the coach swerved into another bend. "Fae folk. The little people." She eyed Amy again. "Be on the lookout for the faerie fort and best ye ask permission before you go for a dander."

Zelda shifted in her seat beside Amy. "How do you recognize a fairy ring? And who would you ask permission?"

The woman was cordial as she eyed Zelda, dressed head to toe in wrinkle-free leopard print. "A ring is but fungi living under t'e ground, mind you, peeping its moldy head to the surface for a breat' of fresh sea air. But do take care, I should say. Many a man of the house has lost his way mistaking a tasty chanterelle for a plate of liberty cap. Mushrooms are often deat'ly."

Deat'ly. Amy smiled to herself. The lyrical Irish dialect left her comprehending about one word out of every five. Maybe one in ten when she was eavesdropping at the pub. The letter h as in aitch, spelled *haitch,* was rarely spoken when it fell in step with the letter t. Tree and three sounded the same. One word out of five was a slim margin from an American southerner's standpoint, but she did grasp they were scheduled to arrive at their resort at tree — as in p.m.

Sammie had schooled them on the vernacular before they left Bluff Springs. Irish born and raised, Sammie ran Crumpets and Cones at the Cardboard Cottage in Arkansas. The long run of letters and strange characters in the Irish language made for a fun, if futile game. They were only going to be in Ireland for two weeks, but they would have good craic. Guaranteed. They had laughed over the colloquial slang for having fun until Genna almost choked on her Irish whiskey-loaded lemonade. Good craic was good fun.

"A faerie fort, on the other hand, is a ring, most likely of stones," the guide said, holding Zelda's attention. "Most likely 'tis the remains of a Celtic castle long gone. And you can be sure the faeries took it over the very moment it went to rack and ruin.

"There are faerie forts over much of Ireland, to be sure, but mostly on private property. So do take care. A farmer and his sheep will have strong feelings about strangers who open the gates to march on in. Not to mention an old ram or bull that come charging at you. If the bull doesn't get you the fae might, if you disturb a single blade of grass within their circle."

"And what would happen?" Zelda asked. "If you were to disturb their circle."

The woman's eyes widened dramatically beneath her dark lashes. "Why, you'd be given a curse, you would. Something horrible it would be. Something unspeakable, even. She might curse you to lose something grand. Or even someone you love!"

"Oh posh," Genna said, flinging her silver braid over her shoulder. "I'm not afraid of some old curse. It's pure blarney."

"I read that if you run into bad luck with a fairy, you just turn your pockets inside out and she will leave you be," Amy offered.

"I've heard that," Rian said. "My grandfather used to say it. You leave a shot of whiskey behind, too."

Zelda giggled. "That might have been his excuse for carrying a flask."

"Who needs an excuse?" Rian countered.

The guide smiled knowingly. "Stick to the trails and you will be right as rain. There's a lovely walk at Glenbeigh County Kerry, not too far from where you're staying. So many a faerie house in those woods no one has surely counted them one and all."

Zelda inhaled with excitement. "Are they really made by fairies?"

"Made by the little folk to be sure."

Genna laughed. "That's a fair enough way to put it."

"We have fairy houses in our town, too," Doris said from the seat behind Amy. "Our school kids make them. In art class."

"The little folk," Genna echoed.

"It's the cutest little surprise you'd ever expect to see when you climb the stairs on the hill behind our library." Doris' eyes were sparkling behind her butterscotch glasses. "My kids had so much fun in that class."

Amy smiled at Doris. She knew the stairs that Doris spoke of. There was a reason Bluff Springs was called the stair-step-town. Stairs made it possible to climb the hills. There were many old limestone staircases that climbed the hillsides, some nearly hidden by overgrown honeysuckle and coral vines. You had to know what to look for, just like looking for fairies or a four leaf clover. Doris was a like a lucky clover. A rare find. Unexpected. A chance encounter.

Doris was the reason why Amy and her friends were on this bucket list trip. At least, she was the instigator. Doris ran the front desk at a hotel in Bluff Springs. The same hotel where Amy was sleuthing for clues in the last murder she found herself investigating. Doris was the one who told her about the big fundraising campaign for their chamber of commerce, encouraging Amy and the Cardboard Cottage businesses to participate. For a small city, Bluff Springs had big aspirations and pockets deep enough to support them.

The chamber capital campaign was an all-hands-on-deck effort to raise the money for much needed renovations to their 19th century address. The Bluff Springs Chamber of Commerce was housed in one of the oldest and showiest Victorian-era buildings in town. It had sprung a number of issues, including a leaky roof. The trip to Ireland was the carrot-on-the stick reward for the campaign participants who raised the most money. An all-expense paid trip. It even included the airfare.

Amy rubbed her eyes as the sunlight bounced off the windows in the van. Outside the wild countryside sped by — an expanse of dark sapphire gray ocean, a patchwork of green hills that marked the boundaries of the farms, and slopes heavily dotted with sheep.

The sweltering summer heat of Arkansas was more than four thousand miles away. The air here was cool like a wet Ozark Mountain spring and the sky never seemed to achieve nighttime. She had checked her watch several times, but even though the sun set officially around ten and rose again before six, the light never seemed to fade from the sky. It created a perpetual twilight that had made sleeping almost impossible.

Her head lolled on her shoulders as sunlight flickered across her closed eyelids. The warm sun lulled her into a trance — awake but not awake, asleep but not asleep.

# CHAPTER TWO

*She stood outside the circle. It was a ring of stones of considerable size. Beside the stones were huge mushrooms covered in purple and white dots. They seemed to glow neon in the twilight, as if the gills of the fungi were breathing. The stones and the mushrooms made a gate of sorts.*

*Something moved in the shadows, and a rabbit darted from behind one of the stones and hopped across the circle.*

*Amy started to follow.*

*"Mind your step, cailín," someone whispered in her ear. "The fae are watching ye."*

*She turned to look behind her at who was speaking, but there was no one there. The wind blew at her copper-colored hair, and she swept the curls from her cheek with her fingertips.*

*The wind circled the stones, turning up dry leaves in their wake, and then brushed through the trees in the outer circle. A circle within a circle, in the circle that was life.*

*At the center of the ring was an even larger stone. A boulder, really. In the center of the rock was a lone tree that had split the stone in two as through all the ages it grew. Hanging from the limbs like ornaments from a Christmas tree were several croquet balls.*

*Croquet balls?*

*Instinctively, she counted them. Twelve in all, two each of blue, red, green, orange, and yellow. Two black ones lay on the ground side by side, as if they were apples dropped from the branch.*

*"Rotten, they are." The voice whispered. "Rotten in the core." Grandmother? Is that you?*

*The leaves rustled in the grass. And suddenly the voice was in her ear again. "Death leaves a heartache no one can heal. Love leaves a memory no one can steal. And they will try. Oh, but they will try."*

*She turned to look behind her.*

*The wind screamed in her face. She felt its icy breath as the wail reached a piercing, keening pitch.*

Amy jerked awake.

"What was that? Did someone just scream?"

"Scream?" Zelda turned and nudged Amy with an elbow. "Not unless that's what you call your snoring."

"I heard the most awful piercing scream!" Amy exclaimed, rubbing at her ears. She touched the earrings Genna had given her, and she treasured, feeling a warm pulse emanating from the gemstones. She reached for the Celtic cross that always hung at her neck. It, too, was warm to the touch.

The guide at the front of the coach eyed Amy closely.

"You heard a scream?" she asked quietly. "From what kind of a creature?"

Amy's eyes flashed, and their eyes met for a moment too long.

"It was just a dream," she answered with a sigh, pushing herself against the warm seat, willing herself to relax.

"The banshee. The *Bean Sidhe*. The woman of the fairies," the guide said with a lilt that begged a question. The blue of her eyes grew dark. "Let's pray it was not the scream of a banshee. She portends a death."

## CHAPTER THREE

The road into the Gougane Barra valley was jaw dropping gorgeous, the sunshine and scenery replacing the chill of her dreamy visit to the circle of stones. The keening that awoke her faded from memory as they rode the black ribbon through the Shehy Mountains of County Cork.

Their guide chattered along the way, a thousand facts and details ready for whomever seemed interested. Amy's eyes were so full of scenery she couldn't listen.

They were used to a curvy ride, but unlike the heavily forested Ozark Mountains in Arkansas, these craggy mountains were stark red sandstone. The road slid around the base of the mountain like a snake. And then suddenly the van dipped down into a glaciated valley, where primordial ice had carved its way screeching and scoring the valley until it melted on its way to sea. The coach bumped along the forested road at the edge of a lake and then stopped.

"Pinch me, I'm dreaming," Zelda said.

Genna reached across the aisle.

Zelda narrowed her eyes. "Don't you dare."

Genna shrugged. "Just being helpful."

"Then slide out of the way," Rian said, motioning Genna to the aisle. "It's time to explore."

The passengers tipped both driver and guide when they disembarked. As they gathered their gear, Amy stood in the sunlight and took in the view of the lake. A rowboat sat empty on the shore. Across the lake, a rock chapel stood at the center of what appeared to be a tiny island, a gentle mist rising from the trees behind it. All the scene needed was an artist at an easel, brush in hand. Instead, there was a man with a camera on a tripod, the long lens pointed toward a pair of swans paddling about in the center of the lake. It was so beautifully idyllic she could still be dreaming. She resisted the urge to pinch herself as she climbed the steps to the hotel, which looked more like a sprawling estate home with plenty of room for visiting family and kin. Their bags were waiting when they arrived at the front desk, but Amy was not ready to settle into her room.

"Should we have a pint and then take a walk? Or should we take a walk and then have a pint?" Amy felt like spinning in the middle of the lobby.

Rian looked at her friend. "I think we should do both." She pointed to an alcove off the lobby with a dark wood bar and beer taps and a shelf full of whiskey. "And then we should do it all over again," Rian added.

"I think I'm going to settle into my room and call my family," Doris said. "I am disappointed that my husband couldn't make this trip, but I'm glad he gets to spend time with the kids. My mom said she'd check in on him daily. I hope that's a good plan."

Amy watched as Doris rolled her suitcase down the hall, disappearing from view.

The foursome gathered at the bar with their Guinness poured and settled. "Cheers!" Genna said. "We did it! Ireland! Here's to friends who know us well and love us just the same."

"Amen," Zelda said and licked the foam from her lips. "And pass the chips, would you?"

Amy reached for the basket of goodies, presumably for hungry travelers caught between meals and kitchen hours.

Zelda ruffled through the basket. "Pringles. Popcorn. KP Salted Peanuts, and Meanies, which are pickle flavored corn chips," she said, reading from the bag. "Salt and vinegar crisps — their word for chips. And scampi fries." She frowned as she read the package. "A cereal snack with a delicious scampi and lemon taste."

"Hmmm, I don't know about that," Rian said.

"Well, I do," Zelda said, ripping into the bag. "I'm always up for shrimp flavored cereal and a beer."

The aroma reached Amy's nose as the bag popped open. It smelled like a tin of sardines. She wrinkled her nose.

"Not bad," Zelda said, smacking the lemon dust from her lips. "Not bad at all."

The door to a courtyard opened, admitting two men to the tiny bar. She would have recognized them as Americans even if they hadn't traveled on the same plane. Noisy. Noisy American men, both lugging clunky golf bags over a shoulder. She had never taken to the sport herself, although Genna claimed the golf course was where most business deals were made. Rian loved a good game of golf, although not for business reasons — she just loved the sport— – but both Genna and Rian had given up trying to teach Amy to play.

Genna leaned in and whispered loudly. "Looks like our compatriots from Arkansas arrived ahead of us."

The door opened again.

"And here comes the ladies auxiliary," Genna added, eyeing them over the top of her glass.

Zelda cut her eyes toward Genna. "Oh, behave. They all got here the same way we did."

"Obviously not," Genna argued. "They've been here long enough for a round of golf."

"You know what I meant," Zelda snapped. "They earned their trip the same way we did. Everybody on the list earned a plus-one guest."

Rian snickered from behind her Guinness. "You and I are the rank and file in this foursome, Zelda. But this time, I brought my earplugs as defense against Genna's snoring."

"Purring," Genna said and faked a smile.

"Our fellow Americans!" The man's voice boomed in the cozy nook of the bar. "What took you so long? We've already had the Full Irish breakfast and nine holes of golf." He put down the golf bag and strode across the floor, his hand outstretched. He stood at least six feet. A big guy. Tall and towering. His black hair was buzzed to within a centimeter of his scalp so that it stood up from his head like hairbrush bristles.

"Richard," Amy said, accepting his handshake and the waft of cologne that seemed to follow him. She noticed that his forearms and knuckles were covered in dark, coarse hair.

"Everyone calls me Dick." He jerked his head. "You met my wife, Eloise."

Amy glanced behind him. Eloise was one of those ethereal beauties, wand thin, fairy-like. Her hair was a natural shade of blonde, the curls cut to frame her face like flaxen lace. She was exactly the type of wife an egotist would want for show and tell, one he could put back in the curio cabinet with his other prized belongings. She smiled at them, but her face looked pinched behind wire rimmed glasses. The dark circles under her eyes said she hadn't slept well last night, either.

She raised her hand slightly. "Hello. It's nice to see you again," she said. Her voice was a thin syrup on pancakes.

"We looked for you at the airport," Dick Collins said. "I thought you would appreciate a ride in our limousine.

Compliments of Bartlestown Bank." His face lit up with pride. "It's not every day you girls get to ride in style, now is it? We had enough room. It would have been tight, but we would squeeze in. Nothing wrong with a little squeeze."

Amy could feel Genna tensing beside her, a caustic comment at the ready. "We stayed in Dublin," Amy said simply. She didn't bother to explain that Rian had insisted they spend their first night pubbing in Dublin.

Gayle Brand stepped forward. "I'm glad you finally made it. I was concerned when we didn't see you here last night. I didn't realize you made other plans."

Gayle was the VP in charge of the capital campaign for the Bluff Springs Chamber of Commerce and the one who corralled the participants toward the goal. Gayle had more than earned a spot on this trip and Amy really liked her. She was smart and friendly and good at her job. She was sophisticated and confident. Her infectious enthusiasm rubbed off on those around her.

What she loved most was that Gayle had freckles too. Freckles seemed unusual for a woman of color. They were subtle, but they were there, and she liked the way they looked on Gayle. Her hair was cropped short and gold hoops dangled from her ears. She was dressed in a trendy sports outfit that outlined her well-toned physique.

"You remember my husband, James," Gayle said, pulling at his arm. He stood wedged between the two golf bags and Dick Collins. He nodded beneath his ball cap. *Woo Pig!* The Razorbacks logo that was as much a staple in Arkansas as rice and rocks, the two things Arkansas had more of than anyplace else.

Amy grinned. James. James Brand. Two letters off from 007.

"We're still waiting for two others from our group," Gayle said. "But they'll be here. They had other plans to work around. And where's Doris? She drove over with you, I hope. Please tell me she's not still at the airport waiting?"

"Doris went to rest and catch up with her family by phone," Amy answered, and she could see Gayle's relief.

"You remember my friends," Amy added. "This is Zelda Carlisle. She owns Zsa Zsa Galore Decor at the Cardboard Cottage."

"Hey y'all," Zelda purred in her Arkansas accent.

"And this is Rian O'Deis. She runs The Pot Shed at the Cardboard Cottage." Rian raised her hand in greeting. "Go Hogs!" Rian cheered, with a nod to James.

"And, of course, you remember Genna Gregory." Amy said, motioning to her friend beside her. "Genna runs everything else."

"Oh, go on," Genna said with a flourish. "I do what I can."

Amy caught the quick look that flashed across Gayle Brand's face. Genna had given Gayle a run for the money. As VP at the chamber, Gayle was in charge of the campaign. Genna was a volunteer. A volunteer who wanted to take over. That was so Genna. Gayle had wrestled the reins of leadership from Genna's overbearing hands several times, but she did so with genuine charm and diplomacy. Genna didn't seem to notice when her focus was redirected, much like a three year old diverted from a jar of treats without throwing a tantrum.

"Amy owns the Cardboard Cottage in Bluff Springs," Gayle said to Eloise. "It's an adorable little group of shops in a quaint Victorian building. She runs Tiddlywinks Players Club. You'll want to put that on your must-do list next time you come to town."

Amy beamed. Tiddlywinks was on her must-do list, a childhood dream housed in a drafty old building with a hefty mortgage. It hadn't come easy. She had worked hard to see it find success. With the help of Zelda and Rian, who rented shops under the same roof, The Cardboard Cottage was doing well. Despite a few mishaps along the way, they were on a winning streak. Sales were up. Business was running smoothly. And now they were in Ireland. All. Expenses. Paid.

"We're looking to buy a second home in Bluff Springs," Eloise ventured, "now that Dick is opening a branch there. We're hoping to find one of those quaint little cottages with gingerbread trim and a porch. Some place with good light for my art studio and —"

"Bartlestown Bank," Dick interrupted. "We've been wanting to open a branch in Bluff Springs for a while now. It's time for us to expand. First thing you do is join the chamber and get to know the movers and shakers. And here we are. I trust you'll be giving us your banking business when we open our doors."

No one seemed ready to commit to that trust, but just then their attention was drawn to the door from the lobby and the young woman who entered.

"*Fáilte!*" The woman said, beaming. "Welcome! *Céad míle fáilte!* A hundred thousand welcomes! We are humbled to have you with us at *Éire Óstán*, the most beautiful hotel in all of County Cork, Ireland! My name is *Muadhnait*," she announced, straightening the cuff of her jacket. "Just call me Mona. It's as near as you will come with the pronunciation. I am the tour and social director, so I'll be taking grand care of you. You've had time to settle into your rooms, I see. So, if you will… follow me!"

Amy glanced at Zelda. They hadn't settled in. They had settled for a pint instead.

"Oh, don't worry," the woman said, seeing Amy's confusion. "Your luggage has already been taken to your rooms. You can collect your room key when we return to the lobby."

"Return?" Eloise asked. "Return from where?"

Amy noticed Gayle's dark eyes were dancing with excitement. She knew exactly what was about to happen. Gayle must have been in on the planning.

"Why, we'll be having a spot of tea on the croquet green just up the hill," Mona answered. "It's a short hike to the plateau, but 'tis a bright and sunny day, and there's nothing better than a brisk walk to cure your jet lag. We'll have an Irish picnic and play a rousing game of croquet. Crooky, as we Irish call it, since we invented the game — although both the French and the English would argue the fact. Croquet isn't as popular today as it could be, I should think, but it is my favorite get-to-know-you game." Mona beamed at the group.

Croquet? The balls hanging from the Hawthorne tree in the dream popped into Amy's head. Hopefully there was no circle of stones on the croquet green. Or screaming banshee wind.

The woman turned and motioned for the guests to follow. "Just leave your clubs at the front desk, gentlemen. We'll be taking grand care of them, then." She smiled, and then marched out of the bar, through the lobby, and down the stairs with a confident and buoyant air.

As Amy crossed into the lobby, she glanced down the hall and saw that Doris would be joining them for tea and croquet, too. The hall was well lighted by a window. A huge hanging pot of something fuscia-pink flowered in the muted sunshine, making the hallway look like a pink tinted sunset. A maid was following a few steps behind Doris, her uniform as distinct to her role at the hotel as the Arkansas Razorback ball cap was to James. Amy heard a sharp intake of breath and turned to see Dick, stopped a few steps behind her, his eyes on the hallway. His face paled.

"Hello, Dick," Doris said. Amy noticed his eyes shifted to Doris, but he didn't smile. "My goodness," she added. "It's just me, Doris. Doris Knight. You look like you've seen a ghost!"

# CHAPTER FOUR

The air felt fresh and heavy with the threat of rain as they followed Mona down a path beside the lake. The shore was full of reeds that rustled when they passed, as if nature's little water creatures hurried to hide themselves deeper within the tall stalks. The resident pair of swans paddled near the shore as the group walked single file and followed them until the path turned upward and away from the lake. The grounds were artfully manicured within the bounds of the property, then wild beyond that. Along the path there were thickets of flowers that were purple and patches of blooms that were pink. Amy breathed the air as they passed a rose garden with its sun-heated perfume. Butterflies and bees bounced from petal to petal without so much as a nod to the strangers walking by.

The croquet green sat on the plateau of a small incline. The grass had recently been mowed, leaving telltale lines in the bright green blades. The course was set up already, with a stand of mallets at one end, the balls lined neatly in front. Nearby, a table set with white linens held plates and platters of food, vases brimming with fresh-cut flowers, and several pitchers of drinks. There were at least a dozen delicate teacups nestled sideways into their saucers, decorative side up. To keep the bugs and such from settling into the cups, Amy guessed, and noticed how none of the decorative patterns matched. That would conveniently help players keep track of their tea.

"How perfect this is," Zelda said as she made her way to the table. "Teatime on the green."

Mona motioned them to the table. "There is not a t'ing better than a cuppa tea to launch a rousing game of croquet," she said. "You'll take it with plenty of Irish cream, for certain." She lifted a teacup and settled the foot into the saucer, then pressed the lever on the silver urn. Amy could smell the rich brew. It was familiar enough. At her shop at the Cardboard Cottage, Sammie served Irish tea with her fresh baked pastries.

"You'll find a plate of scones and berry jam," Mona said, as she handed the cup to Zelda. "Or  Brambrack if fruit cake is more to your liking." She glanced over the spread. "Egg and tomato sandwiches, I see. Always a favorite."

"No cake for me," Dick declared. "I could be allergic. There's probably a walnut in there somewhere."

"More likely a filbert," Mona said. "But in that case, I recommend the soda bread with fresh churned butter and radish."

Amy picked out a bone white cup threaded with delicate shamrocks around the edge, poured cream then tea and took a sip. Zelda was already licking butter from her lips.

"We'll draw for teams and get started soon, but do have a bite first," Mona said, looking directly at Eloise, no doubt taking in her thin, willowy frame. "We won't be dining until nine."

Soon sated by the delicious spread, the group followed Mona's instructions and the Irish game of Crooky Croquet began. The teams had drawn ball colors from a cup. Two players on one ball, each taking turns as the striker, the person striking the mallet to the ball. Amy thought the game was going a bit slow up to now, but she was enjoying the scenery and the frequent trips to the feast on the table. No one would call this a championship play, but what kept it interesting were the rules of Mona's get-to-know-you game.

Before the player struck the ball, he or she had to share something personal about themselves. Ditto when they earned a second shot. It was a great icebreaker. Right up Amy's alley as far as games went. There were all kinds of tricks to get people to talk, as she was learning from her new friend Sam Ford in Arkansas. He was a private investigator, and she made a mental note to tell him about Mona's trick. It was sure to land in his top ten.

Mona and Rian were partners on the yellow ball, the last ball in play. "I don't believe I know an Irish O'Deis," Mona was saying to Rian. "Not as you spell it."

"That's the trouble," Rian said to Mona. "I've been all over the ancestry databases and I can't find a single O'Deis. I know my roots are Irish. My grandfather was proud of that fact. And now, I don't even know where to start looking."

"A DNA test would do the trick for certain," Mona answered.

Rian didn't answer and Amy knew what most likely was zinging through Rian's head. A DNA test would do the trick, sure enough, but Rian's inherent need for privacy and her untethered paranoia would never let her go that route. If all else failed, Rian might consent. But she doubted it.

Mona glanced at Rian. "Could there be a reason the spelling was changed?"

Rian cocked an eyebrow. "I can't think of one."

"Did he say where his people were from?"

"Just that they came from Ireland."

"We're going ancestor hunting," Zelda said. "We're going to find Rian's kinfolk if it kills us." She glanced at Amy. "Well, I don't mean kills us in the literal sense. I just mean we're dedicated to helping Rian find her roots, no matter where it might take us."

"No small task to be sure," Mona said. "There are nearly five thousand miles of shore to Ireland and twenty-six counties in the

Republic. Another six in the North." She leaned on the mallet at her side. "Our counties would equate to your states, I do believe," she added, "although I've never been abroad. How big is your Arkansas, would you say?"

"Not very big," Genna interjected. She had managed to whack Rian's ball out of bounds and was looking smug. "We're in the middle size-wise. You could fit five Arkansas' in one Texas. Not that it's anything to brag about. If you were a Texan."

"Is that really true?" Mona asked.

Genna laughed. "You mean would a Texan brag if given the chance? Oh dear, yes. It's part of their DNA."

Mona looked confused for a moment. She was too young to know much about American sarcasm. And too Irish to know Arkansas sass.

Eloise looked narrowly at Genna. "I was born and raised in Texas."

Genna dropped her eyes, but Amy could see she was holding back a grin.

"But no offense taken," Eloise said, looking at Genna with a thin smile. "I know none was intended. You can't be faulted for your roots, only for what you do with them."

Amy swallowed a chuckle. Eloise focused on her swing, then cracked the ball like she was aiming for Mars and not the wicket six feet away. The ball zipped past the goal, stopping only as it knocked into Dick's shoe. He and James were at the tea table refreshing their Pimm's Cup, the most classic croquet cocktail. The two men had skipped the tea and cream altogether and gone straight for the spiced gin.

"Keep it on the green, Eloise. That's the stuff under your feet in case you were wondering." Dick turned to look at James, as if looking for approval, but the other man didn't respond.

"That may be the only green you recognize," Eloise returned. "You can't even match your socks without my help."

Amy looked at his feet. His socks matched his khaki slacks. The polo shirt tucked neatly at his waist was a bright shade of purple.

"It's your play," Mona said, looking at Dick. As he looked over the course, he scratched absently at his neck, and then looked at James with a questioning frown. "What ball are we playing?" He asked.

James motioned with the head of his mallet. "Green."

Amusement flashed across his wife's lips. Was Dick color blind? Is that what Eloise meant by her comment?  She watched as Dick sauntered over to one of the balls in play and aimed his mallet.

"Wrong one," Eloise said and pointed to the ball next to it. Without looking up, Dick sidestepped to the other ball and casually sent it toward the next wicket.

"Now tell us something interesting about yourself," Mona said lightly, obviously trying to guide him back to her rules.

"I don't know why we're playing croquet when there's a perfectly good golf course on the other side of this hill," Dick said, now aggressively rubbing the skin at his collar. He looked at Mona with a frown. "I'm the president of a bank. What more do you want to know?"

"Why don't you tell them why you only wear purple, Dick," Eloise suggested.

"I like it, that's why," he answered, his voice clipped.

Eloise leaned on her mallet. "And that's why your helicopter looks like a Welch's grape."

"It's the color of my bank logo. Purple's not just a color. It's a symbol of success and I'll have you to know Bartlestown Bank has a five star rating from Bauer Financial."

"You have a helicopter?" Rian asked.

Dick nodded. "Picked it up for song in a divorce liquidation. An old client of mine. What a tragedy that marriage turned out to be. He should have quit when he was ahead."

"He should have quit when he was ahead," Eloise echoed, and Dick gave her a strange look.

Rian turned to Eloise. "Do you fly with him?"

"Not when I can avoid it. That thing is so noisy it rattles my brain. But I agree with Dick. It is the most efficient way for him to travel for his job. The bank president has to be at all the big-wig events and ground breakings. It's a demanding job. Isn't it Dickie?"

"Always on the go," Dick agreed. "Even on vacation."

Gayle Brand stepped forward with her mallet in hand. She was partnered with Zelda on the black ball. "Did I hear you say earlier that your son is at Harvard?" Gayle glanced at Eloise who brightened noticeably at the mention of her son. "You must be very proud," she added. "I know I would be. That says something about your roots. And your status, too." She glanced briefly at Dick. "You must be proud to have Dick Junior at Harvard."

"Don't call him Dick Junior," Eloise spat.

Gayle looked surprised at the outburst. "It's a wonderful opportunity, that's all I meant," she said finally, her composure again in place. "My father was the first in his family to graduate high school. I was the first to graduate college. My twin daughters will graduate college, but they're just starting high school this year."

"Twin daughters! Why didn't you bring them with you?" Mona asked.

"Cheer camp," Gayle replied, looking grateful for the interaction. "They attend every summer and it's a bittersweet slice of heaven. The house is so quiet when they're gone it's a little unnerving."

"But perfect timing for this trip," James added. "We haven't had time alone with each other in a long time." He glanced at his wife and Amy thought she blushed. They weren't alone here, either, but she knew what he meant.

Gayle straddled the mallet and swung deep. The ball rolled through the wicket and tapped the peg.

"You go girl," Zelda exclaimed. "You're a rock star mom with mad wicket skills. I think we're going to win this game!" She turned to Mona. "What do we win if we win?"

"You win the coveted trophy of ice," Mona said. "Although, it's not really ice," she added. "It's some kind of resin, but we are known for our ice sculptures, and we offer these as wedding keepsakes and guest souvenirs." She nodded toward the chapel. "That's the famous St. Finbarr's Chapel. It's tiny and cramped if you have more than fifty to the wedding. But we Irish are used to standing close, you see." Mona grinned. "The chapel is booked for weddings more than a year in advance."

Although the chapel was a good bit in the distance, Amy could understand why it was a coveted wedding venue. From the other side of the lake, it looked like the chapel was floating on an island. From this vantage point, she saw that it stood at the end of a peninsula. A path led to the wide front doors, the perfect wedding walk for a bride. The chapel was not far from the edge of the lake, with a steep gray roof over flat gray stones and large arched windows reflecting in the calm of the water.

Something glinted in the sunlight, and she realized the photographer she had seen earlier had moved to the other side of the lake. The sun was reflecting on the long lens of his camera. He must be shooting pictures of the chapel now.

The chapel wasn't but fifteen or twenty feet wide and maybe twice as long. The rock design reminded her of the buildings in Bluff Springs. It may not have been the same kind of rock, but the skill of the masonry looked similar. Much of buildings in Bluff Springs were built by Irish masons in the late 1800s. Most had stood the test of time. As had this one, here in Ireland.

Amy glanced at Rian, who was gazing at the chapel, too, a curious look in her espresso brown eyes. Maybe they really would find Rian's roots.

"Can we go inside?" Amy asked.

"Why, of course, you can," Mona answered. "When there's no wedding. The door is always open."

"Who was this St. Finbarr?" Rian asked.

"Only the most beloved patron saint of Cork City," Mona answered with a lilt of awe. "They still feast in his honor every September.

"Anyhow," Mona said as she straddled the yellow ball. "My family comes from Galway not Cork." She struck the ball from its place at the boundary of the green and it sailed smoothly toward the proper wicket and cracked into the blue. It was obvious Mona had played a few games of croquet. For her bonus shot, she sent the blue off the course, not as far as she could have, but far enough.

Genna exhaled loudly. "Karma," she said, watching her ball roll away from the target. "You can't ever get away from that stuff."

Mona made her extra shot and the ball rolled within a clear path of the wicket. "There you go," she said to Rian. "You're sitting pretty enough when it's your turn again."

"Pretty enough," Rian said, stuffing the last bite of an egg sandwich into her mouth, then wiping her fingers on her jeans.

Doris moved into play, which put her inches from where Eloise stood. "That's a lovely scarf you're wearing," she said pleasantly. "Did you make it? I understand you like to knit."

"Likes to knit!" Dick chortled with a snort. "That's an understatement. I bought her an entire basement full of yarn and stuff. Tell them, Eloise. Tell them about your obsession." Dick turned to Mona. "She's even been featured in a magazine. My lovely little Eloise." He laughed again. "Likes to knit."

Eloise narrowed her eyes at Dick. "It's a studio not a basement and I'm a fiber artist," she said defensively. "I don't just knit." She glanced at Doris as if looking for an ally while she fingered the scarf at her neck. "Thank you for the compliment, Doris. This is one of my favorites. They call this shade spicy cinnamon, but it's actually the natural color of the wool. It's vicuña from Peru. Do you know it?"

Doris shook her head.

"So hard to find," Eloise added. "A treasure when you do."

Amy caught Zelda's eye. The mention of Peru rustled up memories of their trip to the Galapagos Islands for Zelda's birthday celebration. The cruise had not been the smooth sail they expected it would be, but she had fond memories of the man from Peru that had caught her attention. And she had caught his. Piero. She felt her heart leap at the thought of him.

"I used to macrame," Zelda said. "It's coming back in style, you know, that macrame look. Gen Zs love to decorate with the vintage look. Everything old is new again. Except my girlish figure."

"Are we playing through, or what?" Dick demanded and tapped his foot with the mallet head. "The world is facing economic crisis, and our women are talking about doodahs for the house." He looked at James impatiently. James shrugged and shook his head. "If Reg was here, we'd be playing golf and talking about business."

"Oh, Dickie," Eloise said lightly. "You count money and I count stitches. There's nothing wrong with either and you know it."

"To each their own," Doris agreed. "Everyone has a stress-relief value. I farm chickens and bees in my free time."

Rian perked up. "You farm bees?"

"I'm allergic to bees!" Dick glanced around as if by saying the word he would conjure a swarm. His gaze stopped abruptly, caught by an unexpected movement in his line of sight.

Amy turned to look just as a shadow slipped behind a tree. A squirrel, perhaps.

"Allergic to bees," Doris said quietly, watching Dick over the rim of her glasses. "I didn't know that."

"We're not sure if he really is allergic to bees," Eloise admitted. "I think he's just paranoid about getting stung. Isn't everyone? But then, you never know." She patted the pocket of her jacket. "He always has me carry his EpiPen. Just in case we need it."

"I don't plan on finding out," Dick added. "And I'm not the least paranoid. Although, I'm not even sure you know how to use that device. That Epi-thing."

Amy wondered if she should feel sorry for a small town banker with allergies and a big ego. She didn't. She turned and cradled the shaft of her croquet mallet in her hands. It was her turn to share something personal. There were lots of things she could share, but nothing interesting came to mind. She could tell them that Sparkplug was her nickname when she was kid. But she didn't want them calling her that, even though Zelda called her Sparks. That, at least, was her last name. She could tell them about her dreams, her snippets. Her visions that she couldn't explain. But she wasn't psychic. She didn't talk to the dead. She didn't make predictions or move things with her mind. She dreamed. And yet, sometimes the dreams seemed to come true. She glanced at Genna, who was watching her. She knew what Genna was thinking. Would she or wouldn't she share that little secret?

She hadn't told anyone about her dream in the coach on the way to the hotel. She hadn't told them about the croquet balls hanging from the tree or the rotten ones on the ground. She shuddered slightly, remembering that screaming, icy breath. That soul-stealing scream that had rattled her awake. Could it really have been a banshee as the guide had suggested? Had she really dreamed another snippet? Or was it all that talk about curses and superstitions?

"Get to it, Sparks," Zelda said, nudging the back of Amy's knees with the mallet head. "You're holding up the game. Just spill one of your secrets and hit the ball."

Amy bit at her lip. "I saw a UFO once. I was on my way to New Orleans." She knocked the ball through the wicket.

"I knew it!" Genna blurted. "I knew you had ET in your blood line."

Amy ignored her. She leveled the mallet. "I'm also superstitious." Her second shot went wild.

"I hear that," James said. It was his turn next. "My mother was superstitious. She always spilled a splash of coffee in the saucer before she drank her first cup. Said it brought good luck to the day." He rubbed his hands over his jeans and then grabbed the mallet from where it leaned against the table.

"Something about me. Let's see," he said, tugging at the bill of his Razorbacks cap. "I did hit a home run at Yankee Stadium." He swung the mallet and the ball glided through the wicket with ease. Gayle looked at James as if she were seeing him for the first time. He shrugged at his wife. "I played one game."

"You played baseball?" Rian asked. "At Yankee Stadium?"

James nodded. "That's all there was to it. I am a member of the Cup of Coffee club. It was one and done."

Rian slugged him playfully in the arm. "You're kidding me. The Coffee Club?"

"You know about the Coffee Club?" He seemed amazed.

"What is that?" Gayle asked. She was still looking stunned at this tidbit she didn't know about her spouse.

"That's the club for those who play one game," Rian answered. "They're only on the field for as long as a cup of coffee."

Gayle looked more confused.

"What happened?" Rian asked.

"Busted my foot."

"Too bad," Rian said. "But still," her eyes were wide with awe. "Yankee Stadium. You hit a home run in Yankee Stadium! That's really something."

James straightened his hat. "I did," he said, and a slow smile widened his mouth. "I hit that ball clear into the stands!"

The two of them laughed and Amy knew Rian and James might be talking baseball all week, given the chance.

Gayle turned to Eloise. "Marriage is a never ending surprise, isn't it?"

Amy noticed that Eloise was watching Dick. He was looking off in the distance, a strange expression on his face. Was it worry? Fear? A little of both. He was watching something. Eloise was watching him.

Amy returned her attention to Zelda as her best friend moved into place. One wicket left to go. No one had knocked the black ball out of bounds, and Zelda sent it through the final gate with a loud crack of victory.

"What do you know," Zelda said. "I win the ice!"

## CHAPTER FIVE

Amy was drawn to the window. It was after midnight, but the
sky still had a gray quality to it, the color of pewter with a bit of
pink glow. Even here in the countryside with no streetlights to
ruin night, there wasn't much night to ruin. It had something to
do with the island's position in the northern hemisphere, but the
effect was eerie, and the light was making it hard for her to sleep.

She could see across the lake to the little chapel. The gray
stones were dark, but somewhere inside candles flickered. An altar,
perhaps, with candles that would always be lit for the pious. The
stained glass windows took on the candlelight and illuminated the
colorful arched panels, casting out a hallowed looking glow.

The colors were beautiful, even from this distance. The colors
seemed to dance with the candlelight. She watched for a moment,
mesmerized. And then her eyes stung with tiredness. Her body
felt fatigued, jet lagged, and stiff. The air coming through the
partly open window was cool, and she drank in the scent of the
lake and the mountains and the gardens below.

The front door of the chapel opened, and Amy came alert.
Straining to see, she pressed her forehead against the cool glass.
The figure was unmistakable. He was tall. His hair was short and
dark. His shirt was clearly a shade of lavender, even in the grayish

light. Dick Collins darted out the heavy arched door of the chapel and hurried down the path. She watched as he made his way down the path, following it around the lake toward the front of the hotel. He disappeared from view for a moment, and then he reappeared on the sidewalk out front, and then disappeared again from view.

What was Dick Collins doing in the chapel at midnight?

As she padded to the door, she saw that Zelda was sound asleep. Her quiet snoring sounded much a like cat purring softly. She had her night mask on, and Amy wished she had thought to bring one, too.

She opened the door and peeked into the hallway. There was no one there. Stepping into the shadows of the doorframe, she waited there, watching to see if Dick Collins would pass on his way to his room. She heard the faint sound of footsteps, and her heart began to pound. Should she say something when he passed? Should she ask what he was doing at the chapel so late? He didn't strike her as a religious man who would seek prayer or confessions in the middle of the night. She heard a door open and then close somewhere out of sight. And then there was silence.

Where had he gone? His and Eloise's room was on this wing of the hotel. She was certain of that. She heard footsteps again and shrank against the door, closing it but for a small crack to see.

Eloise Collins darted by on slippered feet, a light rustling as she walked hurriedly down the corridor A door opened. A door shut. And then, silence.

Had she mistaken Eloise for Dick in the dark? Had the figure actually been Eloise? Shadows and distance could play funny tricks. Amy rubbed her eyes as she shut the door. How curious. And yet, none of her business, really. None at all.

She shuffled to her bed and climbed in, put the pillow over her head and begged for sleep.

# CHAPTER SIX

When she awoke, Amy knew something was abuzz. There was a hum under the window on the steps below the hotel. The buzz filtered through the door in the hall. This wasn't the sound of insects. This was the sound of people busy with something important. Something out of the ordinary.

She pressed her forehead against the window. The walkway below and along the path that led to the chapel was full of people. Lots of people.

"What's going on?" Zelda asked, peering from beneath her sleep mask. "It sounds like a swarm of flies in here!"

"There are people everywhere. I don't know what's going on!"

Zelda rushed to the window and peeked out. "A wedding!" She exclaimed. "I bet there's a wedding today! How fun! What craic! Can we crash an Irish wedding?"

Amy eyed Zelda dubiously. Her best friend had a lot of courage and a double dose of moxie that got her — and them — into some tricky situations. She wasn't the kind of person to bully her way into anything, even a wedding. But all Zelda had to do was show up and giggle, and things sort of meandered her way. Good things and not-so good things, alike.

"We can't crash a wedding," Amy said with more annoyance in her voice than she had planned. Maybe it was the feeling that Zelda would talk her into it if she didn't dig in her heels. "We can watch from afar maybe, but there's only room for fifty people in that chapel and I can tell by the crowd it's already over capacity."

Zelda scrunched her nose. "The voice of great reason speaks." She glanced out at the scene with a regretful, forlorn look her eyes. "You are right, of course, Sparks. We couldn't possibly squeeze into the very last pew of that adorable little chapel to watch a real honest to goodness Irish wedding while we are visiting the real honest to goodness Ireland." She glanced once more at Amy. "Right? That is what you mean?"

Amy nodded.

"Well, I don't have a thing to wear to a wedding anyway," Zelda declared and flounced toward the en suite bath.

A knock at the door sounded, and Amy crossed the room, opening the door to see Rian and Genna, dressed and standing in the hallway.

"You're a couple of lazy sleepy heads," Genna said. "We've already had our breakfast and a pint of beer with the bride's uncle!"

"What? Why didn't you wake us?"

Genna shrugged. "We tried. We knocked. You didn't answer."

Amy shook her head. Once she had finally fallen asleep, she slept like the dead. "What time is it?"

"Eight thirty. Or thereabouts."

"What are you guys doing?" Zelda asked as she emerged from the bathroom. "Are you going somewhere? You look like you're going somewhere. Are you going to crash this wedding?" She glanced at Amy. "See, I'm not the only one who thinks it's a good idea."

"We don't have to crash it," Rian answered, "we've been invited!"

"What?" Amy shook her head. "By who?"

"By whom?" Genna corrected.

"By him! The groom's uncle." Rian beamed. "His name is Bryan O'Dea. Can you believe that? He's Bryan O'Dea. I'm Rian O'Deis. What a weird coincidence."

"Do you think he's kin?" Amy asked.

"Kin enough," Genna answered. "He didn't ask Rian how she spells her name, so how would he know? And I don't think we should tell him otherwise. He must think we came all the way from America for the wedding and we shouldn't disappoint him."

"He did seem pleased, didn't he?" Rian asked. "He shook my hand and said something about long lost relations being reunited. Who was I to burst his bubble?"

Amy stepped away from the door and let Genna and Rian inside the room. Zelda plopped down on her bed and Rian sat in the chair by the desk. Genna sauntered to the window and looked outside. Amy stood with her hands on her hips, a little perplexed by the way the morning was shaking loose.

"Didn't we have plans to do some sightseeing today?" Amy asked.

"Don't you think looking at handsome men in kilts constitutes as sightseeing?" Zelda fluffed her dark bob. "It ranks right up there on my list of things to see while in Ireland. I Spy the Irish Guy."

Genna laughed. "And let me tell you," she said in her slow Arkansas southern drawl, "there are plenty of tall, handsome men downstairs. I took notice." Genna looked at Rian. "Did you notice?"

Rian nodded. "Who wouldn't?"

"Old stick-to-her-convention and common sense, Sparks, over here wouldn't," Zelda said. "She was rather combative about my interest in crashing a wedding."

"I surrender," Amy said, lifting her hands in defeat. "I wouldn't think of getting in the way of this fast-moving train. When in

Rome, do as the Romans do. When in Ireland, eat, drink and get married."

Zelda giggled. "Let's just eat, drink, and watch others get married."

"Good idea," Genna replied. "You just got shed of number four and we're not at all ready to deal with number five." Genna paused. "Although, it really is a nice day for a white wedding."

Rian groaned. "And I'm a long lost Celtic cousin from Arkansas."

"Oh, jeez Louise," Amy said. "Today is going to be a humdinger."

# CHAPTER SEVEN

They followed the lovely, yet mournful melody of the piper as he led the guests from the hotel grounds, around the little lake, and up the path toward the chapel. The instrument looked different than the Great Highland pipes of Scotland with its tall drones splayed like proud feathers in a headdress. She knew those bagpipes well. They were played in most of the Bluff Springs parades. This bagpipe certainly sounded different. The drones lay downward across his thigh as he walked. The bag fit under his arm and the piper used his elbow to inflate it with air. There was no blow stick at all. What made it sound so different was the melody. It was softer, sounding more like an oboe to her ear. The song was both rhythmic and harmonic, an octave or two richer than the traditional bagpipe's wail and cry. Someone had a sense of humor. The piper was playing a bagpipe rendition of Billy Idol's 1980s hit, *White Wedding*. Hadn't Genna just said it was nice day for a white wedding?

When he reached the church, the piper stepped aside to let the guests enter. The arched wooden door stood wide open, and she could see the glow of candles and polished wood inside, the stained glass windows shining brightly.

Last night, as she had peered out her window into the semi-dark, the colorful windows had cast their light onto the ground outside. The feeling had been more ominous then, especially after noticing Dick Collins darting furtively out of the darkened door.

Today the chapel was full of gaiety and the promise for the future. The colors in the glass shone within, casting brilliant little rainbows and sending them dancing over the pews like fairies in some storybook poem. She rose on her toes and watched as the chapel filled.

As she had expected, the chapel was well past capacity. There really wasn't room for the four of them to squeeze into a pew to watch an honest to goodness Irish wedding, as Zelda had hoped. They weren't the only ones. Others gathered outside. A group of children formed a circle, and under the watchful eye of the mothers and grandmothers and aunties with them, they were reminded to stay clean and out the lake. The swans paddled over as if to give their blessing, honking and whooping, and fluttering their wings from their place on the lake.

When the piper took up the wedding march the bride suddenly appeared, her gown full of lace in intricate patterns, her dark hair falling in tendrils beneath her veil. An older man stood beside her. He was dressed in a green plaid kilt, his broad shoulders in a dark tweed jacket and his silver hair parted and combed smartly to one side. Amy watched as he tenderly wrapped the bride's hand around his arm, and the two of them entered the church.

Zelda sniffled and then brushed a tear from her eye. "It never fails," she said. "Weddings just make me so happy."

"They make me happy when they happen to someone else," Rian said. "I've never seen the appeal, myself."

"Oh, go on," Genna said. "You're going to hitch up with Dudley Do-Right one of these days. He's gotten under your skin, and you know it."

That was just one of the nicknames they had affectionately given Ben Albright, Rian's boyfriend. Rian once claimed she and Ben as a couple were like Jane Goodall, the anthropologist, and Dave Starsky from the TV show Starsky and Hutch. Genna said Dudley Do-Right and gangster Belle Starr fit them much better. The name stuck to Ben.

Rian shook her head. "Not going to happen."

"You mean you're not going to make him an honest man after all this time?" Zelda asked. "All that sneaking around behind barn doors?"

"We don't sneak around."

"Oh, and the Pope doesn't wear a pointy hat, either," Zelda added. "Where is Officer Handsome anyway? Why didn't he come with us?"

"You and I are the plus-ones on this trip, remember? We came as guests. No room at the inn for Ben."

"Yeah, but Doris had an extra bunk because her plus-one didn't come. Amy could have bunked with Doris, and you could have bunked with Ben."

Rian shrugged. "It worked out just the way it should have," she said. "Besides, he's got a wine farm to watch and bad guys to catch. And I have the three of you to look after. You're always getting into some kind of trouble."

A spark of light caught Amy's eye from across the lake. The hotel sat on the far bank, a sprawling but modest building with two floors and lots of windows. The windows were the hotel's most appreciated claim to fame. Every room looked out onto the view of the mountains and the lake, and every bit of sky that would fit inside the glass panes. The photographer Amy had noticed earlier was once again on the shore, his three-legged tripod leveled on the gentle slope, long lens pointed toward the hotel. Was he shooting pictures of the hotel for a travelogue? Or was he framing the birds on the roof?

She followed the probable line of sight of the camera lens. In an upstairs window, the profile of Dick Collins was visible through the glass. He looked animated in conversation, his hands moving aggressively in front of him. Was he mansplaining? He sure seemed to do enough of that. The woman enduring his distain had to be Eloise, although she wasn't wearing her glasses. The woman stepped away from the window and Amy lost sight of her. At this distance, it was difficult to see her expression, but the camera would have captured it. She pictured Eloise with her delicate, but slightly pinched look. Her sharp cheekbones and high-arched brows made Amy think of how one might describe a pixie or a sprite.

Amy looked back to the photographer. His ball cap was pulled low on his brow as he peered into the camera. Why would a photographer be taking pictures of Dick and Eloise Collins?

"Here they come!" Zelda squealed. "The newlyweds!"

The four of them stepped off the path to let the beaming couple pass and the church let out the guests like ants in a hill. They waited until the last, and then fell into step at the tail end. The piper was just ahead of them, his jaunty, whinny tune following the happy crowd to the hotel.

# CHAPTER EIGHT

Amy's head was pounding. Even though they had not exactly crashed a wedding, they had certainly crashed the wedding reception. Without any excuse, the four of them had joined the party. They ate, drank, and were very merry. They had flirted and flaunted, and Amy hadn't understood ten things that were said to her in passing. The wedding party had moved on in the early afternoon, and the hotel had grown eerily quiet.

Her head hit the pillow with a heavy *thunk* when they returned to their room for a much needed afternoon nap. She hadn't counted three sheep before she fell sound asleep.

It was now late afternoon, and the light blasted through the window like a search beam looking for a runaway. She pulled the extra pillow over her eyes and listened to the *boom boom* in her head. She could taste something hideous on her tongue, remembering the dare to try a platter of something unrecognizable from the wedding feast. It wasn't the raw oysters on blocks of ice, or the mussels steaming in hot broth. The taste on her tongue wasn't from the piles of cakes and treats. This was a slice of something that had landed inside her mouth like a meat and tomato aspic. She asked what it was, but she never quite got the gist. And really, she didn't want to know. Some cultural delicacies were better left a mystery.

Snuggling into the folds of the bed and covers, she willed herself to sleep. Just another hour nap would make all the difference in the world.

The shriek rattled her head like a fire alarm, and she bolted upright in bed.

"Did you hear that?"

Zelda lifted one eye of her sleep mask. "Hear what? Hear you making more noise than is humanly possible? You've been grunting and groaning and whining over there like a lost puppy. Didn't you get a nap at all?"

"I just heard somebody scream," Amy said. "Didn't you hear it?"

"Nobody screamed, Amy. You're hungover in your head. Here." Zelda reached over and handed Amy a bucket of melted ice that was sitting on the floor. "Put your hand it this. It will help. A little."

Amy sat up and pushed off the bedclothes. She hadn't been dreaming. She wasn't asleep. She had been wide awake wishing for sleep when she heard the scream. Or maybe she really had been dreaming. Now she wasn't sure. But the sound that woke her was the same chilling, icy scream she heard on the bus trip to the hotel. The same chilling, icy scream of a banshee, if the tour guide had been on point. The banshee, the woman had said — that portends a death.

There was a rustle outside the door, as if many feet were running down the hallway. Surely the kids from the wedding had all moved on with their parents and nannies. Reluctantly, she rose from the bed and made her way to the shower. Maybe a stream of hot water would cure what ailed her.

What ailed her was too much Irish whiskey. If there was such a thing at an Irish wedding. She and one of the wedding guests —

his name was Sean or Shane or something sounding like that—had found instant friendship and fellowship. She asked him a dozen questions about Ireland, about Irish superstitions, about the kind of games the Irish liked to play, and what she and her friends should see while visiting.

She smiled at the memory as the water cascaded over her. She knew hurling and soccer football would not be games she could add to the shelves at Tiddlywinks game shop at the Cardboard Cottage. They didn't have enough time for a trip to the north coast of Ireland to see the Giant's Causeway, which was one of the places he suggested. And now, even if she did find a lucky a penny Irish Harp side up on the street, she sure wouldn't pick it up. He had told her that fairies were prone to cast a spell on such coins. It was their fun to attach a contract of sorts made between fairy and human so that when the coin was pocketed, the contract went with it. Even though made unwittingly, a contract between a fairy and a human was to be kept. Or else.

"Or else what?" she had asked.

"They might give you donkey's ears and arse!" He had laughed heartily at her expression. All these years she had been picking up pennies thinking she was picking up good luck. See a penny, pick it up, and all the day you'll have good luck. Heads up the luck was hers. Tails up, she always turned it over for the next person to find. That was the way luck worked. Or so she thought. Had she really been picking up spells and contracts all this time? What had she agreed to unknowingly?

"How long does a spell last?" She asked, still alarmed by this news.

"Anywheres from a single day to one t'ousand and one years to be certain. A spell can pass down from one generation to another," he said and laughed.

"Passed down! What kind of spells? What kind of contracts?"

"Oh," he said with a playful smirk, "they crave memory and experience, and the strong emotion of a moment. You see, fairies don't have emotion. They must take it from elsewhere. And so, it could be something like picking a fight with a close friend. Or the loss of a beloved mortal. Or something tender like a first kiss." He looked at her seductively and then leaned in expectantly.

"You're just making fun of me and my gullibility," she said playfully as she nudged him away. "I'm superstitious, but I'm not dimwitted, and you're no fairy king."

"Well, you can't blame a fella for trying," he said and broke into a hearty laugh.

Amy was flattered by his attention if she was honest with herself.

She was toweling off when Zelda banged on the bathroom door.

"I'll be out in a minute," she called, feeling better but not all that generous with goodwill. "You'll just have to hold it until I'm out of here."

Zelda banged again.

"Really, Zelda. Can't you hold…"

"Amy!" Zelda yelled and banged the door again. "It's the maid! She's dead!"

The maid? Amy wrapped the towel around her and opened the door. "What maid?"

"Our maid. You know, the one in the blue uniform. The one with the dark blue stripe down the front."

Amy looked at Zelda in disbelief. "We have a maid?"

"Oh, for goodness sake, of course we have a maid. Who do you think made the bed and tidied the bathroom when we were out. And why aren't you freaking out about it? I said she's dead!"

"What? Where?" Amy looked around the room and then grabbed the bathrobe hanging from the hook on the door. "What are you trying to say?"

Zelda grabbed Amy by the elbow. The door to the hallway was open a few inches and she and Zelda peeked out. In the middle of the hall stood a hotel rolling cart with towels and cleaning supplies and stacks of TP. The woman in the blue uniform was slumped over, her head and arms in the service cart, her feet limp on the floor. One shoe had come loose and was hanging from her toes. The back of her dress was dark with blood.

"No!" Amy yelped. "Not another towel bin!"

"What do we do?" Zelda whispered. "Don't you see it?"

Amy followed Zelda's eyes. On the ground near the maid's feet was an ice pick. The same ordinary kind of ice pick you would use to chip ice at a bar well. The same kind you would use at a raw oyster bar at a wedding reception. The same reception with a good luck horseshoe carved into ice right above the oyster bar. That kind of ice pick. Maybe that very same ice pick!

Amy put her hands to her ears. Zelda was shaking her by the shoulders when she realized the shrieking scream in her head was her own.

## CHAPTER NINE

The posse from Arkansas was gathered in the front dining room. All evidence of the wedding party was gone, and the tables were remade with fresh linens. The bowl of oatmeal with Bailey's Irish Cream and chocolate chips had sounded good on the menu. Now it was a muddy looking puddle in her bowl. It was early evening, time for something more substantial than oatmeal, but it was all Amy could stomach.

The Garda Síochána were gone. The guards had seemed more polite than she thought they would be, but they honorably lived up to their namesake — Guardians of the Peace for the Republic of Ireland. None of them carried firearms, at least that she could see, and they were direct and unassuming in their task to pinpoint the circumstances in the death of the maid. That had not been the case when the four friends were interviewed over the death of Zack Carlisle. That wasn't how they were treated about the death of a yacht dealer from Maine. A towel bin was involved in that fiasco, too, when the four of them ignored protocol and prudence. That had nearly cost them their lives. At least this time they knew to stay out of the crime scene. Even if it did happen right outside their door. She had asked the officer to repeat Garda Síochána — as in *gar-duh sho-hahn-nuh* — a half dozen times until the words finally rolled smoothly from her tongue. This could well be the only Irish she managed to learn while here.

The hallway, however, wasn't a peaceful scene when she and Zelda poked their heads out of their hotel room. Garbed in hazmat suits, four Garda officers scoured the corridor on film and on foot, leaving evidence markers in their wake. The hotel guests were restricted to their rooms until the scene was secured. When the scene was finally cleared, the guests were given disposable booties and room by room, were led to the pub and questioned about what they had seen and heard. By that time the body of the maid had long since been removed, the cart rolled away. Whether the cart was taken in for evidence or returned into service, she didn't know. She didn't ask, although her curiosity wanted to. After what seemed like hours, they were released to the dining room where they were now.

Looking at her friends gathered at the table, she could see they all looked deflated. Not unlike herself. Partly by too much wedding reception and its ever-flowing libation. Partly by the realization that their trip to Ireland had shifted from fun to unfortunate. Very unfortunate for this maid.

Had she really heard the banshee wail before the death occurred? Or had she heard the scream of someone being stabbed in the back? It didn't seem as if either could be possible. No one else claimed to hear any scream at all. Amy thought about her snippet of a dream on the bus. If it really was a snippet. The scene in the hallway outside of their hotel door didn't have much similarity. None, really. Except for that horrible wail. There were no stones in a circle. There were no giant purple mushrooms. No rabbits darting around, not even croquet balls hanging from a tree, or rotten ones on the ground. She pushed the images away determined to get them out of her mind. How silly to think every snippet of a dream foretold a death. It was even more ridiculous to believe she was destined to solve the crime. That was the job for the Gardai.

"I opened the door because I thought someone had knocked," Zelda was telling the group at the table. "That's exactly what I told the police. Amy was in the shower, so I got up and opened the door. And that's when I saw her slumped over her cart. It took me a minute to put it together. Then I saw the …" Zelda stopped and shook her head.

Saw the blood stains and the ice pick at her feet. That's what Zelda meant. It had taken her a moment, too. She had been so overwhelmed by the presence of yet another body in a cart that she hadn't even thought to check for a pulse when she and Zelda were staring at the body in the hall.

"I was still napping in my room," Genna added, "until I heard Amy scream."

"How did you know it was Amy?" Zelda asked.

"I didn't. Not until I opened the door and saw her standing there with her hands over her ears and her mouth wide open. The hotel manager was running down the hall towards us with a look of pure horror on his face."

Amy turned to Rian. "Where were you? Did you see or hear anything?"

"I was out on the grounds with some of the guests," Rian answered. "We finished off a pint and took a walk. Fresh air and all that." She winked and Amy knew Rian had found someone with granny's sweaters. That was Rian's code word for cannabis. Didn't she know how illegal weed was in Ireland?

"I didn't know anything had happened until we saw the Garda cars in the drive," Rian added. "A police car looks like a police car, no matter where you are."

Genna nudged Rian with her elbow. "Did you think they were coming to arrest you?"

"For one quick moment."

"For one quick paranoid moment," Genna added.

Amy glanced at Doris, who was sitting with her hands in her lap, her mouth drawn in a thin line. Her face looked pale, and her eyes were dark behind her glasses. Doris glanced at Dick out of the corner of her eye and then dropped her eyes to her lap.

"Doris," Amy said, catching her attention. "Are you okay?"

It hadn't been all that long ago that a man was found deceased in a hotel room where Doris worked in Bluff Springs. Doris hadn't witnessed the murder, thank goodness, but she had seen the crime scene after the fingerprint team was finished making a mess. Amy knew the incident had left an unsettling impression, and here Doris was again, in a hotel, with another body. This time, it wasn't anybody's husband.

Doris shook her head slightly. "I don't feel well. It must be something I ate."

Or something you saw and shouldn't have. Like a body hanging out of a housekeeping cart. Amy wanted to say that out loud but didn't. Doris' wouldn't have seen the maid draped in the upstairs hall. "What did you tell the Garda Síochána?"

"Not much," Doris answered quietly. "My room is on the first floor. And, well…" she stalled and looked at Dick again.

"But what?" Amy urged. "Please tell us what you told them."

"I told them I saw this maid the day we arrived, and I wondered if it was the same one. She was coming out of the room next to mine and I asked if she would show me how to work the lights in the room. I couldn't figure out how to turn them on. I didn't know you had to insert the room key into the switch by the door." Doris fell silent.

"Is that it?" Amy asked impatiently.

"She didn't answer me," Doris continued. "She turned and went back into the room without saying anything. I thought maybe she didn't speak English. But then later I saw her talking to Mr. Collins."

Dick stood up abruptly, pushing his chair with his knees. He glared at Doris and then at Amy. "I don't know what you're talking about," he barked. "I don't know anything about this… this maid."

Amy noticed Eloise shift slightly in her chair beside him.

"I wasn't even in the hotel when it happened. I was with James on the golf course playing one of the most brutal eighteen holes I've ever encountered. What a challenge! Lost two balls in a sand trap deeper than the Sahara Desert. That course is so narrow and twisty, you can't even see the green from the fairway." He glanced at James for confirmation and then rattled on. "We left the hotel when that noisy wedding arrived. I was gone the whole time. And that's the truth of it. You can take that to the bank!"

Eloise shifted forward. Her face paled.

"Are you okay, Eloise?"

Eloise nodded without lifting her eyes. "I'm fine," she breathed. "I'm just feeling a little strained by … this situation." She lifted her hands and then dropped them into her lap.

"Situation? Oh, shut it," Dick growled. "You don't have anything to add. Nobody wants to hear it if you did."

Eloise seemed to sink down into herself, and Amy felt Genna prickle beside her. His words were more than unkind, and she knew Genna was often quick to defend the downtrodden. Especially since accepting her new role on the board of Project X. That had been the best thing to come about after their misadventure in the Arkansas wine country. Genna's newest passion was serving this non-profit with a clever name. Project X — as in chromosome — was working to lift up economically disenfranchised women in Arkansas. Eloise wasn't that, but she didn't need Dick's callous remarks.

"I was with you all morning," Gayle cut in, her eyes on Eloise. "The two of us were watching the wedding procession from one of the sitting rooms that faces the chapel. James and Dick were out golfing. Oh, and then our last two from Arkansas arrived, so I helped them check in. You were gone when I returned, Eloise. The wedding guests were still at the chapel. You were there, too," Gayle added, nodding to Amy. "I recognized you. I even waved, but you didn't see me. That was silly, really. You wouldn't have seen me. As I told the kind officer, I didn't see anything unusual except a once-in-a-lifetime chance to see a piper leading the wedding guests. That was wonderful. If a bit loud."

Amy nodded. There was a lot of going and coming at the hotel that morning, and there were a good many people roaming the grounds. That included the other couple from Arkansas whom Amy had yet to see. Somewhere in between the "I do" and the last toast to the newlyweds, the maid had found her end. But why? Who would want to stab a maid in the back with an ice pick? Amy considered the question. She considered the probability that the maid was a local resident who knew guests at the party. Maybe there was a jealous girlfriend in the wedding crowd; one who caught the maid smooching her beau. Jealousy was as big a motive as any, and she didn't envy the Garda in charge of unpacking this crime and all its suspects.

"This is a tragedy, but we can't let it spoil our time in Ireland," Genna said, her blue eyes looking for agreement. "I worked hard to earn this trip, and I'll be Humperdincked if I let it ruin Ireland for me."

"A bit insensitive but mostly true," Zelda said. "You did work hard to earn this trip. You all did. I think we should try to have some fun, I think we should try very hard to put this behind us."

"That's the only way I see out of this mess," Dick said. "We have to put bad business behind us. There's not a thing we can do to change what happened. In the banking business we say: write it off. Clear the books. Move on." He glanced at his wife. "That's the only way forward."

"Great! Because tomorrow we have plans to visit a famous landmark," Gayle announced. "Then we will have lunch and do some shopping in a nearby town. Our van is scheduled to leave at eight sharp."

Rian groaned. "Shopping? I'm not into shopping."

"Look at it this way," Genna said, elbowing Rian. "You can visit all the pubs and ask if anyone recognizes you as a long lost cousin. I don't know if you look very Irish, but then, I'm not sure I know what that is. We've already debunked the myth that all Irish have red hair. Haven't we, Amy?"

Amy nodded. She had seen more red heads in Ireland than in Arkansas, but what Genna said was true. Not all Irish were redheads and not all redheads were Irish.

Amy turned to Rian. "Did your grandfather ever say what the family's trade was? Most surnames come from whatever the family did for a living. I don't guess farming is unique enough." Surely Rian appreciated her discernment. Farming was a broad term when it came to Rian O'Deis, who had spent more than a decade growing cannabis crops. Illegal crops. She was now farming vineyard grapes. With legalization laws changing rapidly in Arkansas, Rian had decided to experiment with a line of cannabis wine for the marketplace. The bank and the chamber didn't need to know about that.

"You could be descended from Irish royalty," Zelda chimed in. "Maybe your great grandmother was a duchess disguised as a magazine mail order bride. Or maybe your great grandfather was a bank robber who escaped with the crown rubies and jewels."

"Like there were so many rubies and jewels at the bank of Ireland back then," Genna muttered. "But seriously, Rian, maybe you do have royal blood in Ireland. Wouldn't that be something?"

"They were rock masons," Rian answered simply. "No need to make them more than they were. I'm no Irish royalty. According to my grandfather, his family migrated to Arkansas because they were hired to build. At some point they migrated to Bluff Springs where they built most of what's still standing today. Fires took out the wooden structures, but the rock buildings have endured through time.

Amy nodded. Despite the name, the Cardboard Cottage was a quarried rock building. It had endured, too.

"I don't understand why I haven't found the name O'Deis," Rian continued. "It's not on any immigrant archive I've come across. The name doesn't seem to exist."

"Which makes me wonder if bank robber is even more of a possibility than you think," Zelda declared. "I say he stole the emeralds and fled to Arkansas."

"That make so much sense," Genna added, her tone dripping sarcasm. "This is the Emerald Isle, after all."

"I don't hear you posing any highbrow options," Zelda spat. "And why is it called the Emerald Isle if there aren't any emeralds?"

"That's one I can answer," Gayle said. "From a bird's eye view, Ireland looks like an emerald in the middle of the ocean. A green jewel in a crowning sea."

"Isn't that part of an Americana song?" Zelda hummed a few bars of the *Star Spangled Banner*.

"You're thinking of *America the Beautiful*." Gayle hummed the song. "From sea to shining sea."

Zelda nodded her dark head. "That's the one."

James took off his hat and rubbed his head with his palm. His hair was cut close, but Amy could see the sprigs of gray in the tightly wound curls.

"Since we're talking about ancestors, when I did my DNA profile, I discovered I came from ancient Egypt." He shook his head. "Personally, I have my doubts that kind of knowledge exists, but I admit I've always felt a stirring when I think of the Pyramids of Giza."

"What about you, Eloise?" Gayle asked. "Where did your people originate?"

Eloise was watching Dick, her fingers twisting the tail of the tablecloth.

"Eloise?" Gayle repeated.

Eloise turned her eyes to meet Gayle's and Amy saw something akin to sadness in them.

"What? My people? Oh, my family." Eloise lifted her chin slightly. "We're from Texas. My father was an oil man. I don't mean we had oil. He worked the oil fields. He was never home." She stalled slightly. "I don't know where he came from. Texas is all I know about."

"And it's all you need to know," Dick countered. "You're the wife of a successful banker and that's all that matters."

The waitress appeared and cleared the table of dishes. It was a polite, but firm gesture. Time for them to move on. It had been an exhausting day for everyone, but even more so for the staff at the hotel.

"See y'all at eight sharp tomorrow then," Gayle said. "We'll make a new start on a new day."

# CHAPTER TEN

Amy glanced at the couple seated across the aisle and four seats forward in the coach. They were the pair from Arkansas, the two who had ambled into the resort right in time for a murder. They were the couple Gayle claimed had other plans to work around. Whatever that meant.

She recognized the Bluff Springs Chamber president. Reginald Williams was a somber, spare looking man with pronounced features and a distrustful expression. It seemed odd that with such an unyielding appearance he could lead a membership organization that thrived on the goodwill and good business of his community. But there he was, at the top of the organization hierarchy and probably its paygrade, too. Amy didn't envy Gayle's role underneath him. And, of course he would be on this trip. She hadn't considered that before now, but it would be his presidential perk. Seated next to him was a woman she had never met. His wife, Amy guessed, but no one had introduced her. Not even Gayle, who was always introducing everybody to everybody else. The woman was petite, with a short, blunt-cut hairstyle that made her think of French film stars from the 1990s. Everything about this woman said confidence and class.

The coach sped along the road as if they were on a superhighway and not a thin two-lane road. Even as a passenger, riding on the left side of the road was a source for panic. Amy settled against the comfortable seat, forcing herself to think pleasant thoughts as she looked at the countryside speeding by. Today they would visit a castle — although Gayle would not tell them which one — have lunch at a famous pub, and then shop until they dropped. Zelda was giddy with excitement.

Genna leaned forward from the seat behind Amy. "I bet those two didn't add a dime to the capital campaign," she whispered to Amy. "But they still get to come along for the ride. He strikes me as the kind who rides other people's coattails and enjoys it immensely."

Amy turned to face Genna. "Is that his wife?"

Genna nodded and then whispered close to Amy's ear. "She brokers a big real estate firm. I bet it's killing her to ride with the riffraff," Genna added, a bit too loud. Amy shushed her with a look.

They rode in silence until Gayle pointed out the van window. "Hey, look, you can see the castle from here!" Indeed, they could. It rose from the green plateau like the ancient lookout.

"Where are we?" Amy asked.

Gayle beamed. "It's the Blarney Castle! The most famous castle in all of Ireland. And that says a lot, since there are thousands of castles and castle ruins."

Doris nearly bounced in her seat with excitement. "I get to kiss the Blarney Stone! Oh! It's a dream come true!"

The van let them off at the entrance that was disappointingly modern brick, but a few steps beyond that Amy knew they were in a place of great history. Maybe even magical history. The paved walkway curved its way to the castle alongside gardens and groves and paths that seemed to lead everywhere in all directions.

"Our guide should be here soon," Gayle said, looking anxiously around at the small crowd and then at her boss, as if to assure him he wouldn't have to wait long. "Someone from the Cork Chamber has arranged to meet us and be our tour guide," she said. The older man nodded curtly.

Amy glanced up just as a younger man came through the turn-stile and walked quickly toward them. He glanced at the phone in his hand and with a nearly indiscernible nod, walked directly to the chamber president.

"Mr. Williams," he said, extending his hand. "I am Ian Quinn. I handle community relations with the Cork Chamber. Welcome to Ireland. *Fáilte.*"

"*Fáilte*," the older man repeated. "Call me Reginald. Mr. Williams belongs in the office in Bluff Springs."

Ian smiled. "Reginald, then. And Mrs. Williams," he said, shaking her hand.

"Rebecca," she corrected with a smile. Ian nodded.

"And to you all. *Fáilte*," he repeated, greeting the others as they stood in a semicircle on the path. His crystalline blue eyes looked warmly at each of them in turn.

Gayle stepped forward and extended her hand. "I'm Gayle Brand. We've been corresponding about our trip."

His smile flashed. "Gayle, of course. I recognize you from your photo."

The Irish brogue on a handsome man was almost too much. Amy glanced at Zelda and saw stars shining in her eyes. She had her oversized Fendi sunglasses pushed up on top of her head, her dark bob raked neatly behind her ears. Zelda had opted for yet more leopard print today, and Amy wondered if Ian would notice the cougar in not so subtle disguise eyeing him like prey.

"We are so grateful you would join us," Gayle said. "Let me introduce you to everyone. You've met Mr. Williams and his wife, Rebecca."

Ian nodded in their direction.

"This is my husband, James." She touched the sleeve of his polo shirt. "This is Eloise and Dick Collins, who is a local investment banker and his lovely wife. Doris Knight is one of our most dedicated chamber members. And these ladies are four of our most progressive Bluff Springs business owners. Amy, Genna, Rian, and Zelda."

Zelda stepped forward. "Zelda Carlisle," she purred. "What a beautiful country you have." She looped her hand through his arm. "We're ready when you are," she said, looking up at him. "Show us what you got."

Rian rolled her eyes.

"He looks like Paul Hollywood," Genna whispered to Amy. "How does so much gorgeous fit in one body?"

Amy took a longer look. He did look like a young version of the British baking star.

"If everyone is ready, we can set off," he said, patting Zelda's hand still on his arm. "We'll go right to the castle and hope to avoid a long line, if we're lucky. It's a bit of stroll, but a lovely one. And it's a grand day for a tour." He smiled down at Zelda. Zelda beamed up at him.

They fell into an easy step behind and beside, their destination clearly ahead.

Amy noticed that Reginald Williams was still Mr. Williams to Gayle, even if he wasn't in the office. His wife's first name was Rebecca and that seemed too simple of a name for such a highbrow look. Amy watched as Rebecca walked beside her husband. Her hand rested lightly on the oxblood leather bag draped from her shoulder, the Etienne Aigner horseshoe logo clearly visible. She had on a dark navy drape-style silk pant that rustled softly as she walked, and a crisp white silk blouse. A tiny pearl button closure at her neck was visible inches below her hairline. Not much of a walk in the park outfit. Amy looked down at her own gingham button down shirt and blue jeans. Aside from the Williams couple and Zelda, the rest of them were dressed casual with a capital T for American tourist. Ian was in a chamber branded polo and jeans.

The closer they got, the taller the tower of the castle grew before them. The square battlements at the top looked a lot less like LEGO blocks from this angle, and Amy could see people already lining up on the walkway at the top.

"How do we get up there?" she asked.

"Right up the middle of the castle," Ian said brightly. "Up and around, we'll go some hundred and twenty-seven steps before we reach the top. We'll be eighty-five feet from the ground when you hang to kiss the stone. I hope no one is claustrophobic. It's a bit close. And dark, too."

Amy was mesmerized by his cadence.

"Eighty-five feet?" Zelda screeched. "We're going to hang in the air?"

"You'll be safe. You'll see."

Ian wasn't joking about dark. The smell of wet rock filled her nostrils the moment they entered the castle, and the light seemed to dull right into the stone. The arched openings in the ruins let in heavily filtered light. Wherever the light touched the stone, patches of fern and lichen grew in the castle cracks. It smelled old. Not like her grandmother Ollie's cedar chest old. It smelled like ancient warriors and sun washed rock. Or a mountain after a rainstorm. Or even the frothy white caps on a lake turned up by the wind. It smelled ancient and earthy, she decided, as they climbed the stairs to the second floor.

"It's a tower house, you see, a keep built over five hundred years ago to fortify the lands of MacCart'y of Muskerry. MacCart'y was a powerful dynasty," he explained as they climbed. Stopping near a square of iron grate in the floor, he added, "and this is the famous murder hole."

"A murder what?"

"A murder hole. It made quick business of intruders to the castle. And if you were one— an intruder, that is—you could have all matter of things tossed on you if you entered below uninvited. Things like burning oil or boiling water, or sharp spikes and spears. The legends are wretched. You'd have no more time than to look up before you met your horrible end. You'd never make it safely to this floor, to be certain. Not if you weren't wanted."

Amy shuddered involuntarily. The chieftains certainly took protecting their territory to heart.

"We'll go on then," Ian said. "Single file is all we can manage from here. Stop when you need to catch your breath.  When we get to the top, we may even be able to see the Witches Tree."

"The Witches Tree?" Zelda asked.

"The legend that begat this legend among many others."

"I read about that," Gayle said. "It's a Yew tree said to be over six hundred years old."

Ian nodded. His eyes shone a brilliant blue even in the dusty light. "Legend says this land was the home and bog of the Blarney Witch, who first told the mortals about the magic of the stone and its gift of eloquence. She was saved from drowning by the kind king, and she owed him as much in return. It is said the tree stands beside a stone that imprisons the witch by day and releases her to her woods at nightfall, where she does cackle and call until the first light of dawn. She leaves behind a fire of burning embers in her witchy kitchen before she returns to stone."

"Blarney," Genna mumbled.

"Blarney is indeed the word," he replied. "Or rather, *bhlarna*, from which the name comes. They claim it's a place of the old druids. There's even a circle of stones still standing nearby."

The hair on her neck prickled. "A circle of stones?"

"The Seven Sisters. We'll visit them if we have time. It's a henge circle with trees growing all around."

A breath of wind rushed across her cheek. *And they will tryyyy...* it seemed to say as it passed. She looked up at the opening in the wall above her, pale light filtering through the gloom. The dream of the stones swept through her memory. The wind had rustled the leaves across the grass in her dream, with much the same sound.

They were silent as they climbed the next set of rock stairs, corridors angling abruptly in the narrow tower. People were climbing above them. There were people below them, too, the air filling in and feeling thin as the passageway seemed to grow even more narrow and dark. Her chest felt tight, as if her skin had shrunk a bit. She could hear others breathing, too. What would happen if someone panicked? How would they escape?

The same way they got in. Through these dark, narrow stairs.

She felt someone close behind her and turned to see James. Beads of sweat stood out on his forehead.

"You haven't said much this morning," she whispered.

He glanced at her quickly before his eyes returned to his feet on the steps.

"I'm not crazy about dark, cramped spaces," he complained. His voice seemed louder than intended. Maybe that was a feature built into the castle, too. Not only could someone toss boiling oil onto an intruder, but they could eavesdrop on them all the way to the top.

"I wanted to sit this one out when we hit the first stair, but Gayle said she would kill me if we got all the way to Ireland, and I didn't kiss that stone. Seems like a silly idea to me."

"I heard that." Gayle's voice came from few steps above them. "You need some blarney for that promotion. We both need some blarney luck."

Amy chuckled. "Go forth with gab and use it wisely."

James nodded. "Go forth and get that new job!"

"What kind of job?" They squeezed past the bodies on the stair. A plump man was stalled, his breath heavy and filled with words that even in a foreign language sounded like something you wouldn't say in church.

James grunted. "Can we talk about this when we reach terra firma?"

"Terra firma," someone shouted from below. It sounded like Genna. "I'm ready to kiss that."

They managed to get around the poor man still puffing and swearing and slip into one of the rooms off the stair. The room wasn't much, none of them were. Just a space with an opening in the wall and a stone bench. James stuck his head out the opening and greedily sucked in fresh air.

The group was separated by a few steps on the climb, since not all of them kept the same pace. She hoped they could share the Blarney experience together at the top. Maybe no one would mind if they cut in line a few places to do so.

"Tell me about this promotion," Amy urged, hoping to delay the next set of stairs by at least a few breaths.

"Oh, just another rung up the ladder," he said. "But it's an office position. I've been climbing utility poles for a long time and I'm ready to come in out of the weather. Gayle, well, Gayle wants to lead the Bluff Springs Chamber. She's after the president's job."

She felt her eyebrows rise. "She's trying to oust Mr. Williams?"

James chuckled. "No. He's retiring. Gayle is expecting to be named his successor."

"That would be wonderful!" Amy exclaimed. "She is perfect for that position."

"I know that," James said pointedly. "And she knows that, but there is one person who doesn't."

"Who? Who could possibly object?"

"Dick Collins," he said pointedly. "That's one of the reasons why Gayle made sure he was on this trip. She wants to win his favor. She will. I know she will. Even without kissing the famous Blarney Stone of Ireland." James winked at Amy. "I'm doing my part, too."

"Moral support?"

James nodded. "All that golfing with Dick? It's not about golf."

Amy felt her opinion of James shift ever so slightly. He wasn't just Gayle's plus-one. He was working on his wife's promotion from another angle. The dude-to-dude angle. Mano e mano. Genna was always saying men made their business deals on the golf course. All to be signed, sealed, and delivered at the nineteenth hole. Even on tour in Ireland.

"Well, onward," James mumbled after a final gulp of air. Amy fell into step behind him.

The light grew darker the higher they climbed, and then suddenly they were at the top. Now, they were the tiny people seen from the ground. From this view, the treetops looked like balls of green yarn. She could see the River Martin and the place where it met the Blarney River. She could see the Blarney House and the lake behind, and the gardens spanning in all four directions.

Inhaling fresh air, Amy tilted her head to greet the sun, her eyes closed tight against the glare. The line was still moving slowly, and as they neared the stone she saw why. Not only did you have to hang in the air to reach the stone, but you also had to lie on your back and hang upside down. An attendant held you tight at the waist while you reached for the stone with your lips.

"I sure wouldn't want to climb that twice a day, five days a week," Rian said. "I hope they pay that attendant good money and great tips."

"I am going to tip him twenty euro," Zelda declared. "I'll give it to him before he hangs me over the edge, just to make sure he doesn't drop me."

Amy glanced at Rebecca Williams. No way would this woman get down on the rock. But she looked eager and excited. She was leaning into her husband with a familiar clutch, and Amy saw a tender expression in his eyes.

"Are you really going to do this?" Amy asked her.

Rebecca chuckled lightly, and Reginald put his arm around her shoulder. "I've climbed this far, haven't I? Why would I leave without my lucky gift?"

She looked at her husband and then at Amy. "You're not having second thoughts are you?"

Amy shook her head. "Not me."

"Well, I am," Zelda said. "If I get down there, I'm not sure I will be able to get up!"

"I'll help you," Rian said.

Zelda eyed Ian with a damsel look.

"I will help you, too," he agreed.

"Of course, you will," Genna offered. "You can help all of us old ladies get up from there."

"Speak for yourself," Rian said. "And I think that's the first time I've ever heard you call yourself old."

"It's the first time I've ever hung off a rock a hundred feet in the air."

"Eighty-five," Zelda countered.

"Like fifteen feet makes that much difference," Genna replied. "You'd splat no matter what."

"Has anyone ever fallen through?" Zelda's eye were wide.

"Not since the grates and bars were added," Ian answered. "But before that…" He let his words trail away and the dimples deepened. He was obviously enjoying himself and the attention.

"This is not the time to make a joke like that," Zelda snapped. "Not when I have so much to live for."

"Has anyone ever been pushed? On purpose?" Dick sounded anxious.

Amy turned to see Dick Collins leaning as far away from the edge of the parapet as he could manage and still be upright.

"Aren't you being the fraidy cat," Rebecca said with an audible *tsk tsk*. "Honestly, Richard, if anyone wanted to be rid of you, they have better options than this. There's a murder hole on the second floor and a garden full of poisonous plants down below. No one needs to climb all that many stairs to do you in!"

Eloise gasped, and Amy eyed her with surprise.

Rebecca laughed lightly. "My apologies, Eloise, but I suspect I took the words right out of your mouth."

Zelda giggled. Rian snickered. Genna was just taking a swig of water and nearly choked holding back a snort. Amy caught Gayle covering her smile with a hand. Eloise looked at Dick and then at Rebecca. Eloise's nostrils flared and she giggled through her nose. And then she opened her mouth and threw back her head and laughed like a person gone mad.

"Oh, dear," Eloise said, when she regained her composure some seconds later. "I am so sorry, but that just made my day."

"Well, thanks for ruining mine," Dick sputtered, his eyes trained on Eloise. "Now I won't think of anything else but!"

"Oh, Richard," Rebecca said, her tone a notch shy of contempt, "can't you take a little jesting? No one in their right mind would get rid of you. Why would they? You are essential to how things get done in the world. Where would we be without our Dick?" Rebecca's smile was pure sass. She patted Dick's arm and pulled him closer to her and hence, closer to the edge. "You of all of us should be the most eager to kiss the Blarney Stone of Ireland."

"Why do you say that? What are you implying?"

"Nothing of consequence. It's only that you have a lot of ground to cover before your bank has a successful opening. You still have all the right people to meet. All the right people to talk into moving their money. A little eloquence would certainly be a gift -- even if this is only a superstitious notion."

Dick furrowed his forehead, as if deciding whether he was being encouraged or chastised. "When you put it that way," he said finally. "I could always use more eloquence. It never hurts to have more than you need. Right?" He glanced quickly at the man beside him.

"It never hurts to have more of anything than you need. That's been my experience," Reginald said as he deftly inserted himself between his wife and Dick, a maneuver that caught Amy's eye and a warning look from Rebecca.

Eloise had been watching the parley, the thin smile still on her lips. She turned now to her husband. "Why don't you go first, Richard. You can show us all how it's done."

"Actually, I was thinking I would skip this…"

"You were thinking you could skip this part? I don't think so," Eloise said firmly. Amy caught something commanding in her voice. Something she had not yet heard from Eloise. It was as if she had found a foothold while standing on the parapet of the old castle. A stronghold, even, a place to take a stand.

Eloise grabbed his elbow and pulled herself close. "Haven't we made it this far? Everything is going to turn out for the better. I know it will."

When the long wait was over and it was her turn, Amy scrambled to the ground. Leaning backwards, her hands clutching the bars in a death grip, she settled her hips against the hard stone and let her head fall over the edge. She pursed her lips and kissed the Blarney Stone of Ireland. It was a cold, hard kiss and it was over in seconds.

"Go fort' with the gift of eloquence and be sure to use it wisely," Ian pronounced to her, as he helped her to her feet. "And there is your gift of the Blarney."

"And a bit of flannel, too," Amy said.

"True enough," Ian said with a sidewise look at Amy. "I can see you've been talking with the locals. Flannel and flattery. They do indeed go hand in hand."

# CHAPTER ELEVEN

Amy couldn't help but notice the smudge of dirt on Rebecca Williams' white silk blouse as she followed her onto the coach. So much for park attire *a la chic*. Even Zelda knew better than to wear white to climb an old Irish castle. The group had spent a couple of hours strolling the grounds — thankfully not all sixty acres, but enough to log 10,000 steps on her watch and the start of a blister on her pinky toe.

She was relieved that they had decided against visiting the Seven Sisters Stones. Not that she didn't want to see the famous rocks, but she didn't want to hear more whispers in her head from ancient stones. Instead, the group visited the gardens, including the poison garden full of hemlock and wolfsbane, mandrake and nightshade. The beds were marked with the sign of the skull and crossbones just to make sure everyone knew not to touch. Rebecca Williams pointed out the *Ricinus communis* castor bean, which, as the sign said, was the origin of the lethal ricin.

"As you can see, Dick. We are all only a pinch away from the big sleep," Rebecca said, with a look that struck Amy as rather Machiavellian. She smiled at Dick Collins. "One pinch on the bank board minutes and you'd be history."

Dick didn't laugh at her joke.

They strolled along the Blarney River, tossed coins into the creek for luck, and then shopped at the souvenir boutiques. At last, they said farewell to Ian, thanked him for his grand Blarney tour, and promised to return the favor if he ever made it to Bluff Springs. He said it was on his bucket list. Amy doubted if that was true.

Now headed to a well-deserved late lunch in a neighboring town, Gayle suggested they do some shopping to end the day's activities. Gayle animatedly pointed out different locations on the map. Eloise paid close attention. Dick did not. He seemed to enjoy being in a bad mood.

A cool wind had blown in by the time they finished their meal, and the breeze added a chill to the afternoon as they shopped along the cobblestone alley. Overhead, the colorful flags draped from the rooftops flapped and fluttered. The narrow roads squared off like a maze. There were pubs at every corner, all overflowing and vivacious with song and vigorous laughter spilling into the streets. The group tried to stick together, but Amy lost track of her friends in the bustle of the streets and followed Eloise into a shop of wool goods, yarns and knitting supplies.

"Oh, my, look at this," Eloise breathed as she eyed the shelves. Bright color wares splashed the shelves in tidy piles. "I must buy my son a scarf from Ireland. Massachusetts is terribly cold in the winter."

Eloise fingered the goods. There were piles of scarves and hats in blue weave, piles of green and brown tweed. Eloise landed on a beautiful shade of crimson. "This is a perfect match," she said, then selected a matching hat.

"Did I hear Gayle say your son's at Harvard?"

Eloise nodded. "He's still an undergraduate at Harvard College, but we have big plans for Harvard U."

"You and Dick must be very proud of your of son."

Eloise turned abruptly. "My Richard is not Dick's son," she snapped, her eyes dark behind her glasses. Her jaw tensed and then loosened. Tensed and loosened again. Eloise clenched the scarf in her hands. "Forgive me," she said. "I shouldn't have barked at you. I don't know what's wrong with me. I am so on edge. I can't seem to get any sleep. Maybe it's this pain medication I'm taking." She touched her jaw with her fingers. "I had a dental procedure before this trip, and I don't always do well with medications. They put me a little on edge."

Her smile seemed forced. "Most people don't realize that Richard is not Dick's son. Dickie prefers it that way, and I could never deny Richard's true father, even if he wasn't the man I thought he was." She smiled again and this time it seemed more genuine. "Same names, I know. A funny coincidence."

"Are you enjoying the hotel and the grounds?" Amy asked as they perused the shelves and woven goods. "I think the chapel is quite beautiful. I can see it plain as day from my window. Yours, too, I guess."

"I haven't been to the chapel, yet." Eloise said. "It's still on my list of places to explore."

"Oh!" Amy exclaimed. "I just assumed you had. I saw you pass by me in the hall the other night. I thought maybe you went to the chapel to light a candle."

Eloise turned to Amy and frowned. "You are mistaken, Amy. I haven't been in the chapel."

She turned to the shelves. "Dick claims I sleepwalk sometimes, but I am completely unaware of it if I do." Eloise reached for the brightest shade of purple Amy had ever seen. The color wasn't garish, but it was vivid. It would fit right into Amy's wardrobe. And obviously Dick's, too.

The shopkeeper was watching them with alert eyes. "You have excellent taste," she said as they unfolded the purple scarves. "There are not many who can wear such a hue, but I see you are well suited."

She glanced at Amy and then pulled a tam and scarf in shamrock green from the shelf. "Try this one if you will," she pleaded. "This is a good color for you."

"Actually, I like the purple better. It's my favorite color.

"You and Dick, both," Eloise said. "It can't be for the same reason."

"Is he color blind?"

"Dick calls it color deficient. He can't always tell the difference between red and green," Eloise shook her head slightly. "Not that anyone cares. No one but me, anyway. I'm the one who has to arrange his closet just so. He's terrified to go to the office in mismatched socks."

That's why his wardrobe was purple and khaki.

"This particular shade is most unique," the saleswoman interjected as she tugged at a stack of scarves. "This is called Tyrian purple. The color comes from the Murex snail and has ancient and royal origins. The process of extraction was nearly lost and has only recently been rediscovered as a sustainable resource."

"How do you mean sustainable?" Amy asked.

"Why it's all the rage now," the shopkeeper replied. "Goods from sustainable resources. Taking care of environment and all that. We are famous for our mussels in Ireland. They nearly grow wild on every rock that meets the sea. This type— the Murex— it is not an edible snail, but they are most prolific. Our new generation of young weavers are partial to this sustainable shade. It is a royal color if I may say so. The color of wealth."

"Mussels," Eloise repeated quietly.

"The mussels," the woman agreed. "And snails and cockles and such— they're all in the mollusks family."

Amy selected a tweed hat and matching scarf, wrapping it around her neck in front of the mirror that hung on the wall for that reason. "Shew," she said, sniffing the weave. "It still smells a bit briny."

"That will pass as you wear it," the woman said. "I promise. It's all part of this environmentally friendly processing the weavers now use. No lye, no chemicals, nothing artificial. Your scarf will share its brine with your skin as you wear it, as you will share yours with the scarf. And so, the Wild Atlantic Way will be with you wherever you go."

Amy ignored the not so veiled attempt to hook a tourist with sentiment. "I love it."

Eloise fingered the scarf. "Oh, so perfect," she said, her eyes shining behind her glasses. Her fingers rubbed the soft folds of the scarf.

The saleswoman clasped her hands in front of her. "I am so pleased you found a treasure here in my shop. Now, what else will you have to remember Ireland? You are Americans visiting? Am I right in thinking so? You'll be wanting much more than scarves to remember us by."

It was all the encouragement Eloise seemed to need. Amy watched as Eloise picked out a split reed woven knitting basket, the shape and color of a cantaloupe cut open at the top, and then added a dozen skeins of lambswool. She labored over the rack of knitting needles, picking them up and putting them back, as if weighing them in her hands before making her final choice. She added a card of large needles and another that would make a much finer stitch.

"I think we should catch up with the others," Amy said as their purchases were rung up and packaged in paper totes.

"Oh, you go on," Eloise said. "I want to get a cup of tea and watch the world go by. If you don't mind?"

"You're sure you'll be okay by yourself?"

"I'll be better than okay. I'm a little tired from this morning to be honest. I could do with a rest. Oh, and Amy," she added, touching Amy's arm, "don't tell Dick about the scarves. I want it to be a surprise."

Amy nodded, tucked her scarf around her neck and set off to find her friends.

She heard them before she saw them. A mime and his compatriot had the three of them cornered by a water fountain, all laughing hysterically. The mime was dressed like a frog with short stubby dreadlocks that stuck out from his head, making him seem even more playfully bizarre. The woman with him was dressed like a princess in green and gold. The crown on her head was huge and set askew so that it barely hung to her curls. The frog made an exaggerated attempt to kiss first Zelda and then Genna on the cheek, with the princess shooing him away with overly dramatic gestures. Costume mittens on his feet and fingers were large and floppy,
adding to the fun and theatrics as he hopped and twirled around them.

"Kiss him! Kiss him!" Zelda cried as Amy joined them. "He's really a prince, but his true love must kiss him before he can return to his place at the royal court. He's doomed to be a frog forever if you don't!" Zelda giggled as the frog hopped playfully and the princess chased after him with a peacock feather broom. The frog prince eyed Amy and wiggled his long fingers, beckoning her with an exaggerated pucker to his lips.

"We've just come from the Blarney Stone, so I've had some practice with kissing," Amy said, laughing. She leaned in and planted a kiss on his cheek. He twirled and danced and hopped and then stopped, looked at his floppy frog fingers and toes, wiggled them, and then shook his head sadly.

"Awww…" the crowd sounded in unison as they watched.

"No true love for the prince today," the princess said to the crowd, pretending to wipe away tears. "But tomorrow is another day, and another dollar!" She took off her crown and offered it out for alms as the frog hopped about, making faces at those fishing into their pockets for coins and bills. Amy noticed the crown had a cloth bottom to catch the money as she dropped in a five euro note.

"Where's Rian," she asked looking around.

Genna pointed. Rian was planted at a table outside a pub just opposite the fountain, a pint of Guinness in her hand. She lifted her camera and wiggled her brows.

"Uh oh. Blackmail," Genna said with a chuckle. "You and Zelda will be on the hook for this one!"

"And you think you won't?" Amy asked.

"I did not kiss the frog," Genna announced and laughed. "I've kissed many I can tell you that. And none of them turned into a prince. Not one."

Laughing, they joined Rian at the pub to compare shopping notes. Zelda and Genna had discovered a bath shop that sold seaweed from the bath houses of Enniscrone in County Sligo. The kelp promised to restore vitality and youth, which was right up Genna's alley. From there they discovered a tea shop with all the treats and goodies anyone could ever need for a tea party and then some. Zelda's arms were already laden with packages. No wonder the frog prince had settled his sights on her as a target. Another day, another euro.

Amy showed her scarf. "And what did you find?" She asked Rian.

"You're looking at it," Rian said, tapping the side of her glass. "Best pint in all of Ireland." She motioned to the sign. "At least, that's what the sign says!"

"Have you found anyone who will claim you as kin?" Zelda asked.

Rian shook her head, swinging her brown curls. "Not yet. But I did learn there's an old man who knows about the masons who went to America. He's ninety if he's a day, I'm told, so I'd better find him quick if I want to get any information." Rian motioned with a nod of her head. "They say he has one hand on a pint and the other on the gravestone. Which I guess is their vernacular for really, really old."

"Where are you going to find him?" Amy wondered.

"I'm told to ask for Paddy O'Shaughnessy anywhere in County Clare." Rian said. "I think they were pulling my leg with that name. Limerick is only about two hours from our hotel, so we need to go.

"What I also learned..." Rian continued, after taking a long swig of her beer. "is that Limerick is the home of the famous Limerick Lace, the first Irish Coffee, and the great grandfather of our own John F. Kennedy."

"That's a good connection," Zelda exclaimed. "We may find your O'Deis clan yet!"

They ordered another round and then decided it was time to return to their meeting place. They only made four wrong turns before they saw Gayle waving at them from the van.

# CHAPTER TWELVE

A note was waiting for them at the front desk when they returned to the hotel.

"What does it say," Zelda asked, peeking over Amy's shoulder.

"It says that a Garda O'Shannon with the Ballingeary Garda Station in Kilmore, Co. Cork is requesting our passports," Amy read. She knew she was butchering the names terribly, but Zelda wouldn't know that. "We are to bring them with us before dinner."

"Why do the police need our passports?"

"Beats me," Amy answered. "Maybe it has something to do with the maid."

"Ahh," Zelda said, wiping the day's smudge of mascara from under her eyes. "The maid. I'd almost forgotten about her."

Amy frowned at Zelda. How could either of them forget that horrible scene. Although the woman's face had been facing the trash bin of the cart when she was stabbed, or at least, that's how she landed— Amy had seen enough of her features to recognize her. And since Doris had said she saw her talking to Dick Collins, that meant she spoke at least some English, even if she didn't speak it to Doris. Rather than consider her rude, Doris had assumed otherwise. It was so like Doris to put a kinder spin on a snub. Amy didn't see herself as that charitable if she was in the same situation. Even if the maid did speak English, that didn't mean she wasn't a foreigner. If she was a foreigner, maybe that's why the police were looking for passports.

The thought struck her. Maybe the maid was hiding something. Maybe she was an illegal working at the hotel under an assumed name. In that case she may not have a passport at all. Or maybe she had stolen one from another guest! Maybe that's why the police were looking for passports.

Amy hurried toward the stairs.

"Why are you rushing?" Zelda asked.

Amy beckoned Zelda to follow. "I want to check to make sure we still have our passports."

"Of course, we have our passports. Why wouldn't we?" Realization hit Zelda's eyes. "Ah," she gasped. "You think someone stole our passports? Someone like that maid?"

"I'm thinking maybe the maid was pretending to be someone else."

Zelda gasped again. "You think she's a spy?"

Amy burst out laughing. "A spy? Why would a spy be here?"

"Well, you never know," Zelda said. "Spies are like that. They show up in unexpected places and unexpectedly get killed. I knew there was something odd about that woman."

"Odd? You mean other than the ice pick wounds in her back?"

"She didn't have on the right shoes," Zelda said, her lips pursed in a righteous pout. "She had on a pair of Girotti! What woman in her right mind wears handmade Italian heels to scrub toilets and make beds? I know that brand. I'd recognize that clunky block heel anywhere. She wasn't wearing tights, either. And that's just not a good look for a maid."

Amy stopped at the bottom of the stair and stared at her friend. Behind the stair was a large closet, the door open. Two women were straightening the shelves, folding towels, and replenishing their carts with supplies. They stopped talking as Zelda and Amy approached, intentionally eavesdropping, Amy guessed. No doubt the staff would be all abuzz about the death of the maid. One of their crew. Maybe they were afraid they'd be next. Amy put her finger to her lips.

"Her shoes," Amy whispered as they climbed to the top of the stairs. "One of her shoes had come loose."

"That's why I noticed them," Zelda whispered. "Her uniform didn't fit her either. It was straining against her hips like she had been eating too much banana pudding."

Amy grinned. Too much banana pudding. The wrong shoes. A uniform that didn't fit. A foreign accent someone would recognize if she spoke to them. It all added up. To what? To murder, that's what. If Dick had talked to her, maybe he could identify where her accent was from.

Their passports were right where they left them. Nothing looked out of place in the room, except their bed was now made and fresh towels were set out in the bathroom. The ice bucket had been moved to the table, and two fresh glasses sat beside it. Nothing else looked out of place.

As Amy sat on the bed and looked out the window, she considered her imagination had gotten away from her just now. A spy in expensive Italian leather shoes? An illegal worker with someone else's passport? It all seemed a bit farfetched. The maid was probably a local. Maybe she had plans for the evening and wore her best shoes because she didn't have time to go home and change. Maybe she really did snub Doris by not answering her question, and maybe she was just an unlucky person with an enemy who used the element of surprise to do her in. The maid hadn't seen the ice pick coming. That much seemed true.

"Do you think we should tell Garda O'Shannon what we know?" Zelda asked.

"What do we know? Really? By way of fact. We know we found her right outside of our room. That's something they know already."

"When you say it like that …" Zelda let her voice trail away. "Hey, you don't think they're going to take our passports away from us, do you? Can they do that? Can they do that in Ireland?"

"Unless you've broken a law or they have reason to believe you are about to break a law, I don't think they can."

"Well, we haven't, and we aren't so they can't," Zelda declared with such finality that Amy pitied anyone who would try. Zelda kicked off her shoes and climbed into her bed. "You know, I keep thinking about how that cart was right outside our door. It was just sitting there, waiting. As if someone wanted us to find it first. Like maybe that whole thing was staged outside our door for some reason."

"What kind of a reason?" Amy felt a prickle of dread.

"I don't know," Zelda said and sighed deeply. "Mystery puzzles and brain work are your forte, Sparks. But there's something about that scene in the hallway that strikes me as odd." Zelda glanced over at Amy and raised a brow. "Yes, I do mean odder than an ice pick on the floor at her feet. In fact, maybe that is what's odd. Why was the ice pick on the floor? Why wasn't it… well… you know. Why wasn't it still stuck in her back?"

Amy stroked her chin and wished she could stroke Victor's soft fur. Somehow contemplating mystery puzzles and brain work came a lot easier with Victor purring in her lap. She had left him in good company. A friend and fellow cat lover had taken him in for the duration of her trip abroad. He would be spoiled rotten by the time she got home from Ireland, and he would let her know all about it. Victor loved to pout.

"You know, you may be on to something, Zelda. The shoe bothers me, too, now that you pointed it out. It didn't look like there was much of a struggle out there in the hall. Her face and arms were planted down into the trash bin like she had fallen over into it. As if she landed there from the force of the blow. But if that's the case, why did her shoe come off?"

Zelda nodded. "And the ice pick didn't just fall out, either. What if she was killed somewhere else and pushed into the hall by our door. Maybe she was even dragged to the hall and draped over the cart like yesterday's trash."

Amy nodded. "It's pretty creepy. And if that's true, it explains a few things. Like why we didn't hear anything. Or why she was draped over her tidying cart full of towels and supplies. It also means there was a cold hearted killer somewhere in the hotel."

Zelda shivered. "Eeww," she added. "This makes me think of poor Simon on my Galapagos cruise. I sure hope there's no killer here now," Zelda countered. "There were a lot of people in the hotel for the wedding, but they've all gone home. There must be a lot of suspects on Garda O'Shannon's list. I'm glad we're not on it." Zelda looked across at Amy. "We are not on the suspect list, are we? Not this time?"

Amy plumped the pillows and settled against them, gazing out the window. The roof line of the little chapel rose above the windowsill from this view. That had been a fun day. They had followed the piper with the wedding crowd and joined in the festivities at the reception. There were easily sixty or seventy people in attendance, and any one of them could be guilty of murdering the maid. She still held to the premise that someone caught the maid smooching with someone she shouldn't have, and that had ended her life. Hopefully, it was with neither the bride nor the groom.

She thought about their first evening at the hotel, when she was looking out at the little chapel wishing for much needed sleep in the dusky, almost night sky. What had prompted Dick Collins to visit the chapel in the middle of the night? Why was he so furtive as he made his way to the hotel? And what had made Eloise run through the hall shortly after? Had he been meeting someone in the chapel? Someone he wasn't supposed to be meeting?

She considered their little group from Arkansas. The Williams power couple had not arrived by that time. Or so Gayle had said.

She could cross her friends off that list — none of them would have any reason to spend time with Dick alone in a chapel or anywhere else for that matter. She couldn't see why Gayle or James would meet him late at night. Or Doris. Although, she would need to ask Doris about that, anyway. She had other things she wanted to talk to Doris about, too.

It was entirely possible that Dick was with his wife in the chapel that night. Maybe Eloise went to light a candle and say a prayer at the altar of one of the oldest chapels in Ireland. Maybe Dick went with her and left after an argument. Or because he got impatient. Or maybe because he was just downright disinterested. They all seemed like possible reactions, even probable, knowing what little she knew about Dick Collins. But why would Eloise lie about that?

She could be making more of his furtive behavior than she should be. Perhaps Eloise was running to catch up with him when Amy saw her in the hall. Or Eloise could have been frightened by being left alone in the dark in a strange place and was running to get to safety faster.

Garda O'Shannon could benefit from all of this pondering, but she wasn't about to put herself in the middle of another murder investigation if it wasn't called for. And as far as she was concerned, it wasn't called for. She agreed with Zelda. They were not on the suspect list.

"A nap before dinner?" Zelda asked hopefully, as she reached for her sleeping mask. "We have plenty of time."

Amy didn't answer, but she snuggled into the pillows and closed her eyes. She felt herself slipping into sleep.

*"Death leaves a heartache no one can heal. Love leaves a memory no one can steal. And they will try. Oh, but they will try…"*

"Oh, shut up," Amy said out loud.

"I didn't say anything," Zelda declared.

"Sorry," Amy sighed. "I wasn't talking to you."

# CHAPTER THIRTEEN

Amy and Zelda handed their passports to the officer at the table in the bar and then sat down across from him. He looked at them with questioning eyes. Zelda tapped her fingers on the table when his silence lasted longer than southern Arkansas etiquette considered polite. "Don't you want to ask us what we know?"

"Do you know something?" He asked.

"Well, we know she sure wasn't where she was supposed to be," Zelda proclaimed.

"Why do you say that?"

"Because she didn't get stabbed with an ice pick in the hallway," Zelda snapped, sounding like an accusatory round of Clue.

He leaned forward with interest. "You know where she was stabbed?"

"In the back!"

"I am not an eejit," he warned. "Do not mistake me for one. You say she was not stabbed in the hallway, but how would you know?"

Zelda wagged a manicured finger at the man. "Because one of her shoes came loose and that wouldn't happen unless she was dragged to where we found her. And that means she wasn't stabbed with an ice pick in the hallway."

He paused and his dark eyes bored into Zelda's green ones. "You know for certain it was the ice pick that did the fatal harm?"

"It was on the ground at her feet."

"Yes. That is true. It was."

Amy watched as the man mulled over what Zelda had shared. It couldn't be anything more or less than the police already knew, but something had caught his attention.

"Have you been able to identify who she is?" Amy asked.

He nodded slowly.

Zelda leaned forward. "Is she a foreigner? Is she a spy? Did she steal someone's passport and take over their life?"

Garda O'Shannon's mouth twitched with amusement. "You offer an interesting line of possibilities," he said, dimples showing in his cheeks. "A spy, you say. From another country?"

"Yes!" Zelda exclaimed. "Like somewhere dark and mysterious. Somewhere cold and dangerous."

"But not America?" he asked. "Not a spy from the United States?"

"She wouldn't need to hide her accent for that!"

"She hid her accent?"

"Well, Doris thought so," Zelda claimed. "We have yet to ask Dick about it, but Doris saw him talking to the maid. He would know what kind of accent she had. Now wouldn't he?"

"Dick?" The officer shook his head. "I don't recall…"

"Dick Collins," Zelda said. "Well, his name is Richard, but everybody calls him Dick."

The amused look returned. "Mr. Collins. He contends he never spoke to the maid. He claims he didn't know a thing about her."

"And you believe him and not Doris?"

"You are speaking of Doris Knight?" He fished a passport from the pile at his elbow and opened it, then studied the picture in front him. He turned the passport toward them. "This is she?"

Amy peered at the picture. "That's Doris."

Zelda tapped the photo. "She says Dick was talking to the maid and Doris would never lie."

"And you think this Dick is lying?"

"I wouldn't say he is lying, lying. But… Amy, tell him what you saw the first night we were here."

"You saw something unusual?"

Amy nodded. "I saw Dick coming out of the chapel sometime after midnight. At least, I'm pretty sure it was Dick."

"And why is that unusual? Did you see anyone else."

"Not coming out of the chapel, no. But right after that I saw his wife, Eloise, running down the hallway toward their room."

"His wife? Running toward their room? Was someone chasing her? Is that why she was running?"

Amy wrinkled her nose. "I didn't see anyone chasing her."

"But you saw this Dick? He was also running down the hall?"

"Well, no, I didn't actually see him in the hall. And I didn't see when he returned to his room, either. But he must have."

Garda O'Shannon rubbed the fuzz on the bottom of his chin. "But somehow in your mind you t'ink t'at is related to t'is?" He tapped the passport.

Amy smiled. He spoke like a wind chime. Ting, ting, ting.

He narrowed his eyes at her. "Tell me why you say t'is, so."

Amy bit her bottom lip. Why? What could she say? Because — as Genna would so graciously put it — her spidey sense was telling her it was related. Because a banshee had screamed in her face when she was on the van from Dublin. A banshee had screamed right before the maid was found draped over the cart outside their room. Why? Because her snippets happened when she was attached to the people in her dream. When they were somehow in danger. No, she didn't know this maid, but she did know this little group from Arkansas. And this group had played croquet at the resort. There had been croquet balls in her dream. She was silent, but her thoughts went racing on. This couldn't be a coincidence. Rotten croquet balls. Two of them. That had to mean something.

"I can tell there is much more to this story than you seem willing to share," he said with polite authority. "I should explain how our investigations work here in the Republic of Ireland. If you are withholding information that could prove useful, we can confiscate your passport and detain you indefinitely. And if you invent information that further confuses our investigation, we can arrest you for cause."

Amy frowned. "I don't have anything factual to add and I'm not inventing anything."

"Good." He nodded abruptly. "You are certain you did not know this woman?"

Zelda and Amy shook their heads in unison. "We recognized her from the hotel," Amy said, "but neither of us knew who she was. She was the maid. She wore a hotel uniform."

"And expensive Italian shoes," Zelda added.

He glanced sideways at Zelda as if deciding what information, if any, he was willing to give up in exchange for something more. Amy noticed how very handsome was Garda O'Shannon. Zelda, she was certain, had already taken note.

"Italian shoes, you say," he said finally. "That is curious, given that she was from the United States."

"What?" Zelda cried. "She was from America? How do you know that?"

He leaned back in his chair and then picked up the stack of passports, rapping them on the table like a deck of cards. He took a long time to answer.

"We know because she was a registered guest at this hotel, which has been verified," he said. "It matches the luggage tag on her suitcase."

"But you didn't find her passport!" Amy blurted. "That's what this is about!"

"There is no reason to suspect she is anyone other than who she registered to be." His tone was brusque. "But yes, her passport is missing."

"She really wasn't the maid, then?"

He shook his head slowly.

"I knew that wasn't her uniform!" Zelda exclaimed. "I figured it was too much banana pudding!"

The puzzled look returned to his face. "Pudding, you say?"

Zelda sighed and splayed her manicured hands on the table. "Look, Amy is the one who solves all the crimes we stumble upon because she's the puzzle brainiac, but I am the fashionista. I could tell her uniform wasn't hers because it was too tight. I figured it was because she had been eating too much, like too much banana pudding. Because that will really pack on the pounds quick. If you get into a banana pudding binge, you can kiss your cute little pearl studded Miss Me jeans goodbye. Toddleloo."

Garda O'Shannon's brow furrowed. "Miss me?"

"Oh, but it wasn't pudding," Zelda went on without answering. "I think she took that uniform from the closet under the stairs. I'd say she stole the cart, too, just so she could fool everyone into thinking she was the maid. I mean, when is a maid not a maid?"

Amy's eyes widened as she looked at Zelda. "A maid is not a maid when she is trying to hide who she really is! That's why she was incognito."

Zelda nodded with enthusiasm. "This reminds me of my cousin. She wanted to go to the Grand Canyon with her girlfriends and her husband wouldn't cough up the dough. He said he wasn't going to spend good money to look at a hole in the ground, even if it is one of the great wonders of the world. It is, isn't it? One of the Seven Wonders of the World?"

Amy shook her head.

"It should be," Zelda demanded. "Truly, it should.

"Well," Zelda continued, "She had this brilliant idea. She pretended to hurt her back and told him she needed to hire a maid to keep house until she got better. She let him suffer a little before he was willing to shell out the money, but he finally gave in. But she didn't actually hire a maid, she *was* the maid. She cleaned the house when he was out of the house golfing, and she pocketed the maid's cash that he left on the counter. He never caught on. And that's how my cousin got enough money for her trip. And two more after that! She told him she won it at bingo when he asked her about it, and he believed her."

Amy looked at Zelda. "A maid is not a maid when she's the wife pretending to be the maid!"

"Exactly. I should have pulled that trick for my birthday cruise. Zack didn't want to pay for that, either. But then…" Zelda glanced up when Garda O'Shannon sighed heavily.

"I believe you two have gotten onto a bramble patch," he said quietly, but she could tell he was amused. "We have nothing to suggest she was here with anyone else. She checked in as a single guest. But I will say your observation about her dress is interesting. One of the staff complained of a uniform gone missing. She reported it to her manager and blamed it on one of the other maids who was let go recently. It is quite possible that what you say is correct.

"Still, I will warn you," he continued, his eyes moving purposefully from one to the other. "This is a serious investigation of a very serious crime. You are not qualified nor invited to meddle in the affairs of the Garda Síochána. We will find the culprit. And we will bring him or her to our justice. That is our job. Your job is to be a guest and only a guest enjoying your visit to Ireland. Keep your mischief to yourself, and I'll keep your passports safe to make sure you do!"

"What? You can't do that! We haven't given you reason to take our passports." Zelda narrowed her eyes. "You have no idea who you're dealing with. We're from Arkansas. If we don't want to keep our mischief to ourselves, no one is going to make us. And from what I hear, the Irish are a bit like that, too."

His eyebrows rose in surprise.

Zelda wasn't finished. "And furthermore, Amy has hunted down three — I said three husband killers — and one of them was on my birthday cruise!"

"A husband killer? Is that an American thing?"

Amy's face colored. "No, but it does seem to be our thing. Well, it's not exactly our thing so much as it seems to happen to us. A lot."

The Garda shook his head. "But this guest from the United States was not somebody's husband."

"No," Amy agreed cautiously. "She wasn't, but…" She stopped herself before she could add anything further because that's exactly what she was thinking. The maid wasn't somebody's husband, and that thought sent a shiver up her spine. Two rotten croquet balls had fallen to the ground. If the maid was one of them, that meant there was one more left.

# CHAPTER FOURTEEN

"I'll have a Bloody Mary," Gayle said to the barkeep who was letting the head set and settle on four pints of Guinness. Amy waited patiently on the bar stool beside her.

"With Clamato, if you please," Gayle added.

"I'm sorry. Come again?"

"Clamato. It's tomato and clam juice together. Makes one heck of a Bloody Mary."

The bartender shook his head. "Sorry, we don't have clams. The kitchen has fresh mussels today. Shall I drop a couple in your drink? Reckon it could be the next best thing."

Gayle made a face. "No, thanks. I'll take it ever however you make it."

The bartender nodded. "My pleasure." He began assembling the ingredients and Amy watched as he grated fresh horseradish over the ice, poured in a dash of lemon juice, hot sauce, Worcestershire sauce, salt and pepper and two jiggers of vodka before adding a can of tomato juice. And just before he topped it off with a stalk of celery, he added a healthy shot of Guinness. He beamed as he set the drink in front of Gayle. "My own recipe. The Guinness makes it sing."

Gayle took a sip and blew through her lips. "That would make anyone sing," she said brightly. "Quite a bite of horseradish."

"Too much?"

"Not for me. It's perfect."

"And for you?" He turned to Eloise.

"I think I'll have the same. I never get to have horseradish. Dick is allergic."

Gayle nodded and took another sip while the bartender busied himself with the drink.

"It sounds like Dick is allergic to everything," Gayle said.

Eloise sipped her drink before answering. "If you ask him he is. Anything he doesn't want to eat, drink or do — he's allergic. Especially around the house."

"Let me guess," Gayle said, now chuckling. "He can't mow the grass."

Eloise grimaced. "Not on your life. He complains the grass will give him hives." Eloise took another sip. "Of course, he never complains of hives after golfing."

"Must be another kind of grass," Gayle said lightly.

"Right," Eloise agreed. "The kind of grass you hire people to mow. That's more Dick's style. But he does have allergies and we have to be prepared should he have a reaction. His doctor says that even though he doesn't have a reaction to something one time doesn't mean he won't have a reaction to the same thing later. Vice versa. It's really quite limiting. If I find a nice new recipe to try, Dick's bound to complain. He's pretty much stuck on meat, potatoes and vegetable. That's the breadth of our menu. We do know he's allergic to seafood, so we just avoid it."

"I noticed he didn't eat much of his dinner tonight," Gayle said, obviously trying to be polite. "I guess mushrooms and lamb aren't the right meat or veg."

"What a shame because it was delicious," Eloise said. "Those mushrooms are called ceps. What a fun word to say. I found a cluster of them on the north side in the pines. I can see the pines from the window in my room. It made me wonder if juniper trees really do have berries. You know, the kind they use for gin. Of course, I had to take a walk to find out, and that's when I discovered the mushrooms. It appears to be part of the kitchen garden."

Eloise turned to her drink.

"Did you find them?" Gayle asked.

"What?" Eloise turned to Gayle with a surprised look. "Did I find what?"

"Did you find the berries? The juniper berries. Are they the real thing?"

"Oh, yes, the berries. The junipers are covered in them, but I don't believe they ripen until the fall."

The bartender moved the snacks in front of Gayle and Eloise and Amy recognized the basket Zelda had cruised through their first day in the hotel. Gayle and Eloise poked through the basket for their choices. Then Amy grabbed a bag of crisps with two of the beers. When she returned for the other two, Gayle and Eloise were talking about cooking shows and recipes.

Zelda took a frothy swig of her beer. "Wasn't he just the cutest thing you ever laid eyes on? I wonder if he'll be back anytime soon."

"Are you talking about Garda O'Shannon by chance?" Amy asked.

Zelda nodded enthusiastically. "I wonder if he's married. I'll have to ask him."

"He has grandparents your age," Genna said.

"He has grandparents *your* age," Zelda shot back. "If you're going to knock every fish in the Wild Atlantic, you need to keep it to yourself. I'll bait my hook as I see fit."

"No doubt," Genna replied. "And if he has brothers, uncles and cousins, be sure to invite them over for tea as well."

"That's not a bad idea," Zelda said, ignoring Genna's sarcasm. "We could ask Mona to host a croquet game and invite all the eligible men in County Cork. Wouldn't that be a hoot! It would be a feast for the eyes, for sure!"

"I have a better idea," Rian said. "Let's take a road trip and go Irish hunting. We can hit the pubs on the way to Limerick. We're bound to find every eligible gent in Ireland if we're looking in the pubs."

"I don't think that was politically correct," Genna said, eyeing Rian with surprise. "You of all people should …"

"Listen, if I was eligible, I'd be in a pub," Rian interrupted. "And pubs are quite useful for meeting people. Especially when hunting Irish ones."

"Touché," Genna agreed. "Tell us again who we're meeting in Limerick."

Gayle turned around from the bar. "Y'all are going to Limerick?"

"We were thinking about it," Genna said. "We're planning to rent a car and try our hand at driving on the wrong side of the road."

Rian cleared her throat. "I am going try my hand at it," she declared. "No one is letting Genna anywhere near the steering wheel."

"Just be that way," Genna replied smartly, but she was bluffing. She knew how Rian felt about her driving skills. She often ran afoul of something, whether it be a deer, a tree, or a rusty nail. "But I don't mind being chauffeured around."

"Me either," Zelda added.

"I don't know that I could get the hang of driving on the left," Amy admitted. "I'm afraid I'd be going the wrong way after a turn."

"I got this," Rian said. "You leave the driving to me. Amy can navigate."

"Amy always gets to navigate," Zelda complained.

"Your point?" Rian asked.

"My point is… well… never mind."

"Exactly. Amy is the only the one who can read a map."

"Yeah, but not in Irish," Amy admitted. "The signs are fifty letters long."

"What are you going to do in Limerick?" Gayle asked when their banter had reached a stopping point, and she could interject.

"I'm still looking for my Irish roots," Rian said. "I've got a lead on someone who might know about the O'Deis clan, and I want to ask some questions. We're only a couple hours away."

"Isn't that lovely," Eloise said. "You have roots in Ireland. I remember your saying something about that earlier. I do hope you find what you're looking for."

"I hope we find that Rian is heir to a castle," Zelda put in. "We could all come live in a fairytale."

Rian said," Don't pack your magic wand yet."

"Noted," Zelda agreed. "We don't want just any old castle. The one we walked through today was pretty dark and stinky."

"Hey, look," Amy said, spying a box on the game shelf in the corner of the pub. "There's a box of dominoes. We've never played dominoes in Ireland. It will be a first."

"So many firsts, so little time," Zelda said. "Mix 'em and draw 'em, Sparks. I'm game for a game."

Amy dumped the tiles on the table and spread out the pile. There was a nub of a pencil in the box and scratch pad of paper.

"You want to play?" Amy asked the women at the bar.

"Thanks," Gayle said, "but I promised James I'd let him row me to the middle of the lake to see that pair of swans. He's a hopeless romantic even if he does look like a human bulldozer."

"And I'm not much a game person," Eloise said. "I think I'll take a walk in the gardens and then settle in to read my book. Dick is always chiding me because I've read it so many times, but I can never seem to get enough. *A Tale of Two Cities.* Have you read it?"

Eloise smiled sorrowfully and when no one answered, she continued. "It's such a compelling story of oppression and redemption. And love as the ultimate sacrifice."

Gayle gave Eloise an odd look that Amy couldn't decipher, drained her glass and put a five euro tip on the bar. The drink charge would get added to the room. "Have fun tomorrow. Don't do anything too risky and don't do anything to embarrass us Arkansans." Gayle winked at Rian and she and Eloise left the bar.

Doris didn't answer when they knocked gently on her door a few minutes later. They had checked with the front desk to make sure they had the right room number.

"Shall I ring the room for you?" The desk clerk had asked.

"No, but thanks" Genna answered with a shrug. "We'll just go knock the old-fashioned way."

But Amy's soft knock had not been answered. And then neither was a more insistent clammer on the wood. They were just turning away when the door opened.

"Oh!" Doris exclaimed, eyeing the four of them in the hall. "I thought I heard a knock. I was in the shower. Do you need something?"

"We've come to invite you to go to Limerick with us tomorrow," Amy said. "Rian is taking us Irish hunting and we thought you would want to go."

"Irish hunting?"

"That's Rian's word for it. She's looking for the family O'Deis."

Doris touched the towel wrapped like a turban around her head and then glanced behind her. "I'm just..." Doris sputtered. "There's no..."

"We don't need to come in," Zelda said. "Just meet us in the lobby for breakfast. We'll leave shortly after."

Doris hesitated, then nodded. "Breakfast," she repeated. "Okay, well, until then," she said and gently closed the door.

"Toodaloo," Zelda said under her breath as the four of them faced the blank door. "That was a bit strange."

Amy's mouth tightened around a frown. Strange and stranger. She didn't know Doris well enough to know all of her idiosyncrasies, but she had never known her to be anything but kind and hospitable. "Something is not right," she said as the four of them turned to go.

"Do you think there was someone in the room with her?" Zelda's eyebrows rose under her dark bangs.

"No," Amy said. "She's married. Very, very married."

"We didn't ask her about the room next door. You think it's locked? We could take a peek inside." Rian rattled the knob, but it was locked.

The door to Doris' room opened again. Doris stuck her out of the doorway like a turtle peeking out her shell. "Oh!" She said, seeing them standing at the door next to hers. "You're still here!" She pushed her glasses up the bridge of her nose.

"What are you doing?" Genna asked.

"Me? What are you doing?" The turban had been removed and her hair combed out, but it was still wet from the shower. "Are you trying to get into that room?" She looked at Rian, whose hand was still inches from the knob.

"Is this the room where she was staying?" Amy asked.

Doris hesitated only a moment. "You mean that… maid?"

Amy nodded. "But of course, we know she wasn't a maid. She was a guest at the hotel pretending to be a maid."

"And not a spy," Zelda interjected.

Amy continued, "She was from the United States although I don't think they found her passport. The found her name on a luggage tag."

"I know," Doris said.

"How do you know?"

"I was listening at the door." Doris shook her head. "I shouldn't have, but I couldn't help it. The police were searching in her room."

"Really," Rian sounded incredulous. "You could understand them? Their brogue sounds like a foreign language to me."

"*Gaeilge* is a foreign language," Genna announced.

"*Gwal-gah?*"

"That's how you say it. I asked the barkeep."

They all looked at Doris expectantly.

"I didn't catch all of it, but the door was open, and I just happened to be standing here in my doorway."

Amy put her hands on her hips. "You just happened on purpose to be eavesdropping. Now you sound like us."

Doris shrugged. "It was exciting. I mean, in a horrible, horrible way. I knew I shouldn't be listening, but I couldn't make myself move away. It was as if my feet were glued to the floor."

"What did you accidentally on purpose hear them saying?" Zelda asked.

Doris glanced down the hallway, empty except for the four of them standing there with eager expressions. "What I understood was that someone had already searched her room."

"Well, if that's not spy stuff, I don't know what is," Zelda said with an exhale of satisfaction.

"Spy stuff?" Doris wrinkled her brow.

"No spy stuff." Amy turned to Zelda for emphasis. "Zelda has this romantic notion that the woman was a spy who didn't speak English. We have now debunked that theory."

"The romantic notion may be close enough," Doris said. "And that's what I should have told the police when they asked if I knew anything about this woman."

"Well?" Genna said abruptly when Doris failed to elaborate.

Doris frowned. "I guess it's okay to tell you."

"Of course, it's okay," Genna added. "You're one of us."

Doris nodded. "Someone came to her door the other evening and I'm pretty sure she let him in."

"It was a man?" Rian asked.

"He had a deep voice."

"Did you recognize it?"

Doris paused as if she wasn't going to answer.

"Doris?" Amy pleaded. "Did you recognize the voice?"

"I think it was Dick Collins," she whispered. "I didn't see him. But I smelled him when I came into the hall after he went into the room."

"Oh, for heavens sakes," Genna said. "You can't identify someone by the way they smell."

Doris looked offended. "I guess you're right. But it was a very distinct scent and I've smelled that cologne before."

Amy turned to Zelda. "When is a maid not a maid?"

"When she is Dick Collins' lover."

"What a rat," Genna said.

"Two rats don't make a right," Zelda added, and Rian sputtered.

"I'm guessing that whoever searched her room was looking for her identification so no one would know who she was," Amy said. "I think that's why the Garda wanted to see our passports."

"You already told the police you saw Dick talking to her."

Doris nodded. "When we came back from the croquet game that first day. She was standing by the stairwell, in that little room where the maids keep their supplies. Eloise had already gone up the stairs, and when Dick turned to go up, this woman reached out and grabbed his arm."

"Did you hear what they said?"

"Well, no, I was a bit embarrassed to be watching them, to be honest. He wasn't happy about seeing her. I could tell that."

"He sure didn't like that you told the police about it."

"I know," Doris said, a thin, rather smug smile lighting her face. "It's about time Richard Collins faces the music he's been playing for so long."

Amy nodded. "We need to find out who she was and why she was here."

"Like that's not obvious," Zelda said. "She was here for Dick."

Genna sputtered into laughter and then shook her head.

A movement caught Amy's attention and she glanced over her shoulder toward the lobby. The photographer seemed to be watching them, his ball cap lodged firmly on his head. His gaze shifted away when they turned, but she had the feeling he had been taking pictures of them. But why? Who was he? It was time to find out.

# CHAPTER SIXTEEN

"Why do you think Doris decided not to come with us?" Zelda asked, as the car zipped along the road that led to Limerick. Rian was in the driver's seat and Zelda had her fingertips gripping the headrest in front of her. Amy rode shotgun, with the map Mona had made for her clutched in her hands. It was a narrow country road but with no ocean in sight. If they needed to pull over to let another car pass, at least they wouldn't be staring down at the waves of the Wild Atlantic.

"I don't think she trusts us," Genna said from beside Zelda. "She's used to herding kids that mind their mother, and we're more like feral cats. Or cougars, as the case may be." Genna glanced at Zelda and today's choice in spots.

"She's going to miss out on the best adventure yet," Zelda added, ignoring Genna's comment. "No telling what we will get into hunting the Irish. I never thought of looking for ancestors as much of a quest, but we're going to find them, Rian. And what's more, we're going to discover you're a seventeenth century heiress or something as grand. I can feel it. I can feel luck in my bones."

Amy glanced at Rian. So far, so good. The trip would take them the better part of two hours if they didn't stop along the way, which was a zealous expectation. There would be towns to see and plenty of historic sites and views, all reasons to get out and stretch their legs. Mona had marked several options on the map. As it was, they followed long stretches of countryside dotted with green pastures and sheep with their ever-present splashes of color near their rump. They had learned that this was how farmers recognized their flocks from afar. Along the road were tall hedges of wild fuchsia, with their beautiful droopy blooms of brilliant pink. Amy knew this because they had stopped to look. Rian recognized the flower.

Amy brought up the maid once and was immediately shushed. She brought up the photographer and got three blank stares. No one wanted to explore either topic. If Doris was right, Dick Collins was in hot water with the Gardai. Sooner or later, they would find out that he had spent time with the maid, and he would have to confess why. She wanted to tell her friends about the scream in her strange snippet — if that's what it was — but there seemed no reason to bring it up out of the blue. And the sky was blue. An out of the ordinary blue. A fact that made the day perfect. And after all, the maid was the Gardai's problem. Today the Arkansas four were on an adventure.

"Could they make this any more complicated?" Amy asked, turning the paper sideways. "I don't recognize a single word on this map. And these road signs zip by so fast." The road had started with a solid white line down the middle, but at some point after that last jog to the left, the solid line disappeared, and the road narrowed to not much more than a country lane.

Their journey was not a straight line. Mona told them there were many turns in their destination to Limerick, and no stop lights or stop signs until they reached the city. Just like Bluff Springs. Except not like Bluff Springs, because the wayside markers were in Irish and kilometers, neither of which made much sense. The road went on and on and then all of sudden it would make a swift unannounced turn and a little town would pop up in the place where the roads met. The poles that held the road signs in the bend were stacked on top of each other like popsicle sticks pointing to towns in every direction.

"Did you see that?" Zelda asked, as they whizzed past a marker. "A toy soldier factory. Free admission. Only one in Europe. I didn't know we were actually in Europe. Did you hear me? I said they have toys. Right up your alley, Amy. We should stop."

"No more tea or coffee for you," Genna said. "You're chattering like a Chihuahua."

"Five km," Zelda added. "If we stop here, I won't say another word until we get to Limerick."

Amy chuckled. Like that could really happen. She liked listening to Zelda's enthusiasm bubble over. It was part of who Zelda was. The pot was always full. The rainbow always leading to something spectacular, whether you chased it or not. Zelda's optimism had pulled her out of the doldrums on more than one occasion and the chatter was part and parcel. She knew Rian was eager to get to Limerick and find the old man who knew the O'Deis, but she was also on an adventure with her best friends. There was much to enjoy along the way.

She couldn't believe it when a few miles down the road, Rian pulled in and parked.

The building was a humble stucco structure, similar to the houses they had seen along the way. The Irish didn't seem to go for that keeping up with the Jones idea. The structures were plain, mostly whitewashed stucco with bright painted trim, and enough windows to let in sunlight on a gray day. So far the trim colors had all been basic — red, blue, yellow, and green — the splash of color making them feel like happy homes. Some even had thatched roofs, which seemed cliche but magically wonderful at the same time.

The Toy Solider Factory was a long, low building with an elaborate painted mural covering the walls at the entrance. The four travelers posed for a selfie in front of the fire breathing dragon and then went in.

"Thirty minutes," Rian said, looking directly at Amy. "Thirty and then we're back on the road to Limerick."

Amy eyed the cases of metal figurines. There were tin soldiers and fairies, monsters, hobbits and orcs from J.R. Tolkien's *Lord of the Rings*. "How wonderful," she exclaimed as the elderly clerk approached. "I absolutely have to have this for Tiddlywinks!"

The woman smiled as their eyes met. "We are a true hidden treasure to Ireland," she said. "But we don't often attract visitors from the States. What brings you this way, now?"

"We're on our way to Limerick from Gougane Barra."

"Gougane Barra. Lovely place."

Amy nodded.

"Well then," the woman said, taking Amy by the elbow, "let me tell you the story of Prince August." She began the story of a popular Swedish craftsman who was a tin soldier mold maker that moved to this little town. For years he made tin soldiers, and the craft passed down through the generations. This location was now the only tin solider manufacturing facility in all of Europe, and they sold their casted figures to the four corners of the world. Everything in the shop was Irish made.

Amy swept the room with her eyes. They would be there for more than thirty minutes if the woman pitched her at every showcase, but she didn't want to offend her either.

"I have a toy shop in a little town in the United States," Amy said. "Believe it or not, our state looks very similar to your countryside. I would like to carry some of your pieces in my shop. Can you help me pick out the most popular? I could be here all day if were up to me, but I'm afraid we haven't much time to shop."

The woman's eyes sparkled. "I can and I shall," she said and together they pulled a collection from the shelves. All the while she told the story behind the figures as they moved through the shop. Amy added several do-it-yourself mold kits — mostly fairies and soldiers — and then she spied a wooden chess board with Tolkien-inspired characters from Middle-earth. The chess set would fetch a fair price at Tiddlywinks, and with a first-hand story of its origin to go along with it, it could only add to the sale. Perfect timing for holiday shopping. The counter now piled with her selections, she glanced at her watch. Rian would be motioning them toward the exit at any moment.

"Is there any way this could be shipped to the U.S.?"

"Of course. We post everywhere."

"This will be the first order of many, I promise." After negotiating a discount that included shipping, Amy produced her credit card and wrote down the shipping information.

Rian suddenly appeared beside her. "On the road, soldier," she said. "We have places to go, people to see."

"Nice catch," Amy said to Zelda when they were back on the road. "That was an unexpected find. But if I spend that much at every place we stop, I'm in trouble."

"You don't know what trouble is," Zelda said brightly. "But all the stuff you bought will be a great addition to Tiddlywinks. I didn't see anything that I couldn't live without, but I took lots of pictures of the mural outside."

Selfies, no doubt. Amy checked the map. "Turn right and then turn left, just up ahead," she said. "Oh, and there's a castle ruin not far from here. Mona's marked it on the map."

"Where isn't there a castle ruin," Genna said. "I think we should head toward Limerick and an early lunch. I'm getting peckish."

Zelda nodded. "Agreed. The castle we're most interested in seeing today is the one Rian inherits when she swoops in and claims her clan."

"Dream on," Rian muttered from the front seat, her eyes on the road.

The car was quiet as its passengers watched an unfamiliar world pass by. The mountains of West Cork had since faded to the distant horizon and the road rolled along with a countryside that was now quite flat. They drove through little towns, passed an ancient graveyard, even crossed a one lane bridge over a rumbling, peat-stained creek. The house on the edge of the water looked older than dirt, but it was painted a bright green, and laundry hung on the line in the side yard.

And so, the time passed. A slight right here, a slight left there, a fork in the road and another right. Always moving in a north, northeast direction. No wonder Mona had drawn such a detailed map. When the road finally turned due north, they had passed through only one major city. One legit city. It had an Aldi grocery, a Chinese restaurant, and at least four pubs.

After that, the country road finally gave way to a more typical highway — which meant two lanes and roundabouts— with cars zooming past. And then suddenly, it seemed, they were in the middle of civilization. Limerick rose before them as a bustling big city on both sides of the River Shannon. King John's Castle and riverside fortress rose from the skyline like a stage set for a medieval movie.

"Finally," Rian muttered. "I'm going to find a place to park, and we can walk from here. I don't think I can manage a city of this size behind the wheel."

"Fair enough," Genna said. "There's a big P," she said, pointing. "I think that means Parking lot, even in Ireland."

Rian found a spot and pulled in. She rubbed her hands on her jeans. "That drive was intense."

"So, where do we find this Paddy O'Shaughnessy you're looking for," Amy asked.

"Ask for him by name in any pub," Rian answered. "They'll know where to send us."

"You think they were pulling your leg with that name?" Genna asked.

"Probably," she agreed, "but I'm going to ask anyway."

"Wowza," Zelda said, turning in circles outside the car. "We could have stayed here and had the time of our lives. It's a whole lot different than our quaint little resort in the woods."

Genna motioned to Rian. "Lead the way. You're the one with the agenda."

They set off on foot up the rough brick streets toward the river, the noise of a city blaring around them. They didn't have to walk far.

"Nothing like putting yourself out there," Rian said, as she reached for the door of the pub. The flags of Ireland, the US, and Germany flew high outside the white building. Rian opened the door to Nancy Blakes and Amy blinked in the dark.

Rian ambled onto the bar stool. "I'm looking to find a man named Paddy O'Shaughnessy," she said.

The bartender shook his head. "What would you be wanting the likes of him for?"

"It's a long story and it's been a long drive," Rian answered.

"I have just the thing for that. An early pint of gat? And a day for nothing more."

Rian nodded, even if she wasn't sure what gat was.

"All the way down?" He asked eyeing the other three lining up at the bar. They nodded and then waited as the beers were drawn.

Rian took a long draught. "I've been told this Paddy O'Shaughnessy has knowledge about the men who went to America in the mid 1800s. They were rock masons," Rian added, getting right to the chase. "I'm related somehow but I can't find my direct roots. That's what I'm looking for."

"You and half the world be lookin' for their Irish beginnin's," he said. "No grand luck on those match-up websites, have you then?"

Rian shook her head. "You have to give them a DNA sample. I'm not willing to do that."

He raised a brow. "Wise," he uttered. "There is no telling what kind of conspiracy they would concoct to go along with it. Why, I heard tell of a man stayed hid for decades until his grown children found him out. On one of those sites. One of them DNA kin places, for sure. Not to my liking, either."

"You have any idea where I can find him?"

"Lass," he said. "There is no such Paddy. Or there are millions of such Paddys. You've been Irish-tricked. Someone pulling your leg for a laugh – away with the fairies, will ya. Just what clan would you be looking for?"

"My name is O'Deis."

"O'Dea? Well, your clan is all over County Clare. Turn any corner and you'll bump into them sure as I'm standing here breathing air."

Amy grinned at all the vowels and cadence.

"O d e i s?"

"O d e a."

Rian sighed. "That's the problem. It's not the same name."

The man stroked the bottom of his beard. "I think you're as close as you can get if I was adding the numbers. What's a few letters among kin? There's a place called Dysert O'Dea not far out from Ennis, County Clare. Right nice castle ruin and archaeology centre about the life of Clan O'Dea. It's only about an hour drive north. Menu?" He added. "You can't go traveling on an empty belly, now can you?"

Delighted with the suggestion, they took menus to a table.

"I know it's disappointing," Amy said. "Especially striking out on our first pub stop. But you had an inkling that would happen."

Amy glanced at Rian as she studied the menu. Rian had to be disappointed. She really did want to find her roots. She might have to acquiesce. DNA might be the only way to succeed.

"Fish and chips," Zelda said. "That sounds delicious."

When their food was delivered and they launched into it with vigor, the bartender strolled by with a look of intention.

"Old codger what comes in every day says he knows who you're looking for. Says he knows the whereabouts of a Paddy who clerked the Tithe Applotment Books until he retired an old man. Knows of the whole lot of masons who sailed to America in the time you say. The lot of them came from County Clare they did, to be sure. He's a hundred if he's a day."

Amy noticed Paddy had aged ten years since the last pub visit after the Blarney Castle. The locals in that pub claimed he was ninety if he was a day, then.

"Where do I find him?" Rian asked.

He shook his head. "You'd have better luck him finding you."

"Can I get a message to him?"

"I'll see," he said, and skittered off.

"That's progress at least," Amy said. "I'm sure he knows how to point you in the right direction."

He didn't have an answer, but they left phone a number, email, and address at the *Éire Óstán* along with a tip for great service. It was doubtful someone a century old would have interest in access to any of that, but there wasn't much else to do. There was a lot to do in Limerick, however, so they decided to wander through the streets before heading home.

"Where should we start?" Zelda said, eyes wide. "This is a big city."

"I have an idea," Genna said, motioning them forward "That looks like a walking tour gathering up ahead."

"I don't want to do a tour," Zelda complained. "It's too structured. Not enough window and shop browsing."

"I know that," Genna said, her long strides pulling her away. "But we can tag along behind them so we don't get lost, and if we want to, we can drop into anyplace we see that amuses us."

And so that's what they did. They tagged along a few steps behind the last stragglers in the tour, acting casual when anyone from the group glanced their way. But, other than the guide, who would know? He didn't seem aware they were following.

They passed a museum, a Catholic Church, a medieval ruins, and then came to the Treaty City Brewery. The four of them exchanged looks and parted ways with the tour.

The brewery wasn't medieval, but the building was close to it. They opted to forgo the two-hour brew tour and settled into the pub for a pint. "Looks like we're going to forgo the Treaty Stone," Amy said, opening the brochure she had picked up in the bar. "It's on the other side of the bridge." From the pictures, it looked like Excalibur should be sticking out in the top.

"I'm okay if we skip seeing a rock," Zelda said, flexing her legs. "We have plenty of those in Arkansas."

"It's a special rock," Amy explained.

"Ok, I'll bite," Genna said. "Make it good."

"It's why Limerick is known as the Treaty City," Amy paraphrased from the brochure. "It marks when William of Orange won accession from his father-in-law King James and the Catholics in Ireland were allowed to exercise their religion freely. He was married to Mary Stuart."

"As in Mary Stuart, Queen of Scots?"

"No," Amy said, scanning the brochure. "Wrong century. Mary Stuart number two."

"Well, good for her, "Zelda said, and sipped her beer. "I hope she had a good life."

Amy glanced at Rian, who seemed preoccupied. She had barely touched her beer. "Nowhere does it say Limerick is the home of Irish Coffee. Or Limerick lace. Or even JFK's great-great grandfather."

"I know what I know," Rian quipped. "It's where the name Fitzgerald came from. Somewhere in County Limerick. I looked it up on the guest computer in the library at the hotel."

"Speaking of lace," Zelda said. "I was hoping for a busy alley full of shops and more shops, but I haven't seen anything that's caught my eye."

Genna nodded. "Let's head to the car. My feet are killing me."

When they passed by the museum on their way to the car, the tour group was just returning from their walk. Amy walked over to the guide and slipped a hundred euro banknote into his palm. "You do a great job," she said and rejoined her friends.

# CHAPTER SEVENTEEN

Rian looked dejected when Paddy O'Shaughnessy hadn't materialized. They had stopped by Nancy Blakes pub before reaching the car, but the bartender had no message to give them. He drew a rudimentary map to the Dysert O'Dea Castle and encouraged them to make the journey. "It's only about an hour," he said. "You'll get there in plenty of time to look about."

"We have to go," Amy said. "If you don't do this now, when will we ever have the chance to do it again?"

That settled it. When they stopped for gas, Amy bought a map. Armed and ready to navigate, they headed north by northwest.

The journey toward Ennis was a different drive, passing towns along the way. After at least a dozen roundabouts, they landed on an isolated country lane. The green pastures stretched across the horizon, and the mountains looked like low, dark clouds at the edge of the world. The car bounced onto a worn track, flowering weeds and dainty yellow flowers brushing the undercarriage of the car. Dry stack rock walls bordered them on both sides of the road until they reached a gate and turned in. O'Dea Castle rose some fifty feet from the ground.

"Does it feel like home?" Amy asked, as they left the car.

Rian was silent.  It was not as large as the Blarney castle in Co. Cork, although it had the same castle-fortress shape as it climbed the sky to meet the clouds that had gathered overhead.

Rian stood at the rock wall looking up at the lone flag fluttering at the top. Amy could sense the quiet rush of her inner craving. Was this where it all began? Could this be a possibility? Were these Rian's roots, her beginnings?

Amy glanced at her friend and recognized the deep wonder in her dark brown eyes. She had felt this feeling herself standing in front of the medieval ruins of Limerick. It was a stirring of something ancient embedded in the evolutionary codes of humanity. It resurfaced here as she stood in the shadow of this monolith surrounded by peace. Gone was the noisy city living in modern time. Gone was the hustle of the people on their way to work. Even the sheep in the fields were quietly grazing. It nearly took her breath away. Not because of the majestic views, but because it was ancient. Because it was real. Because it was standing here as proof of history. Proof that humanity advanced from one era in time to another. Year after year. Century after century.

Bluff Springs had recently celebrated its 150th birthday, and here she was looking at a structure five times older. Six centuries had come and gone since these stones were raised. Castles were built to make a stand, to carve ownership of a land and defend it. All to build a people, a clan, a way of life. And here this stood. Still. Even if it wasn't Rian's specific place of origin, it was the genesis all the same.

It was dark and cool inside the castle walls. A few furnishings and artifacts had been gathered to recreate time and place, resurrected with love and toil from a time long since passed. Found in near ruins mid-century, the castle was purchased by an American tourist, John O'Day. Nearly a decade later, its restoration began. By 1988, the building was opened to the public as an interpretive center, with its history researched and restored for curious visitors.

It was a labor of love. A labor of heritage and hermitage, just like the name. Dysert. The hermitage of the clan Deá.

Even Zelda was quieted by the hallowed ambiance. She followed in silence as they walked the grounds with its monuments of historic interest, the remains of the monastic site of St. Tola's Church, and the cross of the crucifixion facing the east. Amy watched as Rian stood before the stone.

"I feel odd." Rian's voice was thick with emotion. "I feel like I'm standing with one foot in this world and one foot in another. I feel like I should say a prayer or something profound. Nothing comes to mind."

"Hail Mary," Genna offered. "That's your go-to."

"Hail Mary," Rian echoed with a nod. "And Amen."

# CHAPTER EIGHTEEN

Amy unfolded the map. "Hey, we're not even an hour away from the Cliffs of Moher. It would be a shame to come all this way and not see them."

"The Cliffs of Moher," Genna exclaimed. "That's on my bucket list!"

Zelda huffed. "Everything is on your bucket list."

Genna turned to Zelda. "The Cliffs of Moher are only the most famous cliffs in Ireland."

"Only the most touristed spot in Ireland," Rian piped up. "Tourists come by the bus full."

"What will we do there?" Zelda asked.

"I don't know," Genna answered, her tone getting testy. "I guess we walk along the edge and look at the Atlantic Ocean. Take pictures. Zen out and listen to the birds."

"The birds?"

"The Puffins." Genna added. "Puffins are those cute little birds that resemble penguins. Like the ones we saw in the Galápagos Islands. The cliffs are home to the magnificent seven. Although I have no idea why."

"You're getting your stories scrambled," Zelda said. "*The Magnificent Seven* was a movie starring a young and dreamy Yul

Brynner, Steve McQueen, and Charles Bronson. Don't you remember?"

"No," Genna answered. "In Ireland, the magnificent seven has something to do with birds."

Zelda frowned. "I'm not all that into birds."

Genna raised an eyebrow. "I've heard they serve cocktails once you reach Hags Head. Can you be into that?"

Zelda nodded.

Amy shook her head. Genna certainly gave the word *bluff* new meaning. There were no bars on the Cliffs of Moher. There was nothing but rock and sea, but Zelda didn't need to know that. Better to let her think cocktails and a nosh were in store after a long, windy walk.

Having read about the Cliffs of Moher before their trip, she had stumbled across ancient myths of mermaids and mystical creatures from the sea. The cliffs were steeped in history about warriors and witches and giants who climbed from one island to the next like steppingstones in a river.

"Which way, Amy?" Rian asked, as they approached another roundabout. Rian was getting the hang of driving on the left side of these narrow roads, and then staying to the left in the roundabout lanes. She certainly seemed more at ease than when they started out this morning.

Amy looked at the map, turned it once and then turned it again. "To the left," she said, pointing. "Yes, left. I think," she added, as the car rounded the curve and skittered off onto the lane. The city traffic dispersed, and another country road stretched before them. Talk of the Cliffs of Moher with cocktails at Hags Head settled into silence as the car zipped along.

"Hey, look," Zelda said as the shore vista came into view some minutes later. "It's the Wild Atlantic. It sure doesn't look very wild. Looks more like a lazy river to me. Where are the cliffs? I don't see cliffs."

True enough, they were driving alongside a flat body of water, but there was a bank on this side of the water and a bank on the other. A fleet of sailboats was moored offshore. Amy frowned. This wasn't ocean.

"Wait," Rian said, looking briefly at Amy. "What direction are we supposed to be going?"

"Due west," Amy said. "The Cliffs are at the west edge of Ireland."

Rian pointed to the indicator above the rearview mirror. "We're going southwest. Are you sure this is the right way?"

Amy glanced at the map in her hands. "We should be on National Road 85. N85. Is that the road we're on?"

Rian frowned. "You're the navigator. Are we on N85?"

Amy turned the map sideways and then turned it again. She traced a finger down from Ennis in Co. Clare to the first body of water she came to on the map. River Shannon. It was indeed southwest of Ennis, and not anywhere near their destination.

"Oh, no. That's the River Shannon. We're headed in the wrong direction."

"Nice job, navigator," Genna muttered. "Now, I'll never get to see the Cliffs of Moher."

"Oh, don't be so glum," Zelda warned. "It's not like we have never gotten lost before. I remember when you…"

"Put a sock in it," Genna snapped.

Zelda pressed her lips closed and folded her arms across her chest. The leopard spots grew large and then shrunk as she moved.

Amy glanced at Rian. "By the look of it, there's nothing but river until we get to the sea."

"And how far is that?"

Amy glanced at the map and exhaled. "I don't know. I can't tell. Wait, there's a ferry landing ahead."

"A fairy landing? These Irish and their winged creatures," Genna muttered. "What is so doggone special about fairies?"

"Not that kind of fairy," Amy said. "Ferry, as in boat."

"A ferry!" Zelda exclaimed snapping out of her pout. "The kind you can put a car on?"

"Where does the ferry go?" Rian asked.

Amy glanced at the map once more. "Across the River Shannon."

"To where?" Genna growled.

"Uhm, to a place called Tarbert."

"They'll have cocktails in Tarbert," Zelda said. "Won't they?"

It was Genna's turn to pout. She folded her thin arms across her chest and sat against the seat. "Whatever," she mumbled.

Rian and Amy exchanged glances and then Rian shrugged.

"It's too late in the day to retrace our steps, Genna," Rian said over her shoulder. "We'll have to come another time."

Amy turned and looked at a scowling Genna as Rian turned into the entrance, following the signs to the Shannon Ferries at the Port of Killimer, and then pulled into the car queue.

Zelda rolled down the window and noisily breathed in the wet, sea air. "This is so much better than walking."

The trip across the Shannon estuary would take a scant twenty minutes. The sky had gotten cloudy since they left the blue skies of Dysert O'Dea, and the wind was blowing across the bow of the ferry with brisk speed. The river stretched its long tongue to the east and to the west. Dark  green water churned beneath the bow as the ferry called the *Shannon Dolphin* chugged along on its watery path toward the other side.

Amy faced into the wind, remembering when they were on the bow of *The Darwinian*. She remembered how the famous Galapagos Dolphins were leaping alongside the ship on either side, with the sun setting in front of them and the moon rising behind. Genna had been in a foul mood then, too, but it was hard to stay angry when such picturesque majesty lay before them. The

Galapagos Dolphin had worked its magic then and Genna's anger vanished. She hoped this "dolphin" would do the same.

She leaned into the wind like a nautical figurehead on the bowsprit of a boat. The wind roared in sharp biting blasts and then something whispered into ear.

*Love leaves a memory no one can steal. And they will try. Oh, but they will try.*

And just as sudden, she was reminded that they had come to Ireland, and murder had followed them here.

# CHAPTER NINETEEN

"Cafe Open!" Zelda sang as they neared a stately rock building and the colorful sandwich board sign out front. Rian pulled in and parked. Zelda was the first out of the car.

"Welcome to Tarbert Bridewell Courthouse and Jail Museum," the woman announced as they entered the dark room. "Will you be wanting the tour?"

Zelda nodded. "First, we'll be wanting a tall cold one in your cafe. Touristing makes me very thirsty."

"Oh, dear. Our cafe has but coffee, tea and baked sweets. And that is a bit plucked over at this time of day."

Zelda's face fell.

"Oh, dear," she said again. It was clear the woman was eager to please. "You can get a pint up the road, there." She pointed in some direction Amy couldn't see. "You won't fail to see it. It is as bright as the day is long. A short walk. Not even a ramble. Just there." She pointed again and then her eyes moved to Amy. Her eyes crinkled into a smile and then dropped to Amy's chest. Amy felt her face flush as she reached for her necklace. The woman's gaze was there. Amy touched the cool silver of the Celtic knot and then rubbed the peridot and tiny diamond.

"Our last tour is four t'irty," the woman said kindly, her eyes still on Amy. "You won't want to leave us without knowing the history of the Bridewell, you won't. There was many a soul whose lives turned a corner in this very spot. Lives were made. Lives were ruint." She glanced once more at Amy's necklace. "Lives were changed forever, you'll see. You'll want to know all about it. Buy your tickets now? Only five euro each for a step back in time."

Amy volunteered a twenty to the counter, suddenly feeling drawn to this woman with deep hazel eyes. The woman's hair was the similar shade of copper that Amy tried so hard to tame. She had gotten used to seeing so many redheads in Ireland, but there was something oddly familiar about this woman. She couldn't pinpoint it, but she was mesmerized by her gaze. It was a peculiar feeling that made her slightly uncomfortable, and yet, she wanted more.

"Four t'irty," the woman repeated. "Last tour. I'll be waiting to show ya."

The Swanky Bar was, as the woman had indicated, impossible to avoid. It rose from the side of the road like a giant sunflower anchored in a nautical-blue painted pot. Sports, beer, darts, and food all day were promised by the signs decorating the front of the building, although the frames of the mullion windows were draped in white lace curtains.

Rian pointed to the mural painted on the wall. "There's nothing like a Guinness at the Swanky."

"Swanky it is," Zelda said, opening the door. "You can't go wrong with lace curtains and a pool cue."

The Swanky was a lot different than Nancy Blake's in Limerick. For starters, the decor was far from trendy. The tables and chairs were a hodgepodge of cast offs, with well-worn seats and tabletops scarred with cigarette burns and beer rings. It looked relatively clean, and it smelled like something wonderful was cooking behind the scenes. She also noticed the dialect of the chatter had shifted. Limerick had one sound. This had another. She had learned that Irish county accents were as different to the regions as they were in the States. You wouldn't call Texas and Arkansas the same southern drawl if you knew better. You wouldn't consider New York and Pennsylvania the same Yankee brogue.

And last but not least, she noticed the locals seemed to have no shy bones when it came to belting out into song. One person would start singing and before long, the whole bar was singing along. This crowd obviously enjoyed their afternoon after work. Pints of beer arrived quickly, and Amy kept an eye on the time. She didn't want to miss the tour. They left after two pints, but not before Zelda had joined some gentleman who was crooning Frank Sinatra tunes.

*"I did it my waaaay,"* a tipsy Zelda sang as they walked to the museum. They were the last tour and the only participants.

"The name Bridewell comes from the workhouse located near Saint Bride's Well in London," the woman explained as she opened a rusty-looking gate with an old-fashioned skeleton key. The gate grated on its hinges with a loud groan and somehow, Amy knew that was done on purpose. It set an eerie stage.

"All the prisons of Ireland were named Bridewell. We have the Crown to thank for this." The guide's expression looked doubtful. "During this era, there were some fifteen Bridewells named after their town. They weren't really workhouses, and they weren't really prisons. They were certainly ill luck for those remanded to its cells. Any manner of things could get you sentenced to a few days or more. No trial per se. If you were arrested you were assumed guilty and the guilty came here to be sentenced and sent away.

The door clanged shut behind them.

"The prisoner's day was regulated by the ringing of bells. The day began at six," she said.

Zelda jumped when a bell rang overhead.

"There was no reason for their day to begin as such. They did not break their fast until nine. They had nothing to do but await the swift execution of justice and the cruel punishment of nineteenth century Ireland." She paused. Another bell sounded. A light flickered on. Now in the spotlight was a bedraggled looking man hunched over a metal bowl, his grimy hand gripping a dirty cup.

"Such was his lot," the guide said, motioning to the waxy looking mannequin in rags. "He was accused of willful trespass and spends his days awaiting trial. Always awaiting trial."

The light went out with a click and another light came on. The spotlight exposed a courtroom drama in full session, complete with an audio of garbled and stilted voices seeming to come from the mannequins of well-dressed statesmen, a jury of angry peers, and one forlorn accused.

The group moved through the exhibits, half in the dark, half in the hot white spotlight, with the audio of horror droning on in the background. It was a chilling and sobering experience. Nineteenth century Ireland was no picnic for the poor.

"This would be one heck of a place to have a Halloween party," Genna said, chuckling under her breath. "You'd have people paying to get out of here!"

"Before I tell you the story of Elva Gráinne and her newborn babe, I want to share something that's not ordinarily seen on this tour. No doubt you can sense in the very marrow of your bones that Tarbert Bridewell has a long and haunting history. It is not uncommon for items to fall from a shelf without purpose or vanish from sight altogether." The woman turned a corner and opened another door. "Just last night we had a group of paranormal investigators in from Dublin. They came together in this very room."

Amy jumped as the wailing on the audio continued in the hall.

"We held a seance. With crystals and Ouija Boards and mediums with glassy dark eyes and metal rods that vibrate in the presence of a spirit." She pushed the door closed behind her and Amy felt the cold rise at her feet.

"I have worked here many years and never have I felt such a chill in my heart as last night. The cold crept in and grew up my legs like a winter wet fog. And there," the guide said, pointing to the window, "there is where we saw handprints on the glass. Handprints as such was made by ice, the crystals bursting into a thousand tiny veins."

Amy shivered. She knew it was the reaction the woman was hoping for.

"They come with great respect, these investigators of the dead. They honor the departed. Come with an offer to help if they can. Come hoping to cross them by. Some spirits go peacefully. And some will not. Those spirits will clang on the bars. They will push and they will shove. They will wrap their cold hands around the heart until you cannot take a breath."

She eyed Amy with dark eyes. "Some see the departed. Some hear them speak." She glanced at Amy's necklace and instinctively, Amy rushed to touch the stone.

"Which are you? Do you see? Or do you hear?"

Amy felt stunned into silence. "I — I," she stuttered.

"Come now," the woman said. "It is one, or it is the other."

"I dream," Amy whispered.

The woman nodded. They were not alone in the room, but it felt to Amy that she and this woman were the only two people there. She looked for her friends standing behind her, watching her with quiet interest. No one said anything, but Genna was right, this would be a spooky place for a party. And a horrible place to have a snippet.

The woman opened the door and the air shifted upwards a few degrees.

"Elva Gráinne wore such a charm." She pointed to Amy's necklace. "T'was her family crest. They were a clan of seers who came down from the mountains at Samhain to celebrate the harvest. And once full with child, the women returned to the mountain caves where they lived. And so, this is how they grew their clan.

"One day Elva came down from the mountain with her babe to aid an old friend who was dying ill at ease. Accused and captured for trespassing, Elva was brought here to await her fate. She was tried and found guilty. She pleaded mercy for her life and that of her child, but she was transported none-the-less."

Amy was transfixed. "Transported? Where did she go?"

"Australia, say some. The Americas, say others. Still some claim she disappeared in a puff of peat smoke."

Amy's eyes widened in the dark. The woman reached into her own collar and pulled out a necklace. It was a small silver Celtic knot inlaid with an emerald stone and a small glittering diamond. "This is the crest of Gráinne. The word for Grace. The rising sun. Every first born is named Elva or Ailbhe, as we say."

"That sounds so much like Ollie! That's my grandmother's name. She's the first born!"

The lantern on the shelf above them rocked violently and then toppled to the floor at their feet. Zelda screeched and grabbed for Amy's arm with sharp leopard painted nails.

"Ow!" Amy yelped.

"Yow!" Zelda echoed. "Get me out of here!"

# CHAPTER TWENTY

"What in the world happened to you?" Amy gawked at the pitiful figure of Dick Collins sitting in an armchair in the hotel lobby. He had one shoe on and one shoe off, his khakis rolled up to the knee on one trouser leg. That leg, resting on the upholstered ottoman, was covered in a compression wrap that ran from mid-calf down to his toes, which were already turning purple. His face and lips were so swollen that his dark eyes were like two slits in a piggy bank. His hands were flesh colored boxing gloves.

"*Mmmer hamble mamber,*" he answered, his puffed lips never separating from each other. He held a glass with his puffed up mitts and fumbled the straw to his lips, grimacing with every move. At least it looked like a grimace.

"Oh my!" Zelda said, arriving behind Amy. She eyed Dick with a sympathetic frown. "You don't look good."

Dick shook his head and his piggy bank eyes disappeared. He thrust the glass out in front of him.

"More?" Amy asked, although the glass was clearly not empty.

He shook his head and groaned. Amy took the glass and set it on the table beside him. It was then that Mona came out of the bar with a bag of ice. She draped it over his ankle and Dick snatched at it before it could slide off, groaning as he leaned forward.

"*Memmer!*" He pressed the ice against his eyes and leaned back in the chair.

"I can get you another one for your face," Mona said. "You really do need to ice that ankle. I don't know what to do about your hands. Are you comfortable enough?"

"*Memmer bamble!*"

Mona turned to Amy and her friends. "I'm glad you've returned safely. Thanks for calling to let us all know where you were. Our roads can be right confusing. Even locals get turned about. I was fretting that something bad had happened. I know Mrs. Brand was pacing the floor."

They had stayed overnight in Tarbert at a local hotel that turned out to have great food and even better music, complete with dancers making a lot of noise on the wooden floor. Good craic. Too many pints after their brush with the strange and supernatural at the jail museum had made the stay over an easy decision. The morning ride to the resort through the countryside of Kerry had been beautiful and blissfully quiet. They stopped for lunch at a cute little cafe on the side of the road, and then spent an hour in the shoppes near Killarney National Park. Zelda was appeased. Genna was still grumbling about the Cliffs of Moher, but a shopkeeper in Killarney claimed the Kerry Cliffs were even better. There was less traffic. Definitely fewer tourists. By the time they finally drove up the drive to the resort, Amy felt as if they had traveled half of Ireland. And yet, she knew they had seen very little of the Emerald Isle.

Mona put her hands on her hips. "As for Mr. Collins here, I understand he took quite a hopper on the stairs. I'm not sure how to get him to his room unless the paramedics will carry him up when they get here. He needs to rest in the quiet."

And not be left in the lobby to moan is what Amy guessed Mona left unsaid.

"What happened to him?" Genna asked.

"We're not certain," Mona answered, nodding at the man behind the ice pack. "It's only happened just now."

Dick peered at them through slitted eyes.

"As best as we can tell," Mona continued as if talking about someone not in the room, "Mr. Collins tripped on the stairs and tumbled down into the lobby." She paused and glanced at Dick. "He must have made quite a racket because one of the maids came out to see what was going on. The front desk was on a break and the concierge was helping a guest elsewhere, so it may have been some time he lay there."

*"Mmmer hamble mamber!"*

"Why are his hands and face swollen?" Rian asked, peering from around Genna's long, thin arms akimbo.

"And where is Eloise?" Genna added.

"I don't know," Mona answered. "Mrs. Collins doesn't appear to be in her room and her mobile is not connecting. We've tried to call her with his mobile, but it just rings steady. As to the swelling of his face, I haven't been able to translate his…"

*"Mmmer bamble bember!"*

"I don't know what that means," Mona whispered to Amy with a distressed look on her brow. "Do you understand what he's saying?"

"No idea, but I think he has allergic reactions to certain things. Maybe he ate something that made his face and hands swell."

Dick lowered the bag of ice and glared at Amy. At least it looked like a glare.

Mona continued. "I've managed to stitch together this much. The concierge claims both Mr. Collins and Mr. Brand arranged a tee time for shortly after breakfast this morning, but only Mr. Collins showed up to collect his gear." Mona lowered her voice. "The concierge said Mr. Collins was particularly annoyed that Mr. Brand wasn't on time and made a spectacle with his impatience. He left without waiting.

"Well, it wasn't more than a half hour or so later that he came zooming in on the golfing buggy, hollering all through the lobby that his hands were on fire. He was wearing his golfing gloves, you see, and he kept trying quite unsuccessfully to pull his hands free. The front desk clerk ended up cutting them off with a pair of shears. And then Mr. Collins blasted on about how she had ruined his expensive gloves! She was a frightful mess of nerves, she was."

Amy glanced at Dick. If he was listening to Mona recount his bad behavior, he wasn't showing remorse. His piggy bank eyes were closed.

"Well, then he must have gone upstairs to his room and tripped on his way down," Amy said.

Mona nodded. "It would seem so."

"So, what are you going to do?" Zelda asked.

Mona shrugged. "The hotel manager is not on the property today, so I am to wait here for the paramedics to arrive. I don't know what they expect to do differently. Haul him off to hospital for a scan, I guess, but I don't think he has broken bones. Although he did howl like a devil while I was wrapping his ankle. I'm not a paramedic, but I knew to get his ankle elevated and iced.

"I hope Mrs. Collins returns soon," Mona added. "She couldn't have gone far. Could she?"

It was Amy's turn to shrug, but the question definitely made her feel uncomfortable. That deep down dread in your belly kind of disquiet. What if something bad had happened to Eloise? What if she was lost? Or injured? Or worse. The death scene flashed in her mind. The scene with the maid who wasn't a maid — not even a spy— but probably Dick Collins' romantic secret that had registered as a guest of the hotel. Except that now she was… dead. Amy glanced at Rian with alarm. Rian nodded.

"I think we should go look for Eloise," Rian said. "Maybe she went for a walk in the woods."

"Or maybe she went to the chapel," Amy offered.

"We should all go look for her," Zelda said. "It's the least we can do."

"It's the least we can do," Genna repeated without much conviction, as she eyed the distressed man in the chair. "I do think the swelling is going down a little, though. At least he's not going to die."

Dick opened his eyes. The slits were getting a little wider.

"Did you trip on something coming down the stairs?" Amy asked.

Dick shook his head.

"You mean you were pushed?" Zelda exclaimed. "By who?"

"Whom," Genna muttered. Zelda shot her a look.

Amy sat down in the chair beside him, and the slits followed her. The taut skin around his eyes was beginning to loosen but his lips were still swollen. It reminded her of the split and swollen lip she had suffered after crashing Zack's Hummer at Blind Bat Pass. When she awoke from the crash and a dark, deep sleep, she was somewhere strange and unrecognizable. Even if she had been able to speak with a fat lip, there had been no one there to hear.

Amy touched Dick's arm and said softly, "Why would someone push you down the stairs?"

Dick opened his mouth, and the words were little more than a croaky whisper. "Trying to… kill… me," he muttered on an exhale of breath.

The room grew quiet. She could hear the whirr of the fan blades overhead and the whooping honk of the swans somewhere far out on the lake.

Mona stared at him in disbelief and then looked at each of them in turn as if looking for moral support. "T'is a serious accusation you make," she said quietly. "Especially after what happened to the other guest from…" She let her words trail off without finishing them. "I'm not sure how to process this at the moment," she continued. "But I think I need to call the Gardai."

"Oh, puhlease," Genna wheezed like an accordion as she shook her head at Dick. "Dick tripped and fell down the stairs. He can't always be blaming everyone else for life's little mishaps."

"Genna!" Zelda exclaimed. "You can't say that out loud. Even if it is true!"

Dick glared at Genna, his mouth twitching slightly under the weight of two fat lips. "Bees," he croaked finally. "My. Room."

"There were bees in your room?" Mona asked with surprise.

"Allergic," he whispered.

"You told us you were allergic to bees," Amy said, remembering the conversation on the croquet green. "Were you stung?"

He shook his head. "Had to. Get. Away." Dick motioned with his hands, flailing as if he were swatting at a swarm of bees.

"Oh, I see," Amy said. "You were trying to get away from the bees and you tripped. But wait, your room is near the end of the hall. You said you tripped on the stairs?"

"Running down," he said. It sounded more like *bubbing bown*. "I was. *Bushed*."

"Pushed? You are quite certain?" Mona's voice was stern, and Amy was surprised at the change in her tone. Dick Collins was testing her patience today. She didn't sound like the cheery social director who had led them to the putting green for cookies and croquet on their first outing.

"You are certain of this," Mona repeated.

Dick sighed. "No." It sounded more like *Bo*.

Mona sighed audibly. "You tripped trying to get away from the bees. No one pushed you."

Dick didn't respond. His attention moved to the window at his shoulder, the crunch of gravel alerting them to an arrival in the drive. A van pulled up and stopped. A siren bleeped once and then died. Mona rushed to the door and Amy rushed to window beside Dick. The medics were climbing out of the van and Amy recognized the Garda who pulled up behind them and stepped from the car.

The medics rushed in and took over. She and the others stood out of the way, out of ear shot of the subject, but close enough to watch, listen, and ponder. He wasn't stung or he would have felt it. And something else caused his hands and face to swell. Had he really been attacked and pushed down the stairs? It seemed unlikely. And yet, there were two black croquet balls on the ground. Two rotten ones. And Dick Collins was definitely rotten.

"He sure has reacted to some allergen," Amy said to Mona. "It was probably something he ate or drank. I wonder what it was. I wonder if he even knows."

"We didn't get that far yet," Zelda said. "We only managed to figure out that he tripped while running to escape the bees. Even if he doesn't want to admit being clumsy on the stairs."

"It could happen to anyone," Mona offered. "What I don't understand is why the bees were in his room."

"Good point," Amy said. "Perhaps the bees came in from an open window."

"I guess it's possible." Mona didn't seem too committed to her words. "Why would he think someone was trying to kill him?"

"Drama," Genna answered, drawing the word out with her slow southern style. "If macho man goes flying down the stairs only to bounce like a golf ball all the way to the bottom, he's sure not going to say it was his own two feet that got in the way. Better to claim killer bees were after him. Better to claim killer bees pushed him down the stairs."

Rian chuckled.

Genna said, "You're picturing that aren't you, Rian?"

"What I'm picturing are those two slit eyes and a pancake mouth. That really has to be uncomfortable. You can't say that was drama."

"Drama with a big dose of Dramamine."

"You mean Benadryl?" Zelda asked. "Isn't that what you take for allergies?"

"Same thing," Rian said. "More or less."

Amy believed Rian. She was a walking RX. "Well, it could be almost anything.  Eloise said he's color deficient — to use his vernacular — which is the politically correct term, I assume. He can't tell red from green and vice versa.  He could have mistaken a red tube of face cream for a green tube of sunscreen and smeared it all over his face. Or something like that."

Rian shook her head. "Wouldn't he read the labels? Especially if he's allergic?"

"Good point," Amy answered. "But I also remember Eloise saying that Dick couldn't match his socks without her help. He's seems quite dependent on his wife's willingness to keep his life in order. Or at least keep his colors in order."

"Did you know Paul Newman was color blind?" Zelda asked casually, as if they were chatting over cocktails in the pub. "He wanted to be a Navy pilot and wound up being famous instead. Just like that. They won't let you pilot a plane if you can't tell port red from starboard green."

"Why do you know that?" Rian asked.

"Oh, let me guess," Genna interjected. "Husband number two was a pilot."

"Close but no cigar," Zelda said. "It was number three." Zelda plunked an imaginary piece of lint from her leopard spotted sleeve. "It runs in the family, you know."

"Being a pilot?"

"No silly, color blindness. His uncle was, too, and he turned out just like Paul Newman."

"His uncle was a movie star?" Amy asked.

"What is wrong with y'all today?" Zelda complained. "Can't you follow a simple train of thought?"

The three of them looked at each other and then burst out laughing.

"Got it," Amy said, gaining her composure. "A simple train of thought."

"Yes it was," Zelda declared as if defending herself from a terrible insult, but with a familiar twinkle in her eyes. "He really was handsome," she added and grinned.

"Paul Newman?"

"My husband," Zelda declared, her tone dripping with mock impatience. "But I agree. Paul was handsome, too."

"Wait," Amy interjected. "Didn't Eloise say Dick had a helicopter?"

"She didn't say he flew one," Rian added. "Just that he had one."

"I can't see any reason to have one if you can't fly one," Genna declared.

"Maybe he found a loophole," Zelda offered. "It wouldn't be the first time, I'm sure."

"Maybe your pilot information is out of date," Genna suggested.

"Are you saying I'm old?" Zelda spat back. "Because you've been 49 and holding for a decade. At least. And that's not even counting the decades before we met."

By this time the paramedics had made their examinations and took Dick's vitals. They had unwrapped his ankle, assessed the damage and bound it again. After going through a litany of nods and negatives, they gave him a shot. The swelling in his face and hands was already diminishing. Dick Collins was beginning to reappear before their eyes. He declined the one-hour trip to the hospital for X-rays and when the subject of getting him up to his room came up, he demanded that someone check for bees.

"I'm not going to my room until the bees are gone," he thundered, now seemingly recovered from his earlier inability to speak.

"I'll check," Mona volunteered.

"I'll go with you," Amy said.

"We'll go look for Eloise," Rian said. "She has to be on the property somewhere."

## CHAPTER TWENTY ONE

"I don't know what to do," Mona said as they approached the landing to the second floor. "I planned a game of blacklight croquet for this evening but now that Mr. Collins is injured, I'm wondering if I should cancel it."

"Maybe you could postpone it until tomorrow. Maybe by then he'll feel up to it."

"You're right. He'll be as right as rain by tomorrow," Mona agreed. "I do hope he recovers quickly so he can enjoy the rest of his stay."

"What's blacklight croquet anyway?"

Mona clasped her hands in front of her. "Oh, it's where all things glow in the dark of a UV light! We really enjoy it when the weather turns Baltic. Guests don't want to get out in that."

As they climbed the stairs to the second floor, Mona shared the backstory on the game room she had been given the permission and budget to build. The resort was miles away from nightlife, so a converted barn next to the garden shed became a game room slash night club. There was a disco ball and DJ station for dancing and karaoke, but the blacklight croquet court was her pride and joy.

"I can't wait to show it to you," Mona added. "You're going to love it. It's so Alice in Wonderland. You seem like an Alice in Wonderland kind of person."

What kind of person would that be?

Before she could ask what Mona meant, they were inside the Collins' suite. The scent of men's cologne was strong, and it looked like someone had gone berserk inside the room.

"Janey Mac!" Mona exclaimed. "This room's in bits! I need to get the maid to tidy before we bring up Mr. Collins."

The bed pillows were tossed on the floor in front of them. A towel lay spread over the rug, a crease running up the middle as if a shoe had caught the edge in a frenzy to get away. One of the lamps was hanging from the bedside table by its electric cord, the bulb shattered into sharp pieces on the floor. The bed looked like someone had used it for a trampoline, and the overhead fan had a tennis shoe spinning in a slow whirl from one of the blades.

"Poor little thing," Mona said, reaching toward the floor. Mona picked up the dead bee with pinched fingers. "Poor bee didn't stand a chance against that trainer." She pointed to the shoe resting nearby, the mate to the one still whirling above the bed.

Amy noticed the window was open the few inches it could be opened. It was the same situation with the windows her room, in that the windows only opened so far, and there were no window screens in this one, either. It was easy to see how a bee had found its way in. Amy closed the window, looking down out at the scenery below, noticing that it was the same view as from her room. The water in the lake sparkled in the sunlight and she imagined the rustle of reeds on the edge of the water, even though she was too far away to hear such a gentle sound. Dark clouds were gathering on the horizon, but for now the sky was bright and sunny.

A bouquet of flowers sat on a tabletop in a glass of water. It was the kind of handpicked bouquet a child would gather, simple and bright and meaningful. A matching glass sat beside it, a drinking glass with a paper cover. The kind you find in a five star hotel. No cling-wrapped plastic here.

There were two armchairs set near the window. On one of the seats, a paperback copy of *A Tale of Two Cities* lay open, well-worn spine up. She picked up the book and scanned the page. Madame Defarge was knitting in her wine shop in Saint Antoine. Wasn't she always knitting? Forever tying those horrible knots. Eloise's knitting basket was beside the chair. The knitting needles Eloise had purchased in the yarn shop were still attached to their cardboard cards, standing among several skeins of yarn. A piece of work was well underway, its gray and crimson zigzag pattern already formed, the first of many rows complete as it lay loose near the top of the pile. Amy picked it up and on impulse put the wool to her nose. It was damp to the touch and smelled like sheep amongst the wildflowers growing on a sunny slope. She inhaled again. Maybe it was laundry soap.

Amy moved to the bathroom. There was a tube of sunscreen on the bathroom counter, and she wondered if this is what gave Dick his fisted hands, fat lip and swollen eyes. She flipped the lid and sniffed. Something generic. Not much fragrance at all. She opened the sink drawer. There were two travel sized packets of Tide laundry soap. A tube of toothpaste. Colgate. A pair of cuticle scissors. There were also two EpiPens each in its hard plastic case. Always prepared. Eloise would be nothing less. Amy resisted the temptation to flip open the outer case and hold the apparatus in her hand, but she could read the directions through the clear tube with its bright orange nose at the needle end. This was serious RX business.

She closed the drawer and moved on to the flowered, zippered makeup pouch that stood on the left side of the sink. A leather case stood on the right. His and hers toiletries, boundaries well defined. She wouldn't unzip the bags and take a peek inside. That was too nosey. The bees would not be hiding in there and she had no business looking through the bags.

She checked the bathroom trash. Without having to dig, thank goodness, she could see it was nearly empty, except for the torn wrapper from a bag of snacks, airline pretzels most likely, or something from the pub basket at the hotel, and the paper cover that matched the bouquet-filled glass. Now glancing at herself in the bathroom mirror, she saw her freckled cheeks, hazel eyes and cascade of red curls she had let run wild while in Ireland. It seemed the right thing to do. She fought the impulse to pull the curls into a knot. When in Rome. Or more appropriately, when in Ireland let your red curls hang free. It was freeing. She fluffed the curls and watched them bounce.

In the refection, her eye caught on the shirt hanging from a hanger on the shower rod. Dick must have spilled something dark on the lavender cuff. Eloise had obviously scrubbed it in the sink until there was almost no stain left. She glanced behind the shower curtain for bees.

"Ah, and here's another, the little bugger," Mona called from the other room. "Right here on the windowsill next to the bed. Dead as ever it could be." Mona held the bee in the palm of her hand. "It must have come in through the open window. If there were more, I'd say they left the same way."

"If we haven't heard them yet, I'd say they've flown the coop," Amy replied. It was then that she heard a buzz and turned to follow the source of the sound. It brought her to the bedside table, the one without the upset lamp. Amy opened the drawer and there was Eloise's cell phone vibrating away against the wood. The phone stopped and Amy closed the drawer.

"Well, that explains why you couldn't reach Eloise. She doesn't have her phone with her."

Amy wanted the discovery to make herself feel better about Eloise's whereabouts, wherever that was. But somehow it didn't.

## CHAPTER TWENTY TWO

Garda O'Shannon had remained after the paramedics left the hotel. She noticed how he singled out the staff one by one — the concierge, the front desk, the gardener, the maids, even the photographer who had been taking pictures of the resort. He had a conversation with Eloise after Rian found her in the woods and brought her back to face Dick and his plight. Maybe plight should be plural.

She wouldn't eavesdrop on the Garda's conversations because it didn't seem possible without being obvious. Besides, he warned her already. Police work was police work. Guests were guests. When their eyes met in the lobby, she could tell he still felt the same way.

Rian had shared with Amy how surprised Eloise looked when she detailed Dick's mishap and tumble down the stairs. "I think she was laughing on the inside," Rian claimed. Rian found her in the woods not far from the hotel. Eloise explained how she had followed the path to the golf green, only to discover a patch of Arum berries in the shade of the woods. She was so excited to find them, she said, that she lost all track of time. She explained how artists used berries like these to color wool and fibers a beautiful shade of crimson. What luck to find them, she said, and she was determined to take enough home with her to make a dye. Eloise held up the bag for Rian to see, the red juice already staining the inside. Dick had chided her about her penchant for all things fabric when he claimed she had a basement full of supplies. Amy didn't doubt that either was true.

Dick refused to return to his room after the paramedics left, even though Amy and Mona had thoroughly checked for bees. With much fuss, he insisted on being moved to another room. One on the first floor. Eloise said the move was ridiculous and insisted on staying where she was— she was already settled in and comfortable. Dick didn't argue about Eloise moving with him and the two of them parted ways. A very married way to solve the issue. Separate bedrooms were not that uncommon for couples who were long past the honeymoon stage.

When she saw Garda O'Shannon again, he was outside Dick's new room. Out of the corner of her eye she watched him knock. Dick let him in. Or so that's what she assumed. She couldn't see from where she stood who opened the door. But she could see Eloise sitting in the chair in the lobby, the same chair the photographer had used to spy on them at Doris' door before. Eloise sat with her knitting piled in her lap, the heavy wooden needles clicking rhythmically as she glared down the hallway at Dick's closed door. Obviously, Eloise was not pleased with this turn of events. Amy wondered if Dick had ordered Eloise to stand guard at his door. If only she could listen in to the conversation. What would Garda O'Shannon make of Dick's claim that someone was after him?

The concierge found a cane in the closet with the spare umbrellas, and Dick seemed to be managing pretty well on his sprained ankle in a hobbled-horse kind of way.

Later, at dinner, Dick complained of a stomachache, still disgruntled about every mishap and discomfort. He griped about the food, his foot, his hands and the itch that followed the swelling. He groused about falling down the stairs and openly scolded

Eloise because she was nowhere to be found when it happened. He also blamed her for the weather which had turned wet and chilly. Eloise never replied. She took it in with a thin, tolerant smile. Dick went on to lament that he would miss a good game of golf with Reg, and that they had very important things to discuss. Important. He had given emphasis to the word. And then he looked at Gayle.

Gayle dropped her fork in her plate and Reginald Williams attempted a withering look, but it didn't land. Gayle was watching James fill her goblet, impatient to bring the wine to her lips. Amy thought her eyes looked on fire. But then, she couldn't be sure it wasn't the reflection from the candles flickering on the tabletop.

When Genna asked why Bartlestown Bank was so interested in Bluff Springs, since it was a small town and rather cliquish toward outsiders — Rebecca chuckled and then suggested that every Arkansas town needed a Sasquatch. James said the Arkansas baseball team already had that mascot. And Genna laughed so hard she nearly spit out her wine. Reginald looked like he wanted to crawl under the table. Rian and Zelda looked as if they were watching a tennis match. But the best of the evening came last. Doris, quiet, humble Doris, with no bone to pick with anyone, shared that in her home when her children behaved badly, they were sent to their rooms.

Dick pretended to be nonplussed by the comments, but he dropped his napkin in his plate and left the table. Amy couldn't help but notice once again his knuckles and nubby dark hair.

It seemed everyone was at the tipping point on Dick's moaning and groaning. Amy didn't understand how Eloise could stand it. If Eloise would only stand up to him, put her foot down, draw the line in the sand. Instead, Eloise seemed resigned to accept his ill-tempered mood as the norm. She left the table shortly after Dick, claiming the need for a walk. Gayle offered to take the tray of remedies from the kitchen to Dick's room. When she returned to join them for their après dinner drink, she said he didn't answer her knock, so she left the tray on the floor by his door.

To their surprise, the after dinner drink was delivered with a note set in a saucer beside the mug. They tore into the black and neon card. *The Blacklight Croquet Ball will commence tomorrow. 4 pm. Sharp. White attire requested. Follow the path to the barn. We'll have good craic!* It was signed, Muadhnait.

After the hectic day they all had, she was glad Mona had postponed the blacklight croquet game. Amy decided the Nutty Irishman made with whiskey, Baileys Irish Cream, and Frangelico, all topped with whipped cream and smashed hazelnuts was the best thing ever. If it hadn't been so caloric, she would have had two.

Sated with a delicious meal and a special invite to look forward to, the four friends enjoyed their evening in quiet. They scattered to their own company, all feeling the need for a bit of space. The trip to Limerick and the spooky old jail had been exhausting. And dangerous. Zelda had nearly drawn Amy's blood with her nails when the lantern fell off the shelf. The welts on her arm were still a bit tender. The night passed without incident, and for the first time since arriving in Ireland, Amy fell into a peaceful sleep. For that, she was most grateful.

# CHAPTER TWENTY THREE

The day dawned with new promise, and they had spent the morning on a wet hike to the waterfall, returned for a late and leisurely lunch. It was now almost four o'clock.

As they approached the old barn on foot, they avoided the ruts made in the mud by Dick and his golf cart. The afternoon brought in more drizzle and the air was downright chilly. Dick wore his purple cap and scarf like royalty, and Amy pulled her own scarf closer, imagining everybody sweating buckets in Arkansas. But not in Ireland. They probably never got a chance to sweat here.

Mona threw open the barn door to greet them.

"Surprise!" She trilled, her energy infectious.

"Would you look at this!" Zelda exclaimed as they entered the rustic barn with its crumbly rock and stucco walls and high tin roof. "It reminds me a little of Lock, Stock and Barrel," Zelda added, looking at Amy with a bit of sympathy. "I mean in an *almost* kind of way."

Amy nodded. It did remind her of her escape room at Tiddlywinks. It was all about making do with what you had— lemonade from lemons. An escape room from a large closet. Or a croquet club from an old sheep barn. As they gathered into the barn, Mona closed the heavy door behind them and turned out the lights. They were suddenly dispersed into darkness. Then Mona flipped another switch, and they were transported to another dimension.

"It *is* Alice in Wonderland," Amy agreed, taking in the painted scenes. The walls were painted in fluorescent colors with scenes one would find in Lewis Carroll's wild dreams. There were giant orange-pink spotted mushrooms — the famous fly agaric with their bright caps and white spots. The painted gills of the fungi seemed to be breathing. A painted tree covered one wall with vibrant green branches with pink and orange and yellow Tinkerbell fairies the size of crows. Three round tables were set along one wall with glow in the dark tabletops and chairs to match.

The wickets, balls, and mallets were painted fluorescent, all mimicking the traditional croquet colors with a bit of reinterpretation. The black ball was painted white. It looked more blueish purple in the UV light. Strings of glow in the dark lights were everywhere — hanging from the rafters, bent along the lines of the wickets, and marking the scoring posts in vivid technicolor.

Mona had asked them to wear white clothing, and now Amy saw why. The lighting put a different perspective on fashion. The twelve of them stood out like glowing ghostly figures.

Zelda laughed and clapped her hands. "Look at the spots on my shirt! Look at your teeth!"

"Look at your teeth," Genna answered. "You can tell who's been using a bleaching kit."

Amy laughed as their brilliant white-blue teeth lit up their dark faces. Everything looked so different in this new light.

"The rules of the game are the same here as on the croquet green," Mona said excitedly. "Pick your colors and then we will have a good luck toast before we play."

A bar in the corner held a variety of goodies and drinks— all glowing like a Franken-science lab. Amy scanned the bar. What in the world would they be eating and drinking that looked like that?

"The bar is stocked," Mona said. "There's a pitcher of gin and tonic already made— that's the one glowing bright blue."

"What's that green stuff?" Rian asked, pointing to several pint jars on the bar.

"That's honey mead," Mona said. "All locally made from Irish honey, of course."

"And what on earth is this?" Genna tapped a large glass of bright purple-pink and yellow ovals floating inside a jar.

"Pickled eggs! The yellow ones are still in their shell. Aren't they bleedin' massive? Utterly brilliant?" The proud angle of her chin said it all.

Dick pulled a wad of bank notes from his pocket. "Look, the euro glows. Glow in the dark money." He pulled another bill from his pocket and Amy sensed his disappointment. The US dollar wasn't so showy.

"Look at your sleeve!" Amy said, pointing to Dick's shirt. "And your shoes! The soles are glowing! Yours too, Eloise!"

Amy looked down at the necklace she always wore at her neck. The tiny stone in the Celtic cross sparkled like Kryptonite.

"This is trippy," Rian said. "I like it."

Gayle clasped her hands in glee. "We should do something like this for a chamber fundraiser. That would be so much fun. And lucrative. We could have a tournament of teams! What do you think Mr. Williams? Mr. Williams? Where are you?"

"I'm right here," he said brusquely. It didn't appear that he had moved but a few feet from the door. "I'm not sure what kind of tomfoolery this is, but I sure hope you don't turn me and Rebecca into hookah-toking caterpillars."

Amy couldn't tell if he was kidding.

"Oh, for the love of fun," Rebecca scolded, her voice playful in the dark. "Lighten up, Reg. No one's turning you into anything. Relax and enjoy the distraction." Rebecca laughed lightly. "If any-one could pull this off in Bluff Springs, it would be you, Gayle."

"I can see it!" Gayle replied.

"That's certainly more your style," Dick muttered. "Entertainment. Running the membership drives. Herding the cats. Keep everybody in their own lane, right, Reg?"

"What does that mean?" Gayle said sharply. "Are you saying I am not qualified to do more? Or more specifically, that I am not qualified to run a chamber of commerce?"

"Dickie, you never said that," Eloise countered.

"Oh, but he did," James said hotly, turning to face Dick. "You just implied my wife isn't good enough to run the chamber. Someday you're going to say the wrong thing to the wrong person and regret it."

"And this may be that day," Genna snapped. "You're outnumbered, and we're all armed."

"No one escapes justice, Dickie," Rebecca Williams said with emphasis. "All deeds find their just deserts."

"I appreciate a good dessert," Zelda added. "Especially one served cold like revenge."

"Let's pick our teams," Mona interrupted loudly, reaching for a bowl of bright strips of paper with an exaggerated flourish. The heated conversation ended as abruptly, and at her turn Amy pulled a folded scrap to reveal a bright orange dot in the center.

"Orange. I'm with you Rebecca."

"Good," Rebecca answered. "A pair of unconquerable women. Now how about a round of G&T, Mona? Make it a double. Our gentlemen need a shot of get-over-themselves libation."

"Oh, let me be the bartender," Eloise said, her blue-white smile shining in the dark. "I love making cocktails. And look how strange everything looks in this light."

By the time they each had a cocktail and were launched into the game, the ruffled feathers seemed smoothed. Amy could indeed imagine a blacklight croquet in Bluff Springs. She loved the idea of creating another game-related fundraiser. Gayle could use her help and expertise, and the exposure would be good for Tiddlywinks. Good for the other businesses at The Cardboard Cottage, too. Zelda would hunt down some kitschy blacklight item to sell at Zsa Zsa Galore Décor. Rian would come up with something trippy to promote at The Pot Shed. It sure wouldn't be her wine — Rian's weed wine was still a long way from marketable. Doris could help, too, if she wanted. Her husband was a crackerjack handyman. He could help design whatever backdrop they needed. Her imagination bloomed in the dark.

"Doris?" Amy asked. "Where are you?"

"Over here," Doris answered. Amy turned toward the voice and Doris waved the tip of her mallet. The brilliant yellow bobbed in the dark.

"You're being awfully quiet," Amy said, waving the tip of her own mallet in the air, leaving orange trails in the dark.

"I'm concentrating on my swing," Doris said. "I'm having trouble getting my bearings. I'm trying to aim for that wicket, but it looks like it's moving."

Rian laughed. "Could be the gin."

The bobbing yellow mallet swung through, and the bright yellow ball sailed toward the wicket and then veered at the last minute.

"Did you just kick my ball?" Doris demanded.

"Wasn't me," Dick said.

"Liar," Doris muttered.

Polite, quiet Doris. Amy turned to play her ball and then suddenly a loud crack filled the room. Glass smashed to the floor. Then came the soft gurgling sound of liquid. The smell of vinegar stung her nose.

"UGH! OOMPF!" It sounded like Dick Collins.

"What's happening?" Amy cried.

Before anyone could answer she heard a now familiar scream. She threw her hands to cover her ears as the horrible, unnatural keening reached an ear-splitting pitch. And then, just as abruptly as it started, it stopped. Silence engulfed the darkness.

"What's going on?" Amy recognized Mona's voice from across the room.

"It's Dick!" Eloise yelled. "He's collapsed! I think he's having an allergic reaction!"

Dick Collins lay prone, his head turned slightly, his cheek against the floor. The wool cap had fallen away from his head, leaving the bristles of his hair exposed. The purple scarf was still wrapped around his neck. All around him were shards of broken glass and slippery wet eggs.

Eloise dropped to the floor and Amy could see the glow of the soles of her shoes as she knelt at his side. In what seemed like one fluid movement, Eloise retrieved the EpiPen from her jacket pocket and jammed it into the outside of his thigh. Even though Amy could only see the trails of color in the dark, she knew that Eloise was holding the injector in place, counting out loud. "One, one thousand, two, one thousand, three…" Amy found herself counting with her, and time seemed to drag. Only seconds passed.

"It's not working!" Eloise yelled. "Nothing's happening!"

A male voice called, "Turn on the lights! Turn off the music!"

Suddenly they were awash in white light.

Eloise let go of the spent pen and it clattered to the floor in the silence that followed. Her eyes were shut tight. Her hands were trembling.

Zelda gasped. "Is that blood? Is that blood on your mallet?"

Amy looked to where Zelda pointed. Doris was holding her mallet in two clinched fists. The end cap was smeared with a wet red stain. Amy looked back to the floor. The back of Dick's head was wet, too.

# CHAPTER TWENTY FOUR

Mona was inconsolable. Amy kept an arm around her shoulder, which was shaking as if she were shivering with cold. Eloise left with Garda O'Shannon, following the body on the stretcher. Dick Collins didn't need the paramedics.

The little group from Arkansas stood outside the barn, looking forlorn and confused by the chain of events. A game of croquet — albeit one set in an eerie light — had turned deadly. No one seemed to have much to say. They stood in the dusky light, their faces clouded with concern, confusion, and maybe a little conflict. None of them had taken Dick's allergies as seriously as they could have. She sure hadn't. She thought it was his ruse. An attention-getting ploy. A way to deflect the world away from all of his insecurities. His air of entitlement sure didn't help. Royal purple logo and all.

Rebecca and Reginald stood off to themselves, their heads bowed in quiet conversation. Gayle clenched her husband's hand. Doris stood alone against a tree just a few feet from the barn. Rian and Genna and Zelda stood nearby. She could guess what they were thinking. Another *wasband*. Another husband that was.

Amy turned toward Doris, whose face was drawn and tight, but in that instant she saw the flicker of decision flash across Doris' face. She watched as Doris pushed away from the tree and approached her.

"I need to talk to you," she whispered. She took Amy's elbow in her hand. "Privately," she added and tried to smile at Mona. It was a sad attempt, her concern creasing every wrinkle in her round, pleasant face.

"I have to tell you something and I don't really want to."

"I don't understand."

"It's something about me and Dick."

Amy's eyebrows rose. Doris led her a few feet away and Amy could feel the eyes of the others watching them.

"You and Dick Collins?"

"It happened so long ago you'd think I'd be over it by now."

Doris stalled. Amy waited.

"I think the police are going to say it was an act of revenge!"

"Doris, what are you talking about?"

"I didn't hit Dick Collins with that mallet," Doris said hotly. "I won't say I didn't think about it. But someone thrust that mallet into my hands right after we heard the glass crash. Right before the lights came on."

"Who?"

"I don't know. I didn't see who it was."

"Where was your mallet?"

"I handed it to my partner to play her turn."

"Gayle was your partner?"

Doris nodded.

"You think she hit him with the mallet?"

Doris shrugged. "I don't know. I didn't see who it was. Someone was standing beside me and then all that glass went crashing to the floor. And then the lights came on, Dick was on the floor, and I was holding the mallet."

Amy sighed heavily. She couldn't remember if the glass went crashing before the fall or after. It happened so quickly, it was hard to remember which sound came first. The only sound she remembered for certain was the scream in her head. And now she wasn't sure whether that happened before or after Dick had collapsed. Time and sequence were scrambling for order in her memory.

"When you talk to the police, will you promise to tell them it wasn't me? I didn't kill Dick. It wasn't me."

"Just tell them the truth," Amy offered. "Be honest. That's all they need."

Doris bit her bottom lip and pushed her butterscotch glasses up on the bridge of her nose. "That's not the worst of it," she whispered. She took a deep breath as if to steel her courage. "I used to work for Dick Collins. My first professional job. At a bank." Doris looked out at the pond in the distance, her memory gathering like the clouds gathering overhead.

"I was married. Our firstborn was about three. We were struggling financially. Trying to save up for a house, a second car, and pay all our bills on time."

Amy could tell Doris was pulling these memories from her mental archives, the way one digs keepsakes from an old cardboard box. It wasn't until the dust was blown off that the contents came into focus. Along with the reason for why such memories were kept at all.

"I never took time off except for what was required by the FDIC. Two consecutive weeks every year. I always arrived early. I always stayed late when he asked."

A knot in Amy's stomach tightened. Not Doris. Not a young wife with a child.

"Dick was new to his job, too," Doris continued. "He was the new branch manager and he really thought he was something special. A big man. A big shot. A man with a plan and no one to stop him."

Amy frowned. Not much had changed since then. Until now.

"He wanted everyone to think he was their friend. Always inviting his employees to his office. But only one at a time."

Doris shook her head. "He wasn't anybody's friend. I knew what he was doing."

Amy was almost afraid to ask. "What was he doing?"

"Fishing for gossip."

"What? Why?"

"Why? So, he had the nitty gritty on everybody. The gossip. The scuttlebutt. The good, the bad, and the ugly. It was like his private spy ring. He was always trying to catch his employees doing something they shouldn't be doing. And not just bank employees. He wanted to know gossip about our banking clients, too. Like who was making big deposits and buying expensive cars. And who was always overdrawn and who was dating who. Who was going through a divorce and who was going broke."

Amy frowned again. "You mean for blackmail?" Somehow this didn't surprise her.

"I don't know why, but I always felt it was his way of manipulating people. For leverage. You know. A way to call in favors they didn't owe. It wasn't all that long before he shot right to the top of the bank."

Doris motioned with her head. "Rebecca Williams was a bank client. I think she was just getting started in real estate. Dick was always pumping me for information about her, too." Doris nudged the rim of her glasses again.

"I never had anything to tell, and I wasn't about to snitch if I did."

Amy noted the emotion still attached to her words. It may have been a long time ago, but the feeling of that workplace abuse hadn't faded much.

Doris quieted for a moment. "My problem started when the bank launched a mentor program. If you were selected, you would spend a year mentoring with leaders throughout the bank system.

It was corporate's way of identifying the most promising new employees." She looked at Amy. Doris' eyes were filled with tears.

"I wanted to be in that mentorship program more than anything. He said I was the ideal candidate. That's what he told me."

"But it didn't happen," Amy ventured.

"No."

"What did happen?"

Doris answered with a hot exhale of breath. "Dick Collins happened. He told me he would send the recommendation letter and all the paperwork that needed to go with it. I even filled out the forms for him. All it needed was his signature and a stamp on the envelope. He told me it was as good as done.

"'*You can take that to the bank*' were his exact words. He said there was nothing left for me to do but wait for the good news. Well, surprise! He never sent that letter of recommendation. He never sent the paperwork, and I don't think he ever intended to. He played me like a fiddle with three strings. And there I was, trusting him with my career."

Amy exhaled loudly. Even listening made her chest ache with disappointment. She'd had her fair share of that, plenty of disappointment from people she'd counted on, believed in, were betrayed by. Who hadn't? It was one of the hard knocks of life everyone experienced at least once. Sometimes more than once.

"I'm really sorry to hear this," Amy said softly and touched Doris' arm.

"I don't know which was worse," Doris added. "Him pretending that it was an honest mistake and *'maybe all for the best'*. Or him firing me when I called him a liar."

"You called him that?"

"Well —" Doris drawled. "Not to his face. Another employee ratted me out."

"I hate this," Amy said.

"Yeah," Doris agreed. "Me too. When I realized he was coming on this trip I wanted to back out. I wanted to tell someone about it, so I told Gayle Brand. I thought she should know."

"And her response?" Amy asked.

"She acted surprised. But also sympathetic to my cause."

Amy nodded. What career women didn't experience the glass ceiling barrier in her professional climb up the ladder?

"She said I shouldn't let him ruin the hard work I put into the chamber campaign." Doris paused then added, "I'm not really sure if telling her was the right thing to do."

"Why do you say that?"

"Because her attitude toward me changed after that. Not that I can say how exactly, but it changed enough to make me feel uncomfortable. You'd think her attitude toward Dick would be the thing to go sour."

"Do you think Gayle told Mr. Williams?"

"I doubt it. Mr. Williams doesn't strike me as the kind of boss who wants to hear a sob story. He's a cut and paste, nail it down kind of guy. No soft edges on that one."

"I agree," Amy said. "Except when he looks at his wife. He's pretty starry eyed then. Did you ever say anything to Dick Collins?"

Doris shrugged. "I said, 'hello, Dick', when I saw him in the lobby our first day here. He didn't smile back. I wasn't surprised. By the look on his face, I wondered if he even recognized me. You know it's been three kids ago. I said, *It's just me. Doris. Doris Knight.* I thought maybe he had forgotten my name."

"I don't believe he was looking at you," Amy said. "I think he was looking at the maid behind you. He told the Garda he didn't know who she was, but I think he did know her. And I think he was surprised to see her here in Ireland."

"Well, that explains his expression. He looked like he had seen a ghost."

A ghost. Or a banshee. She had heard the same scream right before they found the maid in the hall. She heard it again tonight. Two deaths. One slumped over a cart; one shoe on, one shoe off, the back of her uniform dark with blood. And now, another. The back of his head dark with blood. Was it blood? She didn't know. Had he collapsed from an allergic reaction as Eloise thought? Or was it because someone had battered his head with a croquet mallet before thrusting it into Doris's hands?

Dread filled her stomach. That weird dream on the coach from Dublin was beginning to take on the shape of a snippet, with its message an unwelcome foreshadowing of what was then to come.

# CHAPTER TWENTY FIVE

Amy felt Garda O'Shannon's eyes boring into hers as if she were a child being admonished for pulling a dangerous prank.

"We meet once again," he said. "Under no better circumstances. Although I would prefer it to be otherwise."

The comment took her by surprise. So much so that she didn't respond.

"Tell me your version of what happened. That's a tale I be looking to hear," he urged.

She gave him her recollection. The glass crashed. Dick yelled. Eloise pulled the EpiPen from her pocket and stuck his leg. The lights came on and Doris was holding the mallet. It looked like it had blood on it. It looked as if there was blood on Dick's head. There was glass and eggs everywhere, and time had spun so quickly, that no one had time to think.

"Why would someone strike him?"

Hadn't he met Dick Collins? What she said was, "I don't know."

"Muadhnait claims there was tension between the women and Mr. Collins. Can you speak to that?"

"Collins made a tacky comment and they defended themselves. Or rather, they defended women at large. I don't think Dick Collins was used to having women question his words or his actions."

"I see," he said and nodded.

"Whatever tension there was seemed to end quickly. We got our drinks and played a round. Everyone seemed to be having a good time."

"And Mrs. Knight. She had reason to strike Mr. Collins?"

She could feel her eyebrow twitch. "I can't see Doris striking anyone, but if there was a reason, she would be the one to ask."

Garda O'Shannon chucked and his dimples deepened. "You are a coy lass," he said. "I have spoken to Mrs. Knight. She confessed an unpleasant episode in her history with Mr. Collins. She claims vehemently that she did not hit Mr. Collins and has no idea who did. But she was, as others have verified, the one bearing the weapon in her hands. Does this not shock your tender opinion of her?"

"Does it change my opinion of Doris?" Amy shook her head with vigor. "I believe what she told me. Someone put that mallet in her hands on purpose."

"In order to frame her for the injury? Someone who knew of this detail about her and Collins?"

"Or to draw suspicion away from themselves!"

Garda O'Shannon steepled his fingers. "From what I took note, she would have been successful if the lights had not been put on. In the dark, no one was wise to her actions. It was your friend, Zelda Carlisle who made this observation, I am told. It was Mrs. Carlisle who found the body of the … ehm… maid, in the corridor. You see where I am in my thinking?"

"Wait just a doggone minute," Amy spat. "You're trying to pin this on Zelda? Zelda Carlisle didn't kill that maid. Or whoever she really was. And she didn't whack Dick Collins in the head, either! And Doris wouldn't be the one she'd frame if she had!"

The Garda leaned toward Amy. "Then who would she frame for such a crime? If we were bouncing theories and brainstorming?"

It sounded like bouncing *terries* and *brown-storming,* and for a moment she was derailed by the linguistic disconnect.

"Did you see Mr. Collins eat or drink anything out of the ordinary?" he asked.

"I'm not sure how to answer that. Everything looked out of the ordinary under the blacklight."

Garda O'Shannon leaned back in his chair before speaking again. "His wife believed he was having an allergic reaction and the thing that caused his collapse. It seems most uncanny that both would occur at the same time. Whether he ingested something before he was struck is what we will need to determine. If someone was attempting to harm him — as he claimed yesterday afternoon — that is something we will need to ascertain, as well. In your mind are these two occurrences related?"

"What two occurrences?"

"Ehm … the maid and Mr. Collins."

Amy frowned and then shook her head emphatically. "The maid's death was murder. Someone stabbed her with an ice pick. Dick's death was accidental. I was standing there when Eloise plunged that EpiPen into his thigh. She tried to save him. The stuff didn't work."

Garda O'Shannon nodded. "That is true. The epinephrine did not revive him. You are certain of what you saw?" His eyes held hers. "I see I've planted a seed of doubt."

She refused to give him the satisfaction of a response. But he was correct. Not that she had doubt about Zelda's guilt, but he had indeed planted the seed. She had not connected the death of the maid, whose name they still did not know, and the death of Dick Collins. The first death was murder. The woman had been stabbed and rolled into the hallway. Had the police figured out why? Or where she came from? What did they know that she didn't?

Probably a lot.

In her mind, Dick's death was an accident. Something had caused an allergic reaction and the EpiPen Eloise so diligently carried with her had not done its job. How unfortunate. But what if…

The scene in the barn filled her head. The blow to his head could have knocked him out, but could it have killed him? Was that an accident? Or had someone been trying to kill him with the mallet? She tried to remember how things had gone. Had the force of the mallet made him topple to the ground? Had his fall caused the glass to shatter? She remembered the eggs as they floated in the spilled brine. In the blacklight they had been bright neon. In the daylight they were eggs. Just pickled eggs.

Amy looked at O'Shannnon. "Can you tell me what killed him? Was it an allergic reaction or the bash on the head?"

"I cannot tell you," he said sternly. "That is beyond your scope of purpose, Ms. Sparks. At least at the present it is. Details of such nature belong to the Garda Síochána. The Coroner of Country Cork will be the one to determine the cause and manner of death. But still, I am curious to know— how would you explain how you are here in Ireland and your friends are here in Ireland and now… another husband is… departed."

Was he giving her a warning? Was that a cryptic message to say the four of them were under his watch and scrutiny. As Zelda had so willingly shared with him earlier, they had been involved in three other incidents involving husbands. Now there were four.

Amy watched as he put away his notebook and rose to leave. He didn't expect an answer and she didn't have one.

"What in the blue blazes, Sparks," Zelda muttered when Amy returned to their room. "I was hoping to catch O'Shannon's eye and score a dinner date and instead he rode me like a bicycle downhill. He wouldn't give up pushing for details on that mallet Doris was holding and why I noticed that instead of the other thing… the other. You know. The dead guy on the ground."

"What a strange turn of events," Amy answered and plopped into the chair. "What a strange turn. And O'Shannon's not crossing us off his list just yet. We may not be at the top of the suspect list, but we're on it."

The barn wasn't visible from their room, but Amy knew the blacklight croquet barn had already been secured and the Gardai had done their due diligence investigating the scene. From the window in the library, she had watched the men in their protective hazmat suits returning to their van.

Tomorrow she would venture out to see what she could see for herself. Now that this seed of doubt was sprouting. Tomorrow the four of them would need to talk about how they were going to avoid the scrutiny of the Gardai for the remainder of their stay. And that meant they needed to add snooping to their travel itinerary. Tomorrow she would propose an idea that was bobbing around in her head about how to do that. And maybe tomorrow she would tell them about her snippet. Maybe.

She didn't bother to wash her face or brush her teeth. She slipped into her nightclothes and crawled into bed. "What in the blue blazes, Zelda" Amy repeated softly. "What have we gotten ourselves into this time?"

Zelda was already snoring softly from behind her mask.

# CHAPTER TWENTY SIX

After breakfast, Amy expected Garda O'Shannon to be waiting for them in the lobby with another round of questions. But by the time she scraped the bowl of her oatmeal porridge with Bailey's Irish Cream and gooey chocolate chips — now her standard breakfast fare — there was still no sign of him. She was relieved in many ways. The four of them needed to unravel the puzzle they had found themselves in before they blinked any brighter on his radar of suspects. He had no reason to suspect them of anything other than being in the wrong place at the wrong time, but she knew firsthand that investigations like this put everyone in the spotlight of suspicion.

She also was disappointed he wasn't there if she was honest with herself. His dimpled grin was growing on her. And on Zelda, too. Zelda had made more than one flirtatious stab at catching his eye.

Amy, on the other hand, wanted to know what was in that little notebook he was forever jotting things into. She had taken a peek when his head was turned, and decided either the scribble was his own shorthand, or the words were in another language. Probably the latter. Even if she accidentally on purpose got a more than bird's eye view, she wouldn't be able to read his notes anyway.

"Here we are on this beautiful Emerald Isle and once again we are in the thick of it," Genna said, turning to Amy with a mouth full of buttered soda bread. "And yet your spidey-sense hasn't delivered on its creepy night-time visuals." Genna looked at Amy with raised brows. "Or has it? You're not holding out on us, are you?"

Amy wrinkled her nose. Genna had called them her little swami tsunami night sweats when she had been angry at Amy. Actually, Genna had been spit-spitting livid. The sting of that slur had been softened since then. The apology came in the form of a gift of jewelry. Amy loved the earrings with the unusual stone. But mostly the sting had softened because Genna had finally admitted that Amy's snippet dreams might actually foretell some aspect of the future. Not just any future, mind you. A murderous one. With a victim and a bad guy and a slew of really weird clues. At first she had suffered through the interpretation alone, trying to understand the dream and how it all fit the crime. And then she had shared one with Genna. That ended up causing a great deal of anger and angst. Now she was faced with the same predicament. To spill or not to spill? That was the question. The dreams always sounded so strange when she spoke of them out loud.

Genna was watching her. So was Rian. Rian had been a believer from the git-go. She never shamed Amy into thinking she was seeing things that weren't there. Rian knew. Somehow Rian just knew.

Amy glanced at Zelda, who was polishing off her Full Irish — a breakfast of sausages, bacon, eggs, tomatoes, potatoes, and mushrooms, with a thick slice of soda bread slathered in butter. Plus, a side of yogurt. Amy had to admit the creamy homemade yogurt was the best she'd ever tasted. Over the top she drizzled fresh gathered honey, the little bits of honeycomb still floating in the jar.

Zelda looked up, surprised to find all three of them watching her. "What? Why are you all looking at me?"

"We're watching a true master at work," Genna said. "We're waiting for you to fill up."

Zelda dabbed her lips with the white cloth napkin. "Some master the art of cooking. I have mastered the art of eating. One serves the other and vice versa. It takes a village."

"Have you been paying any attention?" Amy asked.

"I can eat and listen at the same time, Sparks. You're going to share your snippet with us because I know you. I know you've been tossing and turning and muttering in your sleep about croquet trees and scary fairies. I've been listening to that every single night. And I am well aware that we have another *wasbund* on our hands. Only this isn't just a husband that was. He was a *husbank*. A husband with a bank full of money. So out with it, Sparks. I'm going to have one more cup of this tea and you're going to tell us what we need to know about your dream."

With that as her encouragement, Amy gathered her thoughts and told them about the dream, the snippet on the coach. It had ended as the icy breath blew in her face and the piercing wail. She had heard that same sound shortly before Zelda found the maid. She heard it again when Dick collapsed. She ended her recounting with a deep sigh, the kind that lifts heavy burdens from weary shoulders. Just speaking it to her friends made her feel a little lighter.

"Two rotten croquet balls," Rian pondered. "I'm going out on a limb here, but I think it means the two deaths are related."

"That's exactly the idea Garda O'Shannon put in my head," Amy added. "I hadn't connected the two, except I knew somehow that if there was one death, there was going to be another."

Rian leaned in and put her elbows on the table. The white linen tablecloth was still cluttered with their spent dishes, but the four of them were alone in the room. "So how many croquet balls were hanging from the tree? I forgot what you said."

"There were twelve in all. Two of each color. At first I thought they were apples, and then I realized they had stripes like croquet balls. The other two were on the ground. The two black ones."

"Twelve," Rian repeated. "The four of us, Doris, and the other six from Arkansas. That's eleven. The maid would make twelve."

"I sure wish we knew her name," Zelda complained. "The maid who was not a maid."

"In my snippet I heard a rustle in the trees, and I thought my grandmother was there with me. I thought I was dreaming of her. But the voice that spoke in my ear was not hers. It was…" Amy stalled. "It was otherworldly, if you can understand that."

"Not a voice in your head, right?" Genna asked. "I mean, you're not hearing those kind of voices now are you? That would be worrisome."

"And what did this voice say?" Rian asked, ignoring Genna's concern that wouldn't seem all that genuine to anyone who knew Genna well.

"It said, '*Death leaves a heartache no one can heal. Love leaves a memory no one can steal. And they will try. Oh, but they will try.*' I remember because I wrote it down and read it over several times."

"I've read that somewhere," Rian said. "Or something similar. When I was researching on the Internet, I remember reading that quote. I think it was an epitaph on an old tombstone."

"Isn't that fitting," Genna declared. "You go digging for your roots in Ireland and we end up digging up another murder."

"I wonder if it's an old Irish saying. I could ask Garda O'Shannon next time I see him."

"Oh, for sure," Zelda said, with a noticeable bite to her tone. "By all means, Amy, you should ask Mr. Dimples what he thinks about your snippety dreams."

Amy turned to Zelda with a furrowed brow. "Ouch. What's that about? My snippety dreams? It's more like snippety you."

"Well," Zelda said with a huff. "We can't all be clairvoyant."

Amy signed audibly. She wasn't clairvoyant. She didn't speak to spirits. And until now, spirits hadn't spoken to her.

"To the matter at hand," Genna said with a stern look at Zelda. "Garda O'Shannon and Mona are the only two insiders at the moment. We can't afford to give them any more reason to put us in their investigative crosshairs. Mona could be valuable to us if we play our cards right. Amy, I'm going to suggest you stay mum about your dream. I mean, to anyone but the four of us, that is."

That went without saying.

Rian tugged at a curl hanging just below her ear, twisting the dark strand absently. Amy could see she was deep in thought. "Did you have a premonition when you walked into Mona's blacklight croquet barn? It's not really the dream scene as you described it. There was no circle of stones. There was no Hawthorne tree growing from a boulder."

Zelda gasped. "But there was a Hawthorne tree! It was painted on the wall. There were fairies painted in the branches!"

"And there were mushrooms painted on the wall, too," Amy added. "Those big fly agaric mushrooms with glow in the dark dots. The trippy ones."

"The trippy ones," Rian echoed. "They also can be deadly."

The four of them grew quiet for a moment and then Amy said, "In the dream, the voice said, *'Mind your step. The fae are watching ye.'*"

"That gives me the willies," Zelda said and shuddered. "The fae are watching us. Everything we've heard about fairies hasn't been all that pleasant. And banshees! Don't even get me started on them!"

Rian was twisting her hair around her finger again. "If we take the four of us out of the croquet ball equation, we end up with seven suspects for the murder of the maid. Doris, Dick, Eloise, Gayle, James, Rebecca and Reginald." Rian chuckled. "Or Reg, as he is affectionately called."

"Affection on that one is a bit of a stretch," Zelda mumbled.

"But not when it comes to his wife," Amy countered. "I've seen how he looks at her. He would Gladiator-up and face a lion if he had to."

"And don't you think that's a little odd for a character like him?" Zelda said. "It's like he has Rebecca on a jewel-studded leash. I'm not even sure if she knows it."

"We need to get to know our Arkansas neighbors a whole lot better," Genna declared, her eyes wide with determination. "We need a few rounds of what I call Sneaky Q&A. You just sneak in a question when they're not expecting it and *whammo*, you get a real live answer. Not some pre-crafted publicity fluff."

"Quite the game plan," Amy said. "Shall we divide and conquer or form a posse?"

"Let's play it by ear," Genna answered. "If you have a chance to nose into somebody's business and none of us are there, do it any-way. *Carpe diem*," she added with a vigorous nod. "And, look! Here comes our first victims. James and Gayle Brand are headed this way."

The couple entered the lobby and before they could approach the front desk or the concierge, Genna intercepted them.

"Top of the morning to ya," James said, his dark eyes full of mischief. "Gayle and I just had another row out to the center of the lake to visit the swans. I think they like soda bread." He glanced quickly at the clerk. "I know we're not supposed to feed them but who can resist?"

Gayle patted her his arm affectionately. Amy had the distinct feeling that the mischief in James' eyes was not just about swans.

"We were hoping to spend some time with you," Genna offered in the southern drawl she used like honey. "What are y'all up to today? What plans did you make for us?"

Confusion flitted across Gayle's face. "Well — according to the itinerary— we were going to drive the Ring of Kerry, but now, considering …"

"Oh my, what was I thinking," Genna drawled. "I didn't mean to sound insensitive."

"No, of course not," Gayle said, forcing a smile. "But Mr. Williams thought it best to cancel our coach tour today. I know you understand. I hope we can reschedule in a day or so." She patted her husband's arm once more. "James is so fascinated by the lake and those swans that we decided we'd spend the day paddling around in that little rowboat. There are several places you can go ashore and explore. We came back to see if we could borrow some rubber boots and order a picnic lunch to go."

"And to drop this off at the front desk," James said, pulling a soggy wallet from behind his back. He was holding it with two pinched fingers.

"What is that?" Amy asked, ignoring the obvious.

James gave her sideways look. "It's a wallet."

"Of course, it's a wallet," Gayle said sternly. "They can see that for themselves."

"What they can't see is who it belonged to," he said, waving it in front of them like a tween with a slimy frog. "It's not just anybody's wallet. It's Caroline Gadling's wallet."

"Who?" Amy asked.

"Caroline Gadling," Gayle whispered.

"I don't know who that is. Is she a local celebrity?"

"You don't know?"

"Know what?" Genna demanded.

"Caroline Gadling is the woman who was … the maid who… the person who…"

"Oh, for heaven's sakes Gayle, spit it out." James turned and looked at Zelda. "She's the person you found outside your door. The one stabbed with the ice pick from the oyster bar, according to Collins. Dick said he saw one of the blokes from the wedding grab it and run. Told the police what he saw. Tell them, Gayle. Go ahead, tell them."

Gayle motioned them away from the front desk and the ears that were obviously listening to every word. "The police asked did I recognize the name of this guest. Of course, I recognized it. I was the one who booked her as the second attendee from Bartlestown Bank."

"Dick's plus-one?" Zelda screeched.

"Hush," Amy warned.

Gayle frowned. "No. Not exactly. I didn't book the two of them into the same hotel room. And of course, I didn't recognize her when we saw her dressed as a maid, because I had never met her. She was just a name on a list."

"No way!" Zelda exclaimed.

"I didn't put two and two together until..."

"Until it was obvious," James interjected. "Doris wasn't the only one who saw the maid and Dick interacting. Tell them Gayle. Tell them what you saw."

Amy thought he was enjoying himself a little too much.

"I saw Dick and the maid together," Gayle said. "I could just tell by their body language that they were not two strangers in the hall."

"Okay, wait a minute," Genna said. "Dick Collins brought both Caroline and his wife to Ireland."

The four of them looked at each other.

"*Deja vu,*" Amy whispered and felt Zelda shudder involuntarily beside her. "When is a maid not a maid?" By now it was a rhetorical question.

"No one could be more surprised than I was," Gayle continued.

"I am now completely baffled," Genna said, folding her long arms across her chest. A bold admission for Genna.

"Let me explain," Gayle said, sweeping her hands as if clearing away the hurly-burly disarray of logic before them. "Caroline was the person who handled the bank's involvement in our campaign. She earned her place on this trip in my opinion, because she did the leg work for the money the bank raised." Gayle put a hand on her hip. "He didn't do much more than show up for the glory.

"I knew it would work out just fine, because she would be the plus-one for Bartlestown Bank. Eloise wasn't coming because she had dental surgery scheduled and couldn't get rescheduled for an earlier date. She didn't want to take a chance on her health flaring up while overseas. I understood that completely. As it turned out, Eloise was able to grab a cancellation and have her surgery in time to make this trip."

"I'd say that's when Dick's plans changed, too," James announced.

"Well, you can't make a promise and then take it back," Gayle continued. "So, I asked Mr. Williams if we could still include Caroline. He was hesitant, but then he said Rebecca thought it was a good idea. At the last minute, Dick sent a message that Caroline would not be coming to Ireland. He said she had used up her vacation time and he couldn't approve her absence at the bank.  It was too late for me to cancel anything."

James nodded.  "We think Caroline decided to surprise him, anyway. He said something on the green about an unexpected guest. I didn't catch his meaning at the time. Now I understand why he shorted our golf game." He paused as the reality set in.

"Wait," Amy said. "You're saying you returned from your golf game early?"

James nodded. "We played nine holes and Dick said he was through. His watch buzzed and his whole attitude changed. I figured it was a text from Eloise. The wedding party was still at the chapel when I dropped Dick and his gear at the lobby, and I went out to the driving range to hit a bucket."

"What a rat," Zelda said. "Why do so many Richards turn out to be such dicks?"

Zelda was probably thinking what she was thinking. That the text wasn't from Eloise, but from this woman who pulled him away from 18-holes of golf for a different kind of game.

Genna nodded her head. "I see it now. This Caroline doesn't cancel her reservations as Dick suggests. She comes to Ireland anyway and pretends to be the maid so no one will know she's here. No one but Dick. Maybe the two of them had a history of checking in for their rendezvous as Mr. Smith and Mrs. Maid. Talk about rats."

Talk about rats. Dead rats. She didn't want to say that out loud. Two rats and two croquet balls, both rotten to the core. But something had gone wrong with that meetup. Something happened to turn an afternoon tryst into a deadly encounter. Like a deadly poke with a pick. But why?

"Where was this wallet?" Rian asked.

"It was floating in the lake. I saw something in the water, rowed over to it and here it is." He held it up, still with two fingers, although if there were fingerprints they would have been washed clean by the lake. "I opened it to see who it belonged to. Gayle recognized the name. I thought she was going to fall out of the boat!"

"I thought I was going to jump out of the boat!"

"You didn't find her passport, too, did you?"

James shook his head. "No, but we're going to go look again. I bet there are all kinds of treasures in that lake. Gayle decided we needed boots for the shore. It's really soggy. And I decided we needed food before we row out again."

"The Gardai will not want you anywhere near the lake," Amy said. "Now that you've found the wallet, that area is considered a crime scene."

His face dropped with disappointment. He glanced at his wife and then at the wallet in his fingers. Gayle shook her head and wagged a finger at James. She must have known what he was thinking. Like what harm could there possibly be in little a delay?

"James Brand," Gayle said sternly to which he shrugged.

"Garda O'Shannon is going to be beside himself with your discovery," Amy said. "I know they've been wondering where her identification was."

"Oh, yes, Garda O'Shannon is going to be beside himself," Zelda said, and Amy could hear the slightest rancor in her voice.

"They will probably dive the lake to see if they can find her passport. And who knows what else."

"What else is there to find?" Zelda asked. "We led them right to the body and the ice pick. What else is left for Garda O'Shannon to discover, huh?" She looked at Amy and raised her brow.

Amy shook her head. Was Zelda serious? Was she really acting jealous about the Garda investigating a murder?

"What else is left for them to discover?" Amy asked pointedly. "Who killed Caroline Gadling?"

"Well, there is that," Zelda said, pursing her lips. "They definitely need to know that."

# CHAPTER TWENTY SEVEN

"Are you thinking what I'm thinking?" Amy asked.

"There's no telling what's going on in that puzzle-brain of yours," Zelda said. "The inside of your head must look like a Sudoku square."

"I'm thinking Dick broke off his golf game to meet this Caroline the maid. Things didn't go as planned. He didn't want her here in Ireland. He didn't know she was coming. He may have been afraid her presence would get him into serious hot water with his wife."

"And you think a little hot water is motive for murder?" Zelda asked.

Amy shook her head. "No, not really, but I have a hunch we are only seeing the proverbial tip of the iceberg. We need to follow in Dick's footsteps the day you found the maid. We know when she was found. We don't know when she was attacked."

"You're always following in the footsteps of a killer," Genna said. "That's not a good plan. It's dangerous."

"Well, what do you suggest? Dick is at the center of this. And now he's gone. How are the two deaths connected? Are they connected?"

"Isn't it obvious?" Zelda asked. "Hubs has a girlfriend on the side and the wife discovers she's not really the maid. The maid winds up dead and then hubs winds up dead. And everybody else lives happily ever after."

Rian rolled her eyes. "That's wrong on so many levels."

"Frankly, I don't see how the two are connected beyond the obvious," Genna declared. "One murder and one accident."

"Or a series of accidents," Rian added. "The last accident was fatal."

Genna cocked her brow. "What do you mean: a series of accidents?"

"Dick had a rough couple of days after they found the maid. Rebecca Williams threatened to do him in with some ricin on his board notes and throw him down the murder hole. Remember that?"

Amy nodded. They had been touring the poison garden at Blarney Castle.

"If I was playing a hand of poker with Rebecca Williams, I'd be nervous," Rian declared. "She doesn't have poker tells."

"Could be the Botox," Zelda offered.

"Could be," Rian agreed. "Could be years of practice."

"If Doris was right, I don't think Rebecca's past is squeaky clean."

"She could be making a power play to keep him in line," Genna answered. "She's on the board of Bartlestown Bank. Has been for years. I can't imagine the two of them see eye to eye on much. She doesn't like him. That much is clear."

"And when were you going to share that little nugget about Rebecca?" Amy demanded, letting her exasperation show. "And how is it that you even know such a thing? She's on the board of the bank?"

"When you're in charge of finding money for a non-profit, you're always looking for people with purse strings and heart. And a healthy ego. The ego is the icing on the cake. Or the Jane Hancock on the check."

"For Project X," Zelda said.

"Project X," Genna agreed. "A little background research and *voila*! You have a self-made woman from humble beginnings who likes to do good in her community. She's a perfect donor candidate. It doesn't hurt that she also owns a chunk of commercial real estate."

"Has she written you a check?" Amy asked.

"Not yet," Genna said. "I haven't asked. I haven't found the right angle. But I will."

Amy thought of Doris and her saga of woe working at the bank. She had mentioned Rebecca was a client at the time. She hadn't mentioned the name of the bank — it might not even be the same one. It didn't matter. The bank could change names, but the people involved could remain the same. Rebecca and Dick had history, and if everything Doris had said about his little spy ring was true, he probably had dirt on Rebecca Williams. And maybe she had some dirt on him.

"A series of unfortunate accidents," Amy pondered out loud. "He got stung by a bee, blew up like a balloon, and then tripped down the stairs."

"And then he got brained with the mallet by Doris," Zelda put in. "That was no accident."

"Yeah, I don't consider being hit in the head with a croquet mallet much of an *—oops, my bad,"* Genna said. "I don't know why Doris whacked him, but I'm sure it felt good."

She could tell them about Doris' experience with Dick. Even though Doris told Garda O'Shannon, Amy didn't know how much Doris left in and how much she left out. It was Doris' story to tell, and she clearly had shared it with Amy in confidence. Doris had been looking for an ally. Maybe even an alibi. Had Doris sought her revenge in the blacklight dark? Was it an impromptu, boil-over reaction from a long unsettled score?

"I think revenge is within the realm of possibility," Rian ventured, her expression rather solemn. "The way I see it, Dick collapsed from the whack on the head and that's when Eloise thought he was having an allergic reaction. She did what she needed to do."

"And what about Eloise?" Genna added. "We haven't seen her since she followed the stretcher out of the barn."

"We haven't seen Mona, either," Amy added. "I think they may both be at a breaking point."

Amy could see her Sudoku grid starting to fill. "Dick told James the maid was stabbed with the ice pick from the oyster bar. He claimed he saw some guy grab it and run. But Garda O'Shannon didn't share that detail with me. Why wouldn't he?"

Zelda narrowed her eyes at Amy but that didn't stop her from thinking out loud.

"While we were crashing the wedding feast, we thought James and Dick were on the golf course," Amy offered. "Dick said they didn't return until after the party disbursed. Today James said they came back early. Who's telling the truth? Where was everybody right before the banshee screamed and Zelda found the maid? Garda O'Shannon must know everybody's wheres and whens."

"Isn't this charming?" Zelda said with obvious sarcasm. "We come all the way to Ireland to be in one of the most gorgeous places on Earth, only to sit around and stew about who knew who and what and when?" Zelda tapped her fingers on the arm of the settee.

Her manicurist had matched Zelda's fingernails to her suitcase *du jour*, which was full of her newest fashion passion: leopard spots. Her nails were tangerine with a little band of black spots crossing the nail diagonally from top to bottom. Zelda looked down at her nails and Amy thought she looked bored. It wasn't her job to entertain anyone, but she felt a pang of guilt anyway. Zelda was, after all, her plus-one and best friend.

"What if we hire a car and go shopping," Zelda offered. "Just because we can't drive the Ring of Kerry doesn't mean we're stuck here with nothing to do."

"I'd be up for that," Rian said. "At least the hire-a-car part. Shopping, not so much."

"I'll see what I can find out," Zelda said, suddenly chipper. She bounded off the settee and headed for the concierge at the front desk.

While Zelda was making arrangements that better suited her mood, Amy and Rian and Genna made plans of another kind. Divide and conquer. Ask questions. Snoop around. Genna would approach Rebecca. Rian would talk with the staff. Amy would catch James and Gayle and grill them again. At the top of her list was what time the Williams' arrived at the hotel. She remembered something about Gayle and Eloise watching the wedding from one of the sitting rooms. Gayle mentioned the bagpipes, which were at the beginning and close of the ceremony. But now Amy couldn't remember whether that was before or after Gayle helped the Williams couple check into the hotel. Had the arrival of the Williams couple triggered a chain of unfortunate events that ended badly for Caroline Gadling? And for Richard Collins, too.

Zelda's displeasure was apparent when she returned from her errand. "No cars until tomorrow. We're stuck."

Amy expected to see Garda O'Shannon drive up at any minute. The Brands had shared their find with the hotel manager, and he had called to report it. The easiest thing to do with Zelda was set her on Mr. Dimples when he arrived. She could shadow him like no one else could. Maybe it would assuage her need to be noticed.

"The three of us are on a mission," Amy shared with her friend. "When he arrives, it would be a big help if you got close to

O'Shannon to find out everything you can. You're good at eaves-dropping."

"Not as good as Genna," Zelda said, "but I can hold my own."

That settled, they went their separate ways with a promise to meet up for lunch where they could compare notes then.

# CHAPTER TWENTY EIGHT

Doris was withholding information and Amy knew it. She didn't know what that information was, but there was something. Doris had a habit of adjusting her glasses when she was uncomfortable, and Amy had noticed there had been quite a bit of that.

Until the Coroner's report, the Gardai wouldn't know the cause and manner of death. Not that Mr. Dimples would share those details with her anyway. But until then, the direction of their inquiry seemed to be headed toward Doris. She was, after all, holding the weapon of malice.

While the four of them were not in the investigative crosshairs, as Genna had so aptly put it, she knew they were under scrutiny. If for no other reason than they had been there, done that — so to speak. How *would* they explain they were all four in Ireland and another husband was dead? Another wasbund. What seemed like a loosely entangled web knitted together because of Zelda's admission, could now make them scapegoats for the investigation team. And yet, if she tried to solve what happened, she could end up pointing a finger at Doris in the process. Given Doris' history with Dick.

She remembered Doris' comment: 'I don't know which was worse; his '*maybe for the best*' statement or him firing me when I called him a liar.'

This was her predicament. If she wasn't supposed to meddle in the investigation, as Garda O'Shannon so clearly put it, why the snippet? Although her angst over these murderous, fortune-telling dreams was nothing new, recent history had given her a different approach. She was beginning to see them as a gift rather than a curse. And that was a big shift in perspective. It was a visceral shift, too — a sort of opening up, a relaxing of, a letting go in her gut. Now they felt … purposeful.

If she didn't do anything but let the Gardai take its course in the investigation, was she about to betray Doris in the worst way possible? She wanted to protect Doris. And her friends. Follow your gut, Sparks. Evidence of means. Evidence of motive. Evidence of opportunity. It was all there, she just needed to find it. Like a puzzle piece you'd swear was missing. And then all of the sudden there it was. That missing piece. Right in front of you.

Maybe she was looking in the wrong place. Maybe there wasn't a connection in the two deaths as Garda O'Shannon had implied. What if the maid's death was a case of mistaken identity? What if Caroline Gadling was in the wrong place at the wrong time? A stroke of very bad luck. Bad fairy luck. Had someone been after the maid — the real maid — striking blindly from behind? The thought made her shiver, and she shook it off.

She started to climb the stairs and then stopped. One of the maids was watching her out of the corner of her eye.

"Hi," Amy said brightly.

The woman's face looked young and carefree. "Something you need, miss?"

Amy eyed the maid's cart. "An extra bar of soap? I dropped mine in the toilet when I was shaving my legs."

The maid ignored the pathetic sounding lie. What an edjit, she could imagine the girl whisper in her head. She smiled politely and handed Amy a fistful of soaps. "Just in case it should happen again," she said cheerfully.

"Actually, I would like to ask you something else."

A shadow crossed over the woman's eyes.

"How many maids work each floor every day? I mean are there several of you?"

"Nah, me an' Bets be it. I take the top up there and she takes the bottom here and we get our bits and bobs in place in no time. Beds, towels, trash, and clean the jacks. Takes no time a'tall when we're not turning the room."

"You're the one taking care of our room upstairs?"

"I would be. Is it a problem?"

"Oh, no, you're doing a commendable job." The woman nearly curtsied. "I was wondering if you saw anything out the ordinary in the rooms in the past few days?"

Amy could see her thoughts turning. "Out of the ordinary?" She spoke slowly.

She needed to be careful. "You know, things out of place or missing altogether?"

"I cannot say. Such as what? Are you missing something?"

"No, everything in our room is where it needs to be." She bit her lip. "What about the guests? Have you seen guests out of place?"

"We see guests everywhere about the hotel, and Bets and me don't say a word, we don't. But when that …"

Amy felt the woman's curiosity rising but it stopped in an abrupt and trailing end. "But when something like what happened happens, that's different, isn't it?" Amy asked.

The maid nodded and Amy saw the conflict behind her eyes. To gossip or not to gossip. Wasn't that a wrangle almost everyone faced when they knew something juicy?

"I promise I won't say where I heard it," Amy offered.

In the brief silence that followed, the maid glanced at her cart and then down the hall. She leaned slightly toward Amy. "Bets says the mister with the nubby hair and dandy ripe air was in and out that room sure as he pleased, he was. Had his own key, he did. And it wasn't even his room. I know because I serviced his room on my floor."

Dandy ripe air. Amy laughed out loud. What a wonderful way to say he was wearing too much cologne — a person of considerable fragrance who left a certain *sillage* in his wake.

"When was that?" Amy asked.

The maid leaned in closer. "The day she were kilt. True enough. He was leaving in a bit of a hurry as Bets was headed in. Had that fur coat of hers all balled up under his arm like he was carrying a lamb, she said. Not that the two crossed paths mind you — Bets was careful like. She said the room was in bits when she got in. Clothes tossed to the four corners.

"Bets came to ask what she should do about it all and that's when we found out she were kilt. Bets told the manger about it, she did. Told the manager about the mess in the room and who made it. Told him she didn't take that fancy fur and she wasn't to be blamed. Didn't want it any of it coming to haunt her none. She does a good job with her cleaning. As honest as the day is long."

Amy couldn't believe what she was hearing. Dick had searched the room. Not only had he taken her passport and wallet, but her fur coat. Had he thrown that in the lake, too?

Amy's heart was racing. So much made sense now. Dick had taken the wallet and fur so no one would know who the woman was. But Dick had forgotten one piece of ID. The luggage tag on her suitcase. It must have been out of sight. Under the bed, perhaps? And what else had he taken? What else would he need to hide from prying eyes?

"Did Bets say anything else?"

The woman nodded. "Plenty to be sure. But not what I will repeat."

What she would give to be a wall with ears near these two, although she wouldn't catch but every third word.

"She's superstitious, Bets is. Says she had an omen he were to be next. And lo if he weren't."

Amy let surprised silence fill in the gaps and the maid turned toward her cart as if dismissed from their conversation.

"Wait! Is there a way to get from one floor to next with a cart?"

The maid pointed to a door Amy hadn't noticed.

"It's a service lift. That's how I get laundry down and our carts to and fro."

"Is there a key?"

She pulled a lanyard from inside her uniform. The key hung from a clasp.

So that's how Caroline and her cart had gotten to the second floor. She had swiped both the uniform and the cart, along with the key to the lift as well. But why? What was she after? If Dick had access to her room, why did she want access to his?

"Is there anyone staying in the last room on our floor?" Amy asked as the thought culled itself forward. Maybe Caroline wasn't hunting Dick at all.

"A gentleman stays in that last suite. With a room full of gadgets that he says not to bother with. Tidy up and be gone, he says. So that's what I do. Clean the jack and make the bed."

"What kind of gadgets?"

"I dunno. Cameras and the like. Keeps the drapes drawn. A right squinter, I'd say.

"Squinter?"

"Me Gran called 'em a Nosey-Parker. A right nosey neighbor watching the goin's on. Squinting out the window, like. I got to get on if you're good, now." She turned again toward her cart as Amy was pondering the Nosey Parker she had never seen enter or leave that last room in the hall.

The woman turned back. "You said, 'people out of place'. The misses next door to the one kilt. Nice lady. Kind eyes. Toffee colored glasses? She came up with a bouquet of flowers when I was tidying for the mister we spoke of."

"The Nosey-Parker?"

"The other one. Said they were for the Mrs. Said, 'could she place them in the room'? I said I would, and she said, 'no, she wanted to do that herself'."

"Did you watch her?"

"I was busy cleaning the jack, so she came in with her flowers. They were left when I came through and she was gone." The woman smoothed her uniformed over her slim hips and Amy was reminded of Caroline and Zelda's comment about pudding.

"But there was a wet spot on the rug," the maid continued, a frown deepening on her mouth. "I wondered had she spilt her glass. But then I remembered there was a wet spot before. I don't know what's going on with the rug. I hope no banshee be spilling her tears, there. That's what Bets be saying."

"Banshee tears?"

"Oh, just the superstitious tales of the shanty Irish. All flannel and flattery. We grew up on myths to keep us in line and not misbehavin'. But it did seem out of the ordinary. It was right before he — well, it was before he took a mad hopper on the stairs. Went headfirst by a look of it. Don't know what he tripped on. Mona had me come up and make his room right all over again. It was a right grand mess."

Amy nodded. "I saw the room, too. I went in with Mona. Shoe hanging from the fan and everything."

The woman nodded. "The room was in bits, it was."

And then Dick moved to another room anyway. Amy's heart was pounding. Doris brought those flowers to the room. Had she brought in the bees, too, knowing that Dick was allergic to their sting? Oh, Doris!

"Well, good day, miss," the maid said as she slid the key into the lift and waited for the door to open. It was all Amy could to do not to follow her and sneak a peek at what a Nosey-Parker's room looked like.

# CHAPTER TWENTY NINE

Amy looked for James and Gayle, but by the time she had gotten the scoop from the upstairs maid, the couple had gone off on a picnic, according to the front desk. The lake was indeed off limits, along with the rowboat and the swans. She knew James would be disappointed. It wasn't lunchtime yet, so she decided to stroll the gardens. Maybe she would locate the couple on the grounds.

The sun was bright today, and the sky a crystalline blue. The sunlight made the flowers in bloom seem even more brilliant than before. She passed a man in a striped work shirt and straw hat that had melded itself to his head over years of comfort and sweat. She wished she had thought to grab her own hat.

"Your gardens are beautiful," she said in passing. He looked up, a bit surprised by her approach, but his expression said he appreciated her comment. His gardens were obviously a source of pride. He touched the brim of his hat politely and spoke. It sounded something like *guru maga hoot.*

She followed the well patterned path that lead through the gardens. One could take several paths while strolling. One path led toward the croquet green where they had climbed for their first-day outing. Another led toward the barn that, with the sun shining on its roof, looked quite innocent in the daylight. There were no markings on the door. No yellow caution tape. Whatever had been discovered inside the barn had been observed, photographed, and catalogued by the Gardai. She could take a peek and see. But she found herself turning away.

The other path led toward the stretch of land that stood out as a peninsula over the lake. The paved path led to the little chapel, the famous St. Finbarr's Oratory chapel, where couples all over Ireland dreamed of tying the knot. She found herself drawn to the structure, with its steep gray roof and flat gray stones and the arched windows facing the lake.

It wasn't a long a walk, but it was a breathtaking one. The dark emerald mountains rose in a circle around her, their rounded peaks covered in trees and a patchwork of color as the clouds and the shadows they made changed the hues from bright green to dark.

She was struck by the absence of sound, although there were natural sounds present. She listened to the pip of a bird somewhere nearby and its mate answering. The rushing sound of a waterfall sounded somewhere off in the distance. She heard water rippling as it pushed gently against the shore at her feet. She looked for the swans, but they were elsewhere.

The absence of sound was the absence of humanity. There were no busy streets with the roar of cars. No bells or blares or sirens. No Harley Davidsons blasting their way through the mountains. No bands. No bars. No people chatter. No motors running. Nothing. Nothing that didn't belong here. She listened to the crunch of her shoes on the pathway. The beat of her gait. The off-click as one heel hit the pavement different than the other.

She was drawn into the simplicity of this moment. She was drawn in to the quiet and everything that lived in that quiet. Thousands upon thousands of trees. Birds by the flock. Flowers stretching their heads to the sun to soak up every ray that splashed down between rains.

She could feel her breath deepen. Her chest opened to let in the air. Let it all the way in. Draw it all the way down to her soul to the place where everything mattered. And where nothing mattered. The place where they were one and the same.

For a flash she thought how wonderful it would be to share this moment with her best friends. And then she knew that it could never happen. That at the very moment more than one stood here, the silence would be broken. The quiet would end. With the very presence of another, the air would change. As though the thoughts inside their heads could change it. It would cease to be as it was right now.

She touched the Celtic knot of her necklace with the tips of her fingers. She was near. She was always near. "Grandmother," she whispered, and the sound of her own voice surprised her.

She opened the wooden door to the church and stepped inside. The quiet followed her in.

In size and appointment, the chapel reminded her of the historic Catholic Church in Bluff Springs. It reminded her, too, of the magnificent hewn rock church that stood on the hill overlooking the wine country of Arkansas. This chapel was smaller. Much less opulent. The artifacts were modest, tucked into the alcoves to be singularly adored, revered, and appealed to in prayer. The air smelled of wax burning and old incense.

There were only a few pews on either side of the aisle. No wonder the wedding had spilled out into the path. She ran her hand over the smooth, polished wood and breathed in the ancient quiet. It was the scent of time that stood still inside this enclave of history, and hope, and hermitage. St. Finbarr had believed in miracles. He made this miracle on the banks of the headwaters of the River Lee. He had so believed in miracles his legend claimed the sun did not set for nearly a month when he died. Lore and legend. Fact or not. She could see why St. Finbarr had chosen to live as a hermit on this island, this tiny island within an island in the vast wild sea.

A sound caught her attention.

"Who is it?" She whispered, daring to break the sacred quiet.

# CHAPTER THIRTY

"Who's here?" Amy repeated when no one answered.

Tentatively she walked down the aisle toward the altar. She recognized the hair. "Rebecca?"

The woman turned to face to Amy.

"Oh, I'm so sorry, I didn't realize…"

Rebecca patted the pew beside her. "Sit, Amy. Come. Sit with me."

Neither said anything for a few minutes and she was satisfied to sit in silence. The quiet of the church soothed her like a soft embrace. It was cool inside the chapel, not from air conditioning — she doubted if there was such a thing in Ireland — but from some ordained architectural knowledge that kept the light in and the elements out.

The altar stood before them. The ornate carved wood was ancient. The censer that hung above it looked as if had come over on a ship from Egypt. The cloth cover on the altar surface was green, decorated with large circles of what looked like embroidered gold. Rian would know all the names of the parts of this sacred center. She did not.

"It is so beautiful here," Rebecca whispered. "The world and its chaos cannot enter here. Can't even cross the threshold."

"Yes," Amy murmured. The quiet enveloped them again.

"He loves me too much," Rebecca said suddenly. She took a deep breath. "I love him, too. Really I do. What's not to love? He's as straight as an arrow."

"He adores you," Amy said. "I've seen it in his eyes when he looks at you."

"Yes." Rebecca looked wistful. Amy hoped they were talking about Rebecca's husband.

"He looks at me with such — with such great need," she said, finally finding the words. "As if he would starve for breath if I were not by his side. It feels unbearably heavy, sometimes. Sometimes I question whether I can breathe myself. Are you married?" She added abruptly.

"Not anymore."

"That can be a blessing. In some ways at least. In many ways I think Eloise is the luckiest."

Amy involuntarily took in a breath.

"Oh, I don't mean to be unkind about Richard Collins," Rebecca said in response. "Poor Dick. No one expected that."

Rebecca paused for a moment as if reflecting on the events of the past few days. "I'm sitting in this wondrous place thinking about how women my age find themselves in a very different place than we thought we would. Every generation is a little different, I guess, but looking at retirement isn't as rosy as you think it is." She glanced at Amy. "I know, that sounds terribly ungrateful, but really, marriage doesn't look the same at this end as it did when we were standing at that end." Rebecca motioned to the altar in front of them and Amy thought of the thousands of couples who had exchanged lifetime vows at that very spot. "I can't picture what the rest of my days will look like. Not the same as they have been, that's for certain. Reg is retiring, you know. Next year."

"At least the chamber will be in good hands," Amy offered. "Isn't Gayle going to be promoted to president?"

"She's expecting it," Rebecca answered. "She's been doing everything possible to make herself the best choice. I certainly think she is, but my opinion only counts behind the scenes. I don't serve on the chamber board. It's a conflict of interest." She glanced sideways at Amy. "Dick Collins opposed Gayle's promotion. Dick was persuasive. He was a solid force to overcome. He liked to use the power of his position and he had his thumb on whomever he wanted to control. Gayle wasn't his only victim."

Amy nodded. Doris either. And now — Rebecca didn't have to say it — Dick was out of the way. Gayle no longer had opposition to her promotion when Reginald Williams retired.

Rebecca sighed heavily. "I can't imagine what Reg is going to do with his days. Take up some ghastly hobby like woodturning or beer making? He's ready to shift into slippers and a housecoat. He's going to be underfoot every day. He's going to follow me around like a puppy on a leash!"

Again, she blew out as if blowing away the thought of Reginald as a dog on a leash. Amy smiled to herself. He'd be an Airedale or a Russian Wolfhound. Or something equally as angular and aloof.

"That's what I meant by Eloise being lucky," Rebecca declared. "She won't have to deal with that. She'll have other difficult things to face, of course, but not a bored husband who bellows when things don't go his way."

Was she talking about Dick or her Reginald?

Rebecca crossed and uncrossed her legs, smoothed the pleats in her pants and then folded her hands in her lap. Her fingers worked the tops of her knuckles. Rian was wrong about her poker tells. This was a woman in conflict.

"My therapist calls it the silver separation. Apparently it's happening all over the free world. Long time marriages of the sixty-plus are changing as they retire. Couples are at a crossroads. Especially us women. We want to reinvent ourselves and launch a lifestyle we couldn't have before now. It's not because we don't love our spouses. It's because what worked in the past doesn't fit the future. The same pieces don't fit this new picture, this new frame. And men don't see it coming. They go blindly into the abyss with a gold watch and a retirement fund."

"I can see that," Amy said quietly. "Men don't want things to change."

"Exactly," Rebecca agreed. "They want Meatloaf Monday."

Amy nodded even though she had never made a meatloaf on a Monday. Or ever.

"We're supposed to stay the same delightful, agreeable girl they married. But that isn't possible. If you can't grow and change you just wither and die on the vine."

"I wish I had sage advice to offer you."

"What a kind thought," Rebecca replied. "And what a mess this trip to Ireland has morphed into for you. You worked hard on that capital campaign. Reg was impressed with your ideas and how you made them happen. Manifest is the word I like to use. You should be proud of yourself."

Amy beamed. She appreciated the compliment more than Rebecca would ever know.

"Did you know I was going to buy that building you're in?"

"You mean the Cardboard Cottage?"

Rebecca nodded. "I was going to turn it into nightly lodging. Something told me to pass. Something told me to let it become something else. That the old building belonged to someone else. Maybe the building itself told me that when I was lurking through those rooms. I'm glad it's yours. It suits you. You've given it an exciting new life."

Amy thought she would burst at the seams. "Oh my," was all she could muster.

Rebecca clapped her hands once and then held them in front her. "I think it's time Reg and I consider a change of plans. I've always wanted to see the whole of Ireland. Scotland, too. Perhaps I'll make a world traveler of him, yet."

"You mean you're leaving?"

"I believe we are."

"Can you leave?"

Rebecca raised a brow.

"Aren't we required to stay until the Gardai complete their investigation and make an arrest?"

"An arrest? Oh, well. I believe the situation has worked itself out on its own. I would say the Gardai have what they need."

"They told you that?"

Rebecca shook her head. "Not in so many words. But what's done is done even if it didn't turn out as I expected. Although Eloise nearly spoiled it with her change in plans. Everything can return to normal now."

Amy's eyes were wide. "What are you talking about?"

"I'm talking about bank fraud. I suspected he was up to more than sexual misconduct, and I was right. I suspected that Dick was using poor gullible, greedy Caroline to cover his tracks at the bank. He probably promised her the moon while he used her to cover his embezzlements and client cons. How do you think he got that helicopter? He certainly didn't take out a loan.

"It didn't happened quite as I imagined, but we had to get them both out of the bank for an extended absence so the discrepancies would rise to the surface. FDIC rules are in place for that reason. That's when bank fraud shows up like a blinking neon light."

Or a blinking blacklight! What had Rebecca done?

"I know what I did was manipulation," Rebecca said quietly, as if talking to herself. "But there was no other way. In the end, well, in the end — I believe a mightier hand was at play."

She rose, crossed herself, and then exited the pew. Amy could hear the heavy wooden door close behind her.

# CHAPTER THIRTY ONE

Amy entered the lobby to the sound of fiddle and flute and rhythmic applause. She could see through to the lobby bar where Rian was sitting. She was actually sitting on the bar, her feet swinging rhythmically against the wood.

Amy turned to the front desk clerk. "What's going on here?"

"The O'Deas of County Clare are in for a *céilí* with all the cousins what could be gathered," the man said brightly. "Your friend has met her clan."

"A *kaylee?*"

"A *céilí* be a gathering for no other reason than to visit with family and friends."

Amy glanced at Rian who was one big happy grin. Beside her on the bar were a dozen pints lined up, foamy heads settling and waiting to be served.

"Can you believe this?" Rian said as Amy approached. "This is the clan O'Dea," she shouted over the happy whine of the accordion in the corner and the roar in the room.

"And why are they here?"

Rian shrugged. "To meet their long-lost cousin from Arkansas."

"Is that true?" Amy asked.

"Who's going to tell them otherwise?"

Amy looked around the small pub that seemed to hold more people than possible. There were only a few tables, but every seat and surface held a friendly face laughing or talking or playing the tune. There were dark heads, red heads, and bald heads. There were dark eyes and green eyes and old eyes. Youngsters twirled ring-around-the rosy in the center of the room, hands clasped together as they spun. The pitch of music and the chatter and the laughter were loud. And cheerful.

Zelda sat nestled in a corner holding court with a table of men, her eyes sparking like emeralds when she looked over at Amy. She lifted her hand and waved. Genna was on the opposite side of the room, arm in arm with a man who was apparently teaching her a dance routine with steps and a twirl.

Amy looked around the room with a full and happy heart. This was the Ireland they had come to see. Oh, the countryside was beautiful with its ruined castles and expanse of green all neatly plotted into squares. The rugged rock mountains were picturesque as they rose toward the sky, with peat-colored water rushing over the edges, down and out to the sea. These were picture perfect backdrop settings of this Emerald Isle. But this, right here in this crowded room, was the spirit of Ireland. The real reason why people came. Not just to see the landmarks that withstood the trials of time. But for the people who called it home. For the culture they lived with family. For this. The clamor of people gathered in one place, comfortable with themselves and anyone else who joined them. For this exact moment, when the tune from the musicians kept time and tempo captive. Toes tapping out the beat. Laughter making the harmony, filling in the space. And stories told to any-one who'd listen. Irish tales of flattery and flannel. Amy let herself fill like a glass, the lyrical brogue and the melodies rushing to her like a warm, welcoming breeze.

No one was on their cell phone. No one was scrolling through their apps or their emails. They were present. They were here to create a good time. *Craic,* they called it. The Irish craic was about fun — whenever and wherever and why ever. Just because. *Céilí.*

Rian handed Amy a pint. "*Sláinte,*" she said, tapping Amy's glass with hers. "I have finally found my roots."

"*Sláinte,*" Amy repeated. "Well done, you."

"Even the O'Dea family bard is here." Rian motioned with her glass. "See that elderly gentleman over there? He's the family historian. Knows everything there is to know about the O'Deas from County Clare. He gave me this book." She held it up for Amy to see.

"'O'Dea'," Amy read. "'The story of a rebel clan'." She grinned at Rian. "Well, if that doesn't fit you to a tee I don't know what would."

"We don't have proof of course, but he suggested the name was altered somewhere on the American side. A typo made early on." Rian pointed to the book title. "'*Ua Déaghaidh.*' That literarily translates to of Day or O'Day as we'd say. Somewhere in transition that little mark over the *é* was confused as the dot over the letter *i*. And then the *a* became the *i* and that's all it took. It's easy to see how the letter *s* was added — it made the O'Dei plural. See?"

"I do see," Amy said. "It's a letter thing."

Rian nodded. "According to the bard, the O'Deas were one of the first families in Europe to have a surname. This book is the history of the clan O'Dea," Rian said beaming. "Right down to the chieftain who now lives in Wisconsin. There's another branch who migrated to New Orleans. And that's getting me closer to home," Rian said, tapping the cover of the book. "It's just a hop and a skip from New Orleans to Arkansas, since it was originally part of Louisiana at that time. All you had to do was paddle up the Mississippi to get to the Ozarks."

Amy watched her friend. She had never seen Rian so animated by history. Or much else for that matter. It did matter, because here, more than 4,000 miles from home, Rian had found her origin, the place where her roots began.

"They had a gathering in 1990," Rian added. "O'Dea families came from all around the world. I wish I had known."

"Next time," Amy said. "I can't think of a better reason for us to come back. You don't own that castle we visited by any chance." She added as a quick afterthought.

"Not by a far stretch," Rian answered. "But I can become a member of The International O'Dea Clan Association. That's good enough for me."

Amy looked over as tables were dragged to the center of the room. A beautiful, tall woman with hair pulled into a thick, dark braid threw a tablecloth over the surface. And then, as if by magic, pots and bowls and baskets of food began to appear. Suddenly there were loaves of bread and crocks of butter. Steaming pots of stew and china bowls clambered into a tall pile as the crowd gathered in. Amy watched as the mountains of food appeared and then disappeared. Evidently, a *céilí* was no *céilí* without sustenance. And lots of it.

# CHAPTER THIRTY TWO

When the feast had been cleared away and the tables returned to their places along the wall, the bard stood. In a strong, clear voice, with all eyes and ears trained on him, he began.

"The legend of the *Ua Déaghaidh,* the rebel clan O'Dea, begins with the king of Scythia — now near modern day Iran — about eight hundred years before Christ. I haven't enough breath left in me to tell that story from beginning to end, but it begins there, nonetheless.

"From Spain, the descendants of this time were told to sail for a green land where they would flourish. It was called Inis Fail — The Isle of Destiny. And sail they did.

"They landed on the wild coast north of what is now Donegal to survey the land for where they would settle. Alas, they were attacked at sea, and returned to Spain. And yet, they were not spurned. Many years later they sailed for Inis Fail once again, but a great storm blew in and flung their ships to the rocks and cliffs from Kerry to Mayo.

Such would be their destiny, you should think. To lie desolate on the shore. But no. We follow *Ua Déaghaidh* through many generations and many wars, as they settled where we live today in County Clare.

"In the early centuries, the lands of Ireland were allotted to the clans of noble pedigree. The chief who gave his own name to this clan was *Déaghaidh*. Day. He is mentioned in Keating's History of Ireland of the year 934. They were one of the first families to adopt a surname when King Brian Boru — the High King of Ireland — made it compulsory for all noble families.

"The O'Deas, as they became known, were lords of land from Northwest Clare from the river Fergus to the East, the Burren to the North and the Atlantic ocean to the West. Known as the Barony of Tullagh O'Dea. The home of the O'Dea, and the hillock where they would come to build their stronghold, the place of their hermitage.

"Sadly, there is much time in our history when warfare and chaos reigns, so. In 1318, the chieftain of Dysert O'Dea fought his fiercest battle. Nearly one hundred men of noble birth perished, but since that day in May, no Englishman held power in County Clare. For more than two hundred years peace and prosperity reigned. By the year 1690, the parish was home to over two thousand families.

"It wasn't to last. But there is tenacity in the veins of the O'Deas clan. There is Will to survive. The passion to live is their destiny. And even though they have since scattered to the four winds, the O'Deas have kept their roots alive and thriving. Including in your America."

He paused and turned a kind smile toward Rian. "Much of the clan lives outside of Ireland, now. We are scholars and architects, politicians and priests. Musicians and poets. We are farmers and industrial workers, shopkeepers and servants. And we welcome you, Rian. This is your family. These are your people. We are your roots. May God keep you in the palm of His hand."

Amy felt her heart swell as she gazed at her friend. Rian's chin trembled as she brought her glass to her lips. She bowed to the bard, and then to the room. "Thank you," she said simply. "I am honored. I am humbled."

"Such news deserves a blessing. And another round," called a voice from the room. "May you escape the gallows, avoid distress and be as healthy as a trout."

Cheers went around the room with a loud crescendo.

Rian laughed and turned to the bard at her side. "I can't match your story but my grandfather O'Deis told this story ever since I was little and sitting on the dock learning to fish. It's the legend of the Blarney Stone of Arkansas."

The listeners cheered and Rian began.

"According to our legend, the Stone of Arkansas was a chip off the old Blarney block."

"Tell us so," one of ladies said. "What would the Blarney be doin' there halfway across the world?"

Rian nodded. "Legend claims that a piece of the Blarney Stone was carried all the way from Ireland to Arkansas in a traveler's pocket. You all would like Arkansas. There are lots of mountains and streams."

"But not as many sheep," Zelda interjected.

"Agreed," Rian said and went on. "This stone in Arkansas weighs more than seven thousand pounds by estimation. Let's see … that's uh … close to three thousand kilograms give or take."

The listeners rumbled with doubt.

"Yes, of course we know he didn't carry that much rock in his pocket. And that's where the story gets good.

"One day a young man was walking in the woods. He was hoping to find the words to ask for his best girl's hand in marriage. He didn't need the words for her. No, she was in love with him, too. He needed the words for her father, who was a stern man not so eager to let her marry.

The listeners hummed with interest.

"So, this young fellow leans against a rock to catch his breath and something catches his attention. And what could it be but a leprechaun!"

The listeners groaned.

"T'aint no such thing as a leprechaun," one of them said.

"No, it wasn't a leprechaun it was a… it was uh," Rian stalled.

"Most likely a Púca," one of the men spoke up. "Thems always bring good and bad at will. Likes to talk with humans about not much of anyt'ing. Seeing how they live deep in the woods. Right rooty looking creature. Always carrying a penny whistle for company."

"I saw one what looked like a dog once," said another. "Had fur was all twisted in knots this way and another! Eyes glowing the color of the setting sun. I said: 'leave me be, Púca, I did. I have no use for ye good or no.' Disappeared right before my eyes. It did. Right when I blinked."

Another said, "Let the woman finish, whatever creature it was after you had one too many pints."

The listeners chuckled.

"This … creature," Rian continued, "told the young man that he rode in a pocket all the way to America clinging to this chip of a rock. Both were tossed in the woods right where they stood. They both went over the hill and down into the holler, as sure as you please.

"But then he fell into a deep slumber and when he awoke some many decades later, the chip had grown into the monolith it is now. The same rock the lad was leaning into."

Rian nodded. "The Púca said, 'Kiss the stone and you will have the gift of gab. Kiss the stone right and proper and the legend of the Blarney will follow you wherever you go for all your days to come.'"

The listeners murmured again.

"And so, he kissed the stone and then he kissed it twice to be sure. And then he became the mayor of our fair city and has never shut up."

They all laughed.

"Did he get the girl?"

"Of course, he got the girl," Rian said laughing. "To her father he gave the most impassioned speech of his life. Not only did he win the girl but the old man's heart. So, if you ever come to visit us, you can kiss our Arkansas Blarney! And you can still hear that leprechaun laughing in the hills. I mean, the Púca, or whatever it is."

There was genuine applause and the hard clink of glasses on the tables.

Genna leaned toward Rian. "Is that a true story? Or is that a crock of rock you just made up?"

"Yes," Rian said, and Amy laughed out loud. Genna wouldn't get any more of an answer than that.

When the murmur from the listeners and the clink of glasses had died down, Amy turned to the man standing beside her. "Have you ever heard a banshee?"

"Banshee." The man repeated. "I have heard it with my own ears, the pitch and keen of the banshee."

"It was a fox, you fool," his wife said and poked him in the ribs. "Or it was the rabbit it were chasing!"

"And how to explain the death of me *Daideó* what followed?"

The woman laughed. "Donkey's years and many a pint."

"True enough," he answered and raised his glass. "It was his time, God bless him. But I'm telling you now," he said and nodded to Amy, "me *Mórai* claimed a banshee lived in the garden down the lane. I was always afraid to see it rise up from the vines and howl when I passed by as a lad. You see that garden was always overgrown from neglect. The way the land fell away, there was a blind spot to it. Me *Mórai* claimed she'd rise up from the hollow spot like a scarecrow, she would. The banshee, I be talking about. Rise up like a scarecrow of a woman with a mossy green frock of shreds blowing in the wind, her hair blowing wild with it.

"There's some what say the cry is only the pitiful wail as she mourns the lost and departed, but others say she portends the death to come. Me *Móraí* was of that ilk. And I come to believe her, I do, as I heard it with my own ears. Saw it with my own two eyes."

"Oh, go on, you," the woman said. "Tell your yarn of the Banshee of Ennis Plow."

And so, he did.

"I have a secret admirer," Zelda claimed.

"Who?"

"I can't tell you."

"Are we playing twenty questions?" Amy asked, trying not to let her annoyance show. "Is that what you're fishing for?"

"No," Zelda fluffed the pillow behind her head. "I'm done fishing. Garda O'Shannon wouldn't bite if he was starving. Now Genna's smitten with an accordion player who likes to dance, and Rian has discovered she's related to all of County Clare."

"And where does your secret admirer fit in?"

"There was a note under the door when I came to change for Rian's party." Zelda dug the note from under her pillow and thrust it out to Amy.

*"There are few things as lovely as a rose in full bloom. If you are so inclined, meet me in the chapel tonight. I have something to show you. You won't be disappointed. Come alone."*

"That is the creepiest love note I've ever read," Amy said. "So inclined? Who says things like that?"

"Aren't you at least a little curious?"

"You won't be going alone, that's for sure. If we let you go at all." Her comment was punctuated with a knock on the door. As she crossed the room, she heard the hushed giggles of her other two friends outside.

"Land shark," Genna said and then snorted into laughter.

"Candy gram," Rian added in a monotone. "Flowers for Zelda Carlisle."

Genna snorted again.

Amy opened the door to see two giddy friends. "Doesn't that skit ever get old?"

"No, it doesn't," Genna scolded. "Unless you're getting too old to remember what humor sounds like."

"Where are my flowers?" Zelda asked, looking disappointed. "I was hoping that my secret admirer really had picked me a bouquet of flowers."

"You're kidding, right?"

Zelda frowned at Amy. "Why would I be kidding about that? It's a perfectly normal thing for a secret admirer to do."

"Secret admirer?" Genna asked.

"More like a secret stalker," Amy muttered. "She got a note asking her to sneak out to the chapel."

Zelda exhaled. "What is wrong with you today, Amy? If I didn't know better, I'd say you were jealous."

Amy turned away. "What are you two after?"

"Rian came to tell you something her cousin shared at the *céilí*, and I came for moral support."

"That sounds like doom and gloom," Zelda replied. "Who needs moral support when you're gossiping?"

Genna shrugged.

"You remember when I mentioned Bryan O'Dea from the wedding? He's how this gathering got put into the works, more or less. He told someone about my search for Irish roots, and that person told someone and so on until it got to the bard, who's in charge of the Dysert O'Dea castle. When I signed the book at the castle registry, I put the resort as our address, and somehow that's how we ended up with today's party."

"That's not the gossip," Genna added.

Rian nodded. "He said he saw the man with the ice pick at the wedding. He saw who took the pick from the ice sculpture at the oyster bar."

"He saw them?"

"He saw *him*. Dick Collins. He didn't know his name, of course, but I knew who he was talking about when he described him."

"Dick was lying!" Amy blurted. "Dick told the Garda he saw one of the men from the wedding take the ice pick and run. Dick took it. I knew it had to be Dick. Especially after what the maid said!"

All three pairs of eyes looked at Amy.

"Oh, right. I guess we haven't spoken since we scattered this morning."

"Out with it," Zelda said, and Amy told them about her conversation with the maid. She told them about Doris and the flowers, and how she had probably brought the bees in on the bouquet. Unwittingly? Maybe. Maybe not. She told them about Dick's access to Caroline's room and how he must have stolen her identification and tossed it into the lake. He took Caroline's fur coat, too, and that, as far as she knew, had not yet resurfaced. It was probably at the bottom of the lake. And finally, she recounted her conversation with Rebecca in the chapel.

Rian twirled a curl in her finger as she listened. "Why didn't he toss the ice pick along with the ID? Why leave the bloody weapon in plain sight?"

"It wasn't bloody," Zelda interjected. "It was on the ground at her feet. Wasn't it, Amy? I didn't see blood on the floor, did you?"

Amy didn't answer. There was something squirming in her mind. Like a worm on a hook. Something struggling to get free.

Something that didn't add up. She wouldn't say it out loud, but it seemed to her that Dick had gotten his comeuppance. Obviously, he had committed a number of sins he shouldn't have. Getting rid of Caroline could have been his last bad act. She remembered Rebecca's parting words: *A mightier hand was at play.*

"I don't think you should meet up with this secret admirer," Amy said finally. "It could be a trap."

"A trap?" Genna probed.

"The maid said there was a Nosey Parker in the room next to Eloise. The real maid. She said he had all kinds of cameras and gadgets in his room. Didn't want her touching any of it."

"I knew there was a spy thing happening!" Zelda declared. "I knew it! Didn't I say she was a spy?"

"Caroline may have been a spy," Amy agreed. "Rebecca knew there was something fraudulent going on at the bank — and it included Dick. Rebecca thought it included Caroline Gadling and she needed them both out of the bank at the same time to prove it. She manipulated this scenario to make sure it happened. Caroline may have sensed what Rebecca was up to. She may have warned Dick about what was going on. She may have tried to bribe her way to a *get out of jail free* card." Amy glanced at Rian and Rian flattened her lips. There was a time when Rian had needed a get out of jail free card, and her friends had driven all the way to the Mexico border with a wad of cash.

"But it didn't go as planned, as it rarely does," Rian said simply. "Caroline didn't get a free card."

Again, the worm wiggled on the hook; an idea struggling to get free. "Unless that was Rebecca's plan all along. She said things didn't go as expected, but maybe they went the way she wanted them to."

# CHAPTER THIRTY FOUR

It was impossible to hide from prying eyes on the walk from the resort and St. Finbarr's Oratory on the shore. The chapel and the peninsular path were visible from most of the hotel's front side windows, as Amy had discovered on her walk earlier. As she took in the environs that encircled the resort then, she noticed a lone figure in the window on the second floor. Eloise was looking out, and Amy could imagine the forlorn feeling that must surround her. She glanced up and saw that Eloise was watching the four of them now.

"Poor Eloise," Amy whispered and with a nod and they all turned to look. The curtains snapped closed, and Eloise disappeared from view.

They had discussed how they could send Zelda on her mission to meet this secret admirer. They couldn't walk together without being seen and they sure weren't going to let her go on her own. They decided they would all go together. The three of them would stay in the pews at the back of the chapel while Zelda met her man at the front, but they would be wary and watching for any sign should they need to spring into action. He would either have to take it or leave it. The choice wasn't his to make.

The scent of candles and old incense seemed familiar when Amy entered a step behind Zelda leading the parade. The chapel was dark except for the glow of the prayer candles in the bye-altar. They slipped quietly into the pews inside the door as Zelda walked toward the altar and the balding head sitting quietly at the front.

"Do you recognize him?" Amy whispered. Rian and Genna shook their heads.

"Hello," Zelda said. The sound echoed to where the three of them sat tense, elbows forward on the pew ahead.

"You've come," was the answer.

"A woman my age can't pass up too many opportunities to be admired, now can she?"

They couldn't hear his answer. In the moments that followed, they could hear nothing but the hum of two voices — one male and one female — talking in low tones. Zelda giggled now and again. Amy could see that their heads were bowed close together. She listened without hearing the words as her eyes swept over the chapel with its artifacts and relics of religion. In the glittering darkness created by the candles, she felt her eyelids grow heavy and her attention drift away. She glanced to Zelda just as the man put his arm around the back of the pew barely touching Zelda's shoulders. He glanced over his shoulder as he moved.

Amy's neck prickled.

She recognized him then, of course. Minus his ball cap, it was the same indistinct and be-speckled face she had noticed behind the camera lens since arriving at the resort. The Nosey Parker with his cameras and gadgets.

Zelda giggled. "Amy!"

Amy jerked. "What?" she whispered.

"You've got to see this. Come up here."

The three of them looked at each other in confusion and then sprang from the pew.

"This is Tom," Zelda said. "And boy does he have something you need to see." Zelda motioned to his camera.

Amy frowned. "You brought Zelda here to look at photos of the resort?"

"No," Zelda said quickly. "Photos of us. That's what he's been doing here."

"I thought you were shooting pictures for publicity?" Genna rumbled. "For a travel book or something."

"Show them," Zelda said. "Show them what you showed me. Especially the ones of that maid… that Caroline. Oh, and show those pictures of me," Zelda added. "I really do need to lay off those scampi flavored fries. They're going right to my ankles. Look," Zelda added, passing the camera to Amy.

The three of them looked into the digital display. It was a picture of Dick leaving the chapel through the very door they had just come through. There was a woman behind Dick and Amy heard herself gasp. She was in the shadow of the doorway, but it was the maid in her uniform. Or rather, Caroline Gadling dressed as a maid, her hands on her hips as if smoothing the wrinkles from her dress. She was putting on her coat and Amy noticed it was a fur. A thigh length fur. Something ridiculously expensive and not at all PETA-friendly. It was obvious she was unaware anyone was watching her, let alone snapping a picture, and the look on her face said nothing holy was on her mind. Even though she was leaving from the same chapel door.

"That was our first night here!" Amy said. "I knew I saw Dick leave the chapel from my window. He was meeting the maid! That proves he knew who she was!"

"Look at the next one," he said. "It was taken the same night."

Gayle Brand was standing in the shadows just outside the door to the lobby. There was plenty of light on the stairs, but she was standing in the deep shadows, as if purposely trying to remain unseen.

"She knew!" Amy said. "She knew Caroline was here. She lied to us. She lied to the police!"

Amy pressed the arrow and photo after photo popped up. They were all pictures of the little group from Arkansas. Many were closeups of Zelda. Amy nudged Zelda with her elbow. Secret admirer indeed.

Amy recognized the group on the croquet green their first outing with Mona. From this angle, they could see Caroline standing behind a tree. Amy had sensed someone watching them that day. So had Dick.

In the next frame Rebecca and Reginald were standing next to Caroline somewhere inside the hotel. The Williams couple may have been the last of the Arkansas group to arrive at the resort, but they had gotten here before the maid was killed, not after. Tom had proof.

Amy stared at the next one. "What is happening here?" James Brand had a golf club in his hand and his face was a wrinkle of rage. Dick stood a few feet from him, leaning against the golf cart, a smug look on his face. Chills went up her spine.

"Are these photos in order?"

"No, but they all have time stamps. They can be put in chronological order."

"I know when you took this one," Amy said, shifting to another frame. "I noticed you on the shore. This is the picture of Dick and Eloise up in their room. It was just before the bride and groom left the church. Dick said he was golfing and yet, here he is."

"Look more closely," Tom said. "He's talking to someone. It's a woman. But the reflection in the window goes right across her face."

Amy gasped. "Is that Eloise? Or is it Caroline Gadling?" She remembered how animated the conversation appeared from below. She had assumed the woman was Eloise. Why wouldn't she? "I can't tell if this is Eloise or Caroline. Or could it be Rebecca?"

"Where was Eloise when this was taken?" Rian asked. "That would help pinpoint who this is."

"She was somewhere in the hotel with Gayle," Amy answered. "Do you know where?" She turned to face him.

"No," he said. "That's the thing about taking pictures. You can only be in one place at a time."

The next picture was of her friend Doris Knight in the sunny garden where the old gardener had been pruning. Doris had a small bouquet of fresh snipped flowers in one hand. The other hand was holding a glass over a rose bloom.

"That's Doris," Rian said. "She's catching bees!"

Amy pressed the arrow quickly.

In the next shot, Eloise and Doris were in the lobby of the hotel, one coming and one going, their faces turned slightly to greet each other in passing. Doris held the bouquet of flowers, and the glass and Eloise held a pair gloves.

Rian tugged at a curl. "Why are you showing us these pictures?"

"I shouldn't be showing you these pictures," he said. "It's not protocol. But I can't get rid of this feeling that you are in danger. I don't want you to get hurt," he said looking directly at Zelda. "I was hired to shoot this event — this group from Arkansas. And so far, two of you are dead."

# CHAPTER THIRTY FIVE

Tom claimed he didn't know who his client was. He said he rarely did. He worked as a semi-retired freelance photographer for a firm that specialized in investigating fraud. They handled mostly insurance fraud, he said. White collar stuff. Not the guy who claims he can't lift his five pound chiweenie and then enters a Bass Pro tournament. They laughed at his unexpected humor and the creepy Nosey Parker vibe faded. Maybe he was a better secret admirer for Zelda than they thought.

Zelda didn't seem disappointed he wasn't all roses and wine. He promised to send her photos suitable for framing and she was thrilled. One would most likely be that rose in full bloom he alluded to in his cryptic note under the door. He seemed smitten, and his attention seemed to satisfy Zelda's bruised ego.

"That photo of us walking up to the barn bothers me," Genna said. "It's eerie. We looked like kids headed for Disney World with an all-day pass. In hindsight, it was more like the stage set for American Horror Story. You know the one, that Cabinet of Curiosities episode. We even have our own fortune teller." Genna glanced at Amy. "If you had been inside the building, Tom, you may have caught that whole shenanigans on film."

Amy looked at the photo again. What he caught on film were the excited expressions of a group of friends from Arkansas. Except they were not all looking chipper. Dick was scowling from under his purple tam as he reached for the cane in the golf cart. Eloise had her hands stuffed in her sweater pockets as though her fists were full of rocks. Doris looked like a bird about to take flight at any moment. Her arms were aloft at her side. Gayle and James were watching Dick, while Rebecca and Reginald looked directly into the camera as if they knew they were being watched. Reginald's expression was unnerving.

"He knew you were watching," Amy exclaimed.

Tom nodded. "I believe he did."

"Which means Reginald Williams could have been your client," Rian said. "But what was he looking for? Where were you when you took these?"

"On the upstairs balcony. I overheard Mona talking about the blacklight croquet game to one of the employees. She was making sure the food and drink would be in place on time. That's how I knew where you'd be. Check that next frame again," he added. "Look close."

Reginald's gaze had shifted. He was now looking at Dick and there was no mistaking the hatred in his eyes or the set of his jaw. The camera caught the rawness of his expression. If he knew he was being photographed, he didn't care.

"Yikes," Zelda said. "If looks could kill."

"I don't mean to scare you, but I saw that expression more than once. Isn't he the head of this group? There's something sinister behind that man's somber mask."

"He looks like a real *Phantom of the Opera* kind of dude in this picture," Rian said.

"Yeah," Amy agreed. "And Rebecca is his Christine. Look how he has hold of her hand."

"I wonder did he think there was something going on between Dick and Rebecca?" Amy offered. "Perhaps he hired you to catch them in the act."

"He spent a pretty penny to do it, if that's the case," Tom said. "A trip to Ireland doesn't come cheap."

"No, but the chamber was already booking this trip. So, what's one more on the list? It's just one more added to the chamber's dime," Amy said. "And if Rebecca knew about you, maybe you were meant to shoot two birds with one stone."

Tom looked at her funny.

"That is not what I meant," she said, backpedaling.

"I'm flattered you've been looking out for us," Zelda said with a toothy Zelda smile. "Just remember to catch my best side from now on."

"You need to be careful," he warned. "My gig is over. I've been called back to the States. I got a message at the front desk that the contract has been satisfied. I'll be leaving tomorrow."

"What a shame," Zelda said. "We still have several days left and I would have welcomed the distraction."

Tom blushed beneath his whiskers.

Amy gave Zelda the side eye to see whether she was batting her lashes. It wouldn't be out of character.

They waited until Tom packed his field bag and left the church.

"What do you make of this?" Amy asked.

"What do you make of it?" Rian replied.

"Rebecca wanted to catch Dick and Caroline," Amy said. "She wanted evidence and she made sure she got it."

"And that means Reginald was only a step or two behind," Genna interjected. "He may look like he wears the pants in their marriage, but Rebecca wears the shoes. No mistake about that. Reginald treads where Rebecca leads."

"That look!" Zelda exclaimed. "Disturbing to say the least."

"Rebecca is the reason Caroline and Dick were in Ireland at the same time," Amy declared. "She admitted that, and the photo proves she knew Caroline was here. Reginald knew it. He had to know. Rebecca used this trip to Ireland to catch a thief. And now that both thieves are out of the picture, the photographer and the Williams' are headed home."

"Don't you think it's odd that he took so many photos but never caught the killer?" Rian offered. "It's like he knew where not to be."

"Or maybe he did catch them and didn't show us," Zelda countered. "Maybe that's why he was alarmed for our safety."

"Rebecca may be at the epicenter, but Gayle and James are in her wake," Genna added. "Gayle had an ambitious agenda and Dick was in the way."

"And James has a swing," Rian noted. "Plus, a temper. We saw it in that photo, and we all saw it spike when Dick made that comment in the barn."

"Not his first misogynistic rodeo," Genna muttered. "Dick, I mean. Not James."

Rian nodded. "The other thing we know is that they knew who Caroline was. At least some of them knew she was here."

"You're right," Amy agreed. "And they all kept her secret. They let her play her little maid game so it wouldn't spoil their plans. Maybe she was trying to stay off the radar to protect herself."

"Or maybe she was just flirting with disaster," Zelda said. "If I was going to play maid, I would have packed a better fitting uniform. And some real maid shoes. That spy in maid's clothing wanted to surprise him. And he didn't like it."

Amy nodded. "Caroline went to his room when we were watching the wedding procession. He said he was golfing, but he wasn't."

No one needed to state the obvious. They sat in silence in the chapel. No one seemed eager to leave.

Amy assumed the police interviewed all the guests on the premises the day of Caroline's death. Even though the wedding party was gone when they found the body, protocol would require the Gardai to track them all down. That's probably when Bryan O'Dea shared what he saw — the man with the ice pick. She wished she had known that earlier. She would have asked O'Dea some questions. No doubt Garda O'Shannon had.

Tom said he had been interviewed by the police and was asked for copies of his photos. He gave them a memory stick with the time stamp included in the data. Somewhere in those photos there was evidence that Dick Collins had stopped Caroline dead in her tracks. No, there was no smoking gun. They didn't see a picture of him holding the weapon or rolling the cart to the hallway. But there was enough evidence to give the Gardai a timeline. They still didn't know what killed Dick. Was it an accident as they all presumed? Or was he another victim?

Dead men don't tell tales.

The worm finally wriggled off the hook. The squirming idea finally caught. Two croquet balls rotten to the core. Two deaths. Two murders. She could see no other way to go from here. If Dick killed Caroline, who killed Dick?

Rebecca popped into her head. Why would she want him dead? Why not just get him fired him and let justice take its course?

Because Dick spied on people's dirty little deeds, that's why. And Rebecca had a dirty deed to hide. That had to be it.

Genna interrupted her thoughts when she rose from the pew. Amy followed her friends out into the daylight. Listening now for the sounds from her solitary walk earlier, she could only hear the chatter in her head. Gone was the sense of peace. Now unease was rising. If Tom the photographer was right, the four of them could be in danger. What did they know that put them in harm's way? What was she missing? Had Zelda inadvertently given the killer's identity away? Had she shared too much with too many? Had they witnessed something without knowing it?

Even Doris seemed suspect. She was so angry with Dick that she could have set the bees loose in his room. She may have been so overcome that she swung at him with the mallet. But Doris didn't mean to kill him. Somebody was hoping it looked that way.

Drat that O'Shannon! He was playing the cards so close to his chest. He already knew this. He had to. Not only did he know, but he had photos to connect the Arkansas dots. And that included four friends who found themselves involved in yet another murder. O'Shannon let her believe what she wanted to believe. And yet, he pointed her in a different direction. Not one murder and one accident. Two murders. He wanted her to know that. He wanted her to see the connection without telling her what the connection was. Was he worried about them, too? Who else should be worried that they could be next?

Amy glanced up to the window where Eloise looked out at them earlier. The curtain was drawn. She couldn't help but wonder what role Eloise played in this. Did she have any idea about their fraudulent schemes at the bank? Or Dick's infidelities? Did Eloise have any inkling of what her trip to Ireland would become?

She thought of the childlike joy in Eloise's face as she rummaged through the bins of yarn and stacks of tweeds on their visit to the wool goods store. Eloise chose red hats and scarfs for her son at college, purple for Dick, and finally a basket of goodies for herself. She had labored over her purchases, as if buying yet another card of knitting needles and a dozen skeins of yarn was an unnecessary indulgence. But she did not seem like a woman who knew about her husband's sordid affairs. She did not look like a woman troubled by a maid who wasn't a maid. As she thought about it now, Eloise didn't seem troubled by anything. She seemed content in her perfect little life as a banker's wife, with all the time and money needed to make art and put a son through college. A very expensive college.

There was a happy jig playing as background music when they entered the hotel lobby. They passed the front desk and the now familiar face. Dick's golf bag was still leaning against the wall. Would Eloise donate the clubs to the resort? Or would she ship them home? It didn't seem worth the effort. Amy turned and the others kept going.

"Hey," she said to the clerk. "Have these golf clubs been here all the time?"

"I believe they have. Why is that, do you ask?"

"Do they belong to Dick Collins?"

The clerk flipped the luggage tag. "Richard Collins," she said without emotion.

"No one has touched them?"

"I can't say, miss. I'm not here 'round the clock."

"Were you here the day he fell down the stairs?"

A tiny grin turned the corners of her mouth. "I was here."

"Were you the one who helped cut off his gloves?"

She hid her amusement well. "I was."

"What did you do with them?"

The woman turned and reached into the top pocket of the bag, pulling out a pair of gloves.

"May I?" Amy held out her hand and she placed them in her fingers. She brought them to her nose and sniffed. She turned them upside down and shook them and a flutter of fine dust fell from the fingers. She bent down and swiped her finger in the powder that settled to the floor. Peanuts. Someone had put peanut dust in his golf gloves. No wonder his hands had ballooned. No wonder his eyes and lips had swelled. He had been lucky that day. He had been lucky that for him peanuts were not deadly. But then, he wasn't that lucky.

"Did Collins have a key to another room?"

The clerk's eyebrows raised all the way to her hairline. "He took a second room after his fall. Is that what you are referring to?"

Amy shook her head.

The woman hesitated before speaking. "He had only the keys to his rooms. At least, no more were assigned."

"Thanks," Amy said and turned away and then turned back again. "Have you seen Mona today?"

"She's in the library. She calls it her office since that's the only place she can connect her computer. Just on the other side there."

Mona was hunched over her computer in the dimly lit room when Amy entered. The curtains in the windows were drawn but there were several reading lamps placed at strategic spots beside comfortable chairs.

"Hey, Mona," Amy said as she approached. The woman turned and raised her brows in surprise.

"Miss Sparks!"

"Call me Amy and how are you doing, Mona? I know this had been a rough week for you."

"We have words for weeks like this," Mona said. "Nothing I can repeat here."

Amy nodded. It would be a doozie whatever the word was.

"Is there something you need?"

"When you were researching things that glowed in the dark, what did you discover? What glows under a blacklight and what doesn't."

Mona frowned.

Amy could see the trepidation on her face. "This is important, or I wouldn't ask."

Mona sighed and turned to her computer, clicking a document on the screen. "I did research online and then we tested things in the blacklight to see how it all looked."

"What kind of things?"

"Stuff from the bar. Different drinks. Food from the kitchen. I dragged all matter of things out there to see what we could create. Do you want me to print this list?"

Amy nodded.

"Are you looking for something specific?"

"No. Yes. I don't know."

Mona chuckled. "I can tell you it was quite an experiment to find the right glow and colors. But I don't think we'll be playing any more blacklight croquet. Not after what happened."

"That's really too bad," Amy said and meant it. "It wasn't your fault. Who could have known?"

"I know. We've had hundreds of games and nothing bad has ever happened." Mona looked at Amy with a cocked chin and curious look. "What are you looking for? Really."

"Does blood glow in the dark?"

Mona shook her head. "Not unless you add that stuff the forensic teams use. Luminol, I think they call it. Otherwise, it just looks black."

"So, things that don't glow in the dark look black. And things that do glow take on a whole new dimension."

"That is what I found to be true," Mona agreed. "We used a number of odd items to add depth to the art. We found ordinary things that look different under the blacklight. In the daylight you can see our creativity for what it is."

Amy nodded. "Like the mushrooms and the fairies. They looked amazing."

Mona beamed with pride. "The only drinks we found that has any presence at all was tonic water and honey mead. Since we have plenty of both, we decided those would be our drinks of choice. You can add tonic to anything to make it glow. No one seems to mind our limited menu. Oh, and tomato juice glows yellow, but it's not very bright. We nixed the Bloody Mary idea. It's one of the bartender's signature drinks, but it just didn't have the color zing."

Mona handed Amy the paper from the printer. "Vitamins glow? Medications, too?"

Mona nodded. "Couldn't figure out how we could use any of that."

"And chlorophyll glows red?"

"Yes, but you can't put enough lettuce in a sandwich to make much impact. You really have to extract the chlorophyll and that's gets all manky."

Amy didn't know the word, but she could guess what it meant. "Huh," she said as she read. "Soap and laundry detergents glow."

"Oh, on everything," Mona said. "On your hands, in your hair, on your clothes. Anywhere you haven't rinsed well enough you glow like a spotted blue beacon."

"My necklace glowed," Amy said. "I see here that diamonds shine blue. I remember noticing that everyone's rings and earrings were tiny specs of florescence. The white around Zelda's leopard spots were brilliant."

Mona nodded. "That's why I asked you to wear white. White is the easiest color to shift in that light, and in that way I can see everyone clearly in the dark."

"Did you see people clearly? I mean could you tell who was who?"

"I can't say as I was paying much attention," Mona answered. "I was fairly unnerved by the argument that flared up at the start and … well, you know exactly what happened after."

Amy nodded. Except she didn't know exactly what happened. It all happened so suddenly. It all passed so fast. "Were you able to tell the police the order in which things occurred?"

Mona eyed Amy carefully. "You were there. You don't remember?"

No, she wanted to say, there was a banshee screaming in her ear. "I can't remember whether the crash was before or after Dick fell."

"Oh, it was after," Mona said. "There was a loud whack as someone hit their ball and then he made an odd sound and then the urn of eggs went crashing."

Amy nodded. "Do you remember what color mallet Doris was holding when the lights came on?"

Mona thought for a moment. "It was green. Wasn't she green?"

"Her partner was Gayle."

"Oh, well then it had to be yellow. They were the yellow team. You were the orange. You and Rebecca Williams."

Amy nodded. "What color did you play?"

Mona's brow wrinkled and her eyes narrowed. "I drew the white," she said. "I was partners with Mr. Collins. Is that of significance to you?"

Amy shook her head. "Nope. Just curious, that's all."

Mona shut the lid to her laptop computer and turned to face Amy. "In Ireland we say that curiosity killed the cat. I would be careful if I were you. The Garda Síochána say this was a crime. A crime," she repeated slowly. "I'd be careful with your curiosity, if I were you."

# CHAPTER THIRTY SIX

Tom's pictures scrolled through her head in a semi-state of dreaming as her brain tried to make sense of what didn't make sense. Even Zelda had tossed and turned and huffed and puffed. The warm day had brought in a heavy fog that settled over the lake and the wind bayed like a lonely dog. Even the roof of the chapel had disappeared from view. The morning dawn had come and gone without her notice and by the time she finally got out of bed and dressed, Zelda was gone.

She would catch up with her at breakfast. She took her time getting ready for the day. She made a cup of tea in the electric kettle and sat in the window to drink it. When she finally reached the dining room, no one was there. The breakfast spread had already been removed. Not even a crumb of bread was left behind.

Odd. Where had everyone gone?

She retraced her steps and through the lobby. The front desk clerk smiled. "Good morning, miss. It's a grand day. Enjoy it so."

She nodded politely without speaking and went out into the daylight. The feeling that nudged her out the door and down the steps felt like walking in a dream. A lonely dream at that. It was as though she was being called to find solace in the fresh air and the gardens. She touched the Celtic knot at her neck and felt a surge of warmth.

Her feet followed the path and then, as if her feet were on their own, she turned toward the path that led to the barn. Glancing up ahead, she noticed the barn doors were shut. The wind was brisk. The sky bleeding through the clouds was a grayish shade of blue. The leaves on the trees rustled as she passed beneath them. Unlike last night, the sound of the wind in the leaves was a gentle melody now. She perked her ears to listen. She felt tentative. Unsure. Cautious of the wind turning into a howl. She recalled the man's story of the garden where the banshee rose like a scarecrow to mourn the departed. She wished that she had someone with her instead of going off alone. But there had been no one around and she couldn't stop her feet from moving in this direction.

As she stood before the heavy wooden doors, she realized there was nothing to keep her out.

She didn't bother with the lights. She let the dim settle over her eyes until she could see in the dark of the interior. The tables and chairs were stacked against the wall. The bar was empty of its colorful accoutrements. The room still faintly smelled of vinegar, but there was no evidence of the spill. The croquet balls and mallets were gone. Dusted for fingerprints? Examined for blood? Measured and marked for their role in a crime?

The wickets were still in place. As were the creative scenes on the walls. Now, with the magic of the blacklight gone, the Hawthorne tree looked like a schoolkid drawing with glow sticks and fuzzy pipe cleaners glued to the wood. The giant mushrooms no longer seemed to breathe, and the cotton ball dots looked sad and out of place. It was no longer a Wonderland. And she wasn't Alice. What had Mona meant by that?

A shuffle made her heart leap. She turned toward the sound and there, in the shadows, stood Eloise Collins.

"Oh!" Amy exclaimed when the pale face turned to her. "You scared me. I didn't know anyone was here!"

Eloise nodded slowly, and suddenly Amy felt her heart sink with a great ache. It felt icy hot and heavy. She remembered a similar feeling when she had fallen out of tree as a kid. She would never forget how she had gasped for air but could only fill her lungs with a searing hot ache that stretched across her shoulders. It was this weight that she felt here in the room.

"She shouldn't have done that," Eloise said, her voice sounding like an echo from far away.

"Who?" Amy asked.

Eloise didn't respond.

"Who, Eloise? Are you talking about Doris? I don't think Doris meant to hit him. I'm sure it was an accident."

"An accident," Eloise repeated and then fell silent. Amy realized that in her grief she wasn't going to make a lot of sense. Now she wasn't sure what to do. Leave Eloise here alone in the dark? That didn't seem right. She hadn't seen much of Eloise in the past couple of days and no one seemed surprised that she was keeping to herself. They had left her to be on her own. And now, Amy felt a little guilty for not being more present.

"I know how hard this is," she said. "What can I do to help?"

Eloise turned dark eyes toward her. "It's too late for help. What's done is done."

The shiver went up all the way her spine. Hadn't Rebecca Williams said the same thing?

"Have the police given you any new information?" Amy ventured. "Have they determined the actual cause..." Amy let her question end there.

"I was right there," Eloise said suddenly. "You saw me. Everybody saw me. I had the EpiPen ready in my pocket. When he dropped to the ground I knew what I had to do."

"Then it really was an allergic reaction?" Relief flooded her. Doris, at least, was in the clear.

"I saw you walking to the chapel," Eloise said suddenly, her voice more upbeat. "Everyone likes that chapel. Even that man with his camera. He was there."

Should she tell Eloise who Tom was and why he was here? That he had been hired to follow the tourists from Arkansas — mostly likely and more specifically — Richard Collins. Tom had not known who the client was that hired him, but two and two made sense. Tom was here to catch something nefarious in the works. He was here to get evidence on film. Had he captured Caroline in Dick's room just moments before her death? All while Eloise and Gayle were watching the wedding procession and the wailing bagpipes come and go.

The vacant look had returned. The look was disconcerting.

With Amy's urging, Eloise finally agreed to return to the hotel. They went into the library and once Eloise was seated in a reading chair next to the peat fire, Amy went off to find them a cup of tea.

"You are so different than Dick said you were," she said, smiling up at Amy as she accepted the cup and saucer. "You're not at all rebellious and unyielding. I think you're the opposite. You remind me of Lucie Manette. You know who I mean? Lucie, from *A Tale of Two Cities*. She was the golden thread that wove her family together. You're the thread of your little group of friends."

Eloise looked out the window for moment as though lost in thought. "Lucie was a such a lovely girl," she said before taking a sip of tea. "But not all love can transform a jackal to a hero. Isn't that what made Madame Defarge so bitter? There are some hearts that cannot be turned. Not in the real world. Not as long as there are Evrémondes and Gadlings."

Amy felt her eyes widen. She did know who Caroline was! She did know the maid!

"Did I ever tell about my son, Richard?" Eloise asked, a light taking over her face. "He's away at college. Harvard. Harvard College, I mean. He's still an undergraduate — a straight A student."

"I know you are proud of him," she said. "The two of them were close?"

"Not so much," Eloise said. "Dick insisted Richard go into banking. He wanted him to follow in his footsteps; take over a branch when he graduated college. Richard has other aspirations." Eloise beamed. "He wants to be an academic. He wants to make his mark on bright young minds."

The faraway look returned as Eloise sipped her tea. "Isn't that always where contention lies— the conflict that often arises between ambition and the person who's paying the bills?"

She knew Eloise wasn't expecting an answer and Amy watched as she set the cup on the table with measured movement. "I wish I had my knitting," she said, patting her lap. "I feel at a loss when I don't have my yarn and needles. I feel bare, like I've forgotten to dress." The light glinted off her glasses. "Isn't that silly? Dick would say I was silly. Dick says all women are silly."

Before she could respond, a shadow passed across the door and suddenly Genna was standing in the doorway.

"There you are!" She said brightly. "I went to find everybody, and they've all disappeared!"

"Disappeared? You found me."

"Well, yes, that's true. And Rian's in the shower," Genna admitted. "That's why I came down here. She said she'd meet me in the pub. But where's Zelda?"

"I haven't seen her."

Genna set her arms akimbo. "Where did she go?"

Amy shrugged. "She was gone when I got up."

"She went shopping with Rebecca and Doris," Eloise interjected. "I heard them talking about it. I thought she was going to ask me to go. And I was relieved when she didn't."

"Who are you talking about?" Amy asked.

"Rebecca Williams. She hired a car to take them shopping so the three and them could get better acquainted."

Amy felt something stir in the pit of her stomach. "She told me she and Reginald were leaving the resort."

"Well, the three of them left this morning. Maybe an hour or so after breakfast. Rather impromptu and impetuous, it seemed to me."

"Was Mr. Williams with them?"

"I don't believe so. But I haven't seen him, either."

"Do you know where they went?"

"I don't recall the name. Some little village Mona recommended. Is something wrong?"

"No," Amy answered a bit too quickly. "Nothing wrong with a shopping trip. Zelda will love it. I just didn't realize they were going."

"Ditto," Genna said with a slight huff. "I could have done some shopping. Although, it would be marathon shopping since we're talking about Zelda."

"Well," Eloise said, rising from her chair. "They're certainly in capable hands. I've known Rebecca a long time. She's always impeccably well-groomed and attired. It's all about appearances, isn't it?"

Eloise dropped her gaze and Amy wondered if there was a dig buried in her comment.

"Oh, dear, I'm getting another headache," Eloise said and lifted her hand to her brow. "I don't think I'll be down for dinner tonight. Thank you for the tea," she said, turning to Amy. "And for being kind. I'm glad you aren't how Dick described." She glanced at Genna and smiled thinly. "I don't suppose you are how he portrayed you, either."

Genna frowned and Amy shook her head before Genna could ask for an explanation. There would be time for that later.

"I don't have a good feeling about this," Amy said, when Eloise left the room.

Genna arched her brow.

"I can't get over this feeling that Rebecca is the mastermind behind this trip to Ireland," Amy shared. "And I have a feeling Doris and Zelda are playing right into the palm of her hand."

# CHAPTER THIRTY SEVEN

When Zelda and Doris didn't show up for dinner, Amy's stomach turned to knots. Neither were answering calls, but cell service had been spotty throughout the trip. Even though they all had upgraded to international calling, their phones didn't connect with regularity.

"Do you think we should call Garda O'Shannon?" Amy asked her dining partners. The three of them had taken a table in the corner because James and Gayle had taken a table for two. Of course, there was no Rebecca, but there was also no sign of Reginald, either. That made the knot tighten a little more.

"Call the Garda and say what?" Genna ventured between bites. "That three shopaholics are on the loose somewhere in Ireland?"

"I could tell him what I know," Amy answered. She could hear how plaintive her voice sounded. It matched the tightness in her chest. "We can't go looking for them ourselves and Mona's already gone home. We don't even know where to look. At least O'Shannon would be able to … "

"To what?" Genna interrupted. "Put out an APB? A BOLO? A Silver Alert?"

Amy glared at Genna. "That sounds ridiculous."

"Doesn't it though," Genna replied, pulling another piece of soda bread to her plate, then slathering it with butter one torn bite at a time. Dinner was braised pork belly served in a sauce that rivaled anything Paula Deen put on the table. Calories included. There were steamed carrots and potatoes swimming in the broth and plenty of bread to soak it up with. It was delicious, but she was struggling to swallow even tiny bites. Judging by their dedication to the plate, her friends didn't feel the same foreboding.

"Besides," Genna continued, "what do you know that Garda O'Shannon doesn't?"

"It's more what he knows that we don't," Rian replied. "He has Tom's photos, the weapons, and all the witness accounts. He probably knows the manner of death for both victims by now. Whomever he suspects, he's watching them closely."

Amy glanced at the table where James and Gayle were canoodling over their wine.

"Maybe we should talk about this elsewhere," she said. "Just in case anyone is listening."

"I don't think those two are aware anyone else is alive," Genna said. "I've never seen a married couple with such devotion to each other. I think they genuinely like each other's company."

"Imagine that," Rian said.

"You enjoy Ben's company," Amy said. "How is that different?"

"We're not married, for one. As long as we keep it that way, I may continue to enjoy Ben's company."

"Don't you ever get romantic ideas about setting up house and picking out furniture?"

Rian eyed Amy with alarm. "That's your idea of romance?"

"No, but nesting is the natural order."

"Among birds, maybe. Men, not so much."

"I disagree," Genna put in. "Men nest. They just do it differently. We're all fine linens and scented candles. Men are all about lawnmowers and tools."

Rian rolled her eyes. "That's so sexist. I have a shed full of tools."

"You have a shed full of tools your grandfather left behind," Genna retorted. "You inherited his nest along with your cabin on the pond. "

"I'm the one who keeps them rust free and the blades sharp."

"True enough," Genna acquiesced. "I have a garage full of tools no one has touched in eons."

Amy suffered through another delicious bite then turned to Rian. "When you were researching about Limerick, where did you access the Internet? My phone isn't doing anything but spinning in space."

"Mine, too," Genna said.

"In the library. There's a guest computer on the desk. It's a little slow, but it gets there eventually." Rian lifted a brow. "What are you looking for?"

"I want to Google us and see what comes up."

"Google us?" Genna asked. "Why?"

"I don't mean us as in the four of us, although it would be interesting to see what O'Shannon found on the Internet about us. I bet he searched our names after we gave him our passports. I've never Googled myself. Have you?"

Genna nodded. Amy wasn't that surprised. "I want to see what I find about the others in this Arkansas group. You said you found stuff when you were researching for Project X, but you didn't have murder on your mind then."

"No, I didn't," Genna said. "I was looking for money."

"That's what I'm looking for, too," Amy added. "Money is not the only motive for murder, but it ranks in the top ten. I want to see if I can find money attached to specific persons."

"Let me guess," Genna whispered. "Collins, Williams, Brand, and Gadling."

"Egad. Sounds like a law firm," Rian interjected.

Genna chuckled. "Or an unlawful firm."

"It sounds like a late night project to me," Amy added. "There's no way I'm going to sleep until Zelda is safe and snoring from behind her mask. I don't know where the three of them are or what they're doing, but it better be good craic. Because if Rebecca kidnapped them to keep them quiet, she's going to find herself on the wrong end of right!" Amy slapped the table with her fork.

"*Sshh*," Genna whispered. "You've caught the attention of the lovebirds."

Amy glanced over at their table. Gayle and James were staring at the three of them now. "Sorry, we got a little carried away," Amy said.

Gayle smiled and nodded, but there was something odd in her expression. Amy remembered how Doris felt after sharing her story with Gayle. On one hand Gayle had been reassuring. And yet, Doris was left with an odd feeling. Amy felt that way now. Were they overlooking the obvious? Who had the most to gain in this scenario? Not Rebecca, unless her dirty deed was really, really dirty. Certainly not Doris. No, with Dick out of the way, Gayle stood to gain the most. Is that why she was hiding in the shadows that night? An opportunity to strike out? Had something happened then that made her shrink into the dark. Had she waited for an opportunity to strike again? Like at the blacklight croquet game? That was certainly one way to climb the corporate ladder. But what about Caroline? What would be her motive there? Were there two motives for murder, or one?

Amy checked her watch. It was past nine-thirty. Still no sign of Zelda.

"Let's go to the pub where we can talk without ears," Amy said, motioning with a nod to the couple, who had since returned their focus to each other, but were still close enough to eavesdrop.

Rian scraped her chair back from the table. "I agree. A drink will make us think better after all that food. Shall we have a Nutty Irishman all around?"

"All around," Genna agreed as they left the dining room. Amy could feel the Brands watching them leave.

They lined up on the barstools and the bartender's brows rose in anticipation.

"What a pleasant surprise," he said. "Three surprises, I should say. A pint each? Or a brilliant little night cap? Something to help ye sleep?"

"Nutty Irishmen times three," Genna said. "We're in a drinking kind of mood."

When the drinks were poured, Amy signed the room receipt and added a healthy tip. Maybe the bartender could be bribed. She slurped at the whipped cream. "Do all the drinks get charged to a room?"

"When you are a guest at the hotel, they do. Otherwise, the bar is cash and credit."

"Has anyone ordered your famous Bloody Mary in the past few days?" Amy ventured.

"I have served many. It's a guest favorite, you know."

"And what about room service? Do you keep track of that, too?"

"When it includes drinks from the bar, I do." His eyebrows knitted. He seemed too polite to be curious. "But when drink goes out with food it gets charged through the kitchen."

"I think you know what I want to ask."

He nodded. "And I think you know I won't be asking about your business, will I? Nor will I be able to answer you about mine. We do have policies. Hotel rules about privacy."

"If I were to ask whether a Bloody Mary went out on room service, would you be able to answer? Or not?"

He nodded. "Or not."

"To a room on the first floor or not?"

"Or not," he said.

"So, not to my room. And not to theirs." She motioned to Rian and Genna, who had taken their drinks and moved to a table by the window. "They're in room 16."

"Correct. No, to either," he said, obviously enjoying their verbal game of cat and mouse. "The hotel has four rooms on that wing. And four on the other."

Amy paused. "You mean the other wing of the second floor."

"There are four rooms on that wing, as well."

"I get it," she said. The bribe had worked. Sort of. He had given her just enough information to put an idea in her head.

"What was that all about?" Genna asked

"Just a wild hair," Amy said as she settled in a chair beside them. "Dick Collins was allergic to horseradish. I know this. Eloise knew this. Gayle knew this. The bartender's Bloody Marys are full of horseradish. I was wondering whether someone took the liberty to send one to his room, but evidently not. The Brands and the Williams are both staying on the other wing of the second floor. From what the bartender didn't say outright, the drinks went to their room, not to Dick's."

"Too easy anyway," Rian said. "And way too easy to track down. Besides, Dick wouldn't drink it."

"You're right," Amy agreed. "He wouldn't ingest anything out of the norm. Unless it was properly disguised. He wouldn't be able to tell if it was tomato juice or a green smoothie by looking at it. Being color deficient," she added. "And if we know anything about Dick's behavior, he wasn't the adventurous foodie type. Although someone could have extracted the horseradish and added it to his drink later."

"Still too easy," Rian said. "Horseradish is hard to disguise. He would taste it with his first sip."

"Maybe that's all it took."

"We didn't have a Bloody Mary at the croquet game," Genna said. "We drank gin and tonics. And there's no way you could get away with putting horseradish in that."

Amy set her drink on the table, noticing the ring the cup made. She reached for a coaster and set it under the glass. It didn't remove the ring, but it removed it from sight.

"Why wasn't there blood on the floor?" She blurted.

Genna and Rian turned to stare.

"Think about it. I don't recall seeing blood anywhere except for the back of her dress. How did that happen?"

"It means the killer was tidy," Genna said.

Amy exhaled. "No, it means she wasn't killed in the hallway."

"We knew that already."

"Wouldn't there be a trail from wherever she was pushed with the cart?" Amy asked.

Rian shrugged. "Unless the weapon was left in place. That would staunch the wound. And it would cease altogether when the heart stopped."

"This is not after dinner conversation," Genna muttered. "I'm starting to feel queasy, and I want to talk about something else. "

"But the weapon wasn't left in place. It was on the floor," Amy declared, ignoring Genna's plea. "It was laying there in plain sight. It sure didn't fall out on its own. We're missing something." Amy tapped the table with her fingertips. "I need to make sense of this because otherwise I'm going to panic about Zelda and Doris being kidnapped."

She drummed her fingers again. "Dick didn't know Caroline was going to be in Ireland. He tried to prevent her from coming, but Rebecca out maneuvered him. She needed Caroline and Dick together. Caroline arrives; he's not happy about it."

"He knew that with both of them out of the bank at the same time, their fraud jig was up," Rian added. "But then it's too late and he knows it."

"He blames Caroline," Amy added. "Always blaming someone else for his own misdeeds. And then he stabs her in the back."

"That fits," Genna put in. "*Quid pro quo.*"

Amy shook her head. "Except when they met in the chapel, that sure looked like a lover's meet up. Do you think Caroline was smart enough to figure out that Rebecca had set her up?"

Genna scoffed. "She was smart enough to disguise herself as the maid. She had to know that if anyone recognized her, she'd be in boiling hot water."

"With who?" Rian asked.

"With Dick, for one. He didn't want her here. He told her she couldn't come. Eloise, for two, especially if she knew they were having a little game of hide the putter."

Amy frowned. "Gayle for three, because she didn't cancel Caroline's reservations and she may have suspected all along that Dick and Caroline had something going on. Maybe she wanted to out his bad behavior in front of Mr. Williams."

"And then there's Rebecca," Genna added. "If she was telling you the truth, Caroline might have caught on to what was happening. Maybe Caroline told Dick that night in the chapel that he was being watched."

"Or maybe Caroline confronted him," Amy added. "Maybe she made herself a very disposable kind of employee."

"All of this is plausible," Rian agreed. "And now I see why you're freaked about Doris and Zelda's absence, Amy. If Rebecca felt she was being backed into a corner, no telling what she might do. If something happened to her plan to catch Dick and Caroline red handed, then she might resort to a completely different approach."

"You mean murder," Genna said. "Two murders."

Rian nodded.

"When I asked Eloise what the police knew about Dick's death, she said he had an allergic attack. Well, she didn't say that exactly," Amy admitted. "But that was the gist."

She paused to gather her thoughts. "Back to our timeline. Dick is angry to find Caroline in Ireland. He meets her in the chapel. Gayle knows about that because she's hiding in the shadows in Tom's photo. We don't know why. The next day Dick goes golfing with James, who probably knows all about Caroline by now because Gayle has told him. Dick leaves the golf game early — even though he claims he played eighteen holes."

Rian nodded. "James was his alibi."

"Except that he wasn't, really. They parted ways. Eloise was with Gayle somewhere watching the wedding. Dick returns to the hotel and lets Caroline into his room. They have words which Tom catches through the window. That's evidence because the picture was taken during the wedding. But then, Dick stabs her with the ice pick and drags her to the hallway."

Rian shook her head. "Nice theory but let me poke some holes in it — no pun intended.

Genna groaned.

"The timing is off," Rian continued. "The maid wasn't in the hall when you returned from the wedding reception. O'Dea didn't see Dick take the ice pick until the party at the hotel was well under way. You saw Dick arguing with someone not long after the bride was walked down the aisle, but the photo isn't clear enough to be accurate. It could have been almost anyone."

"Oh, you're right, it doesn't fit." Amy shook her head slowly.

"Well, that leaves one question," Genna said. "Who do we think Dick was arguing with in his room?"

The three of them looked at each other. "Rebecca!"

"Rebecca and Reginald had just arrived on site," Amy said. "Maybe Rebecca confronted Dick and Caroline together. Maybe they were all three in that room. Caroline had to have been killed not long after that."

"And where was the body hidden?" Genna asked. "Assuming that's what happened."

Amy's eye widened. "In the elevator? Did Tom the Nosey Parker have a picture of that? What if he caught the killer in action? What if that's why he tried to warn us? Maybe he thought we were too close to the truth!"

A loud noise made them turn to the bar. Reginald Williams was righting the bar stool he had just tumbled over. His thin, angular face was awash with alarm. He smoothed his hair, adjusted his glasses, and strode from the room without a word.

# CHAPTER THIRTY EIGHT

The three of them looked at each other. "How long was he listening to us?" Amy asked.

"Long enough," Rian answered.

"I don't think he liked what he heard," Genna said. "We touched a nerve."

"More than a nerve," Amy added. "That look! What *was* that look?"

Rian twisted a curl. "He either got a rude awakening about his wife and her schemes, or he wasn't expecting anyone to uncover it. I'm wondering if *he* was the one who hired Tom the Nosey Parker. What if Reg was keeping tabs on his wife because he thought *she* was having a toe to toe with Dick."

"Rebecca hated Dick," Amy said.

"She pretended to hate him," Genna said. "He made it easy."

"What do you think Reg will do?" Amy asked.

"What can he do?" Rian answered. "Play dumb and innocent. That's what I would do."

"Like he would stoop that low," Genna added.

"We need to find out who else knew about the fraud investigation," Amy declared. "I'd like to know what Eloise knows about everybody else, too. I have the impression Dick told Eloise a lot of things from the inside of the boardroom. Not because he wanted her to know, but because it made him feel all the more superior. I know he shared his opinions about us with Eloise. They weren't all favorable, mind you. Let's take Eloise an after dinner drink and do a little welfare check. Maybe we can get her to share some of Dick's spy ring gossip."

"Another Nutty Irishman times four," Genna said as she approached the bar, bearing an empty mug. "On a tray if you please. This time we're taking it with us."

"Four, you say?"

Genna nodded.

"To what room should I charge this?"

"Mine is fine," Genna said. "Room 16. Heavy on the whipped cream and the hazelnut sprinkles, please. That's the best part."

Amy focused on carrying the tray and four mugs as they climbed the stairs to the second floor. Room 17 was their destination. Two down from Amy and Zelda's and next door to Rian and Genna's. Nosey Parker had been on the other side in Room 18.

Rian knocked on the door. Amy looked at Rian half expecting her old, familiar SNL routine, but Rian stood poised. A few seconds passed and Rian rapped again. They heard shuffling on the other side and then the door opened.

"Oh!" Eloise said as she greeted the three of them. "Is something wrong? It's so late!"

"We brought you a nightcap," Amy answered. "I know you said you weren't feeling well, and we wanted to check in on you."

Eloise looked at the tray and then at Amy. "But there are four drinks!"

Amy smiled warmly at Eloise.

Genna nudged the door open with her fingertips. "No one enjoys drinking alone. That's what friends are for."

"Friends?" Eloise asked, her brow knitted over her wire rimmed glasses.

"If we aren't friends yet, we will be after these Nutty Irishmen," Genna added, stepping into the doorway. Eloise had no choice but to step away from the door and let them in.

"Set that tray right here," Genna said to Amy, motioning to a table. Amy recognized the flowers in the glass. They looked less perky than before, but they were still a bright spot in the room. After setting down the tray, she handed a mug to Eloise.

"*Slainte*," she said, taking one for herself. Rian and Genna followed.

"*Slainte*," they said in unison as Eloise looked at them over the top of her mug. After a couple of minutes of awkward silence and it was clear they were there to stay, Eloise motioned them to sit. Eloise perched on the foot of the bed, while Genna and Rian settled in the two armchairs. Amy sat on the window seat and turned to look out the window. She recognized the view. She and Mona had explored this room the day Dick was chased down the stairs by bees. The room itself was tidy now. Beyond tidy, really. The bunched up towel on the floor was gone and, as Bets the maid would say — so were the banshee tears. Nothing seemed out of place or out of order. Except it no longer smelled like cologne. Amy noticed the gray and crimson knitted piece was a good bit longer than before. It lay on the top of the basket as if Eloise had set down her knitting to open the door.

"Here we are!" Eloise breathed into her warm drink. "I hope you have enjoyed your visit to Ireland. It's a very charming place. Usually." Her eyes darted briefly to the door and then to her guests.

"It's certainly been out of the ordinary," Genna said. "We weren't at all expecting ..."

"Eloise," Amy interrupted with a glance at Genna. Straightforward wasn't the best approach here. She scanned her memory for the query tips that Sam Ford had shared. Don't rush the approach. Don't dance around it until they get suspicious. Frame your question and never predict the answer.

"We haven't been as attentive as we should have been," she began. "We've been preoccupied with our own agenda and haven't been there for you. We decided that wasn't right. We're here to remedy that." At least it was ninety-nine percent true.

Eloise looked relieved.

"This can't be easy to weather on your own," Amy said.

"Especially since you're a long way from your good-old-girl network in the States," Genna interjected. "I know when I was facing this same situation I needed a lot more support than I received."

Eloise looked closely at Genna. "This… this happened to you?"

Genna nodded. "Twice. God rest their souls."

Eloise clutched the cup in her hands, casting her eyes to the floor.

"It's a journey," Genna added softly. "You don't bounce back overnight, and especially if police are involved. The police like to ask questions. They like to rake up dirt. You know what I mean, don't you?"

Eloise nodded.

"They always take more than they give."

Again, Eloise nodded.

Amy wondered if they were still talking about the police.

"That's why we thought you might want to talk to some friendly faces," Genna added. "Maybe get things off your chest, if you need to."

Eloise sighed heavily. "I did call my son and tell him about it. He wanted to fly over and take care of me, but I said everything was taken care of, really, and there was nothing for him to do. I didn't want him leave school." Her voice rose an octave. "He has to stay in school. He has to stay there!"

"That's wise," Amy encouraged. "You don't want his grades to suffer."

"No." Eloise said flatly. "No, he must be protected from everything that's happened. He simply cannot be involved in any of this. My Richard cannot be harmed by what's happened!"

Rian cradled her mug. "Will you return home as planned? Have the police said you could leave?"

"Garda O'Shannon is so polite," Eloise said. "He's a perfect gentleman. Always asking his questions in the most kind and caring way."

Amy wondered about that. He hadn't always seemed so kind to her.

"They said they confirmed Dick had an allergic reaction to something he ingested. They may never know what caused it because we don't know the extent of his allergies. It's an arduous process to uncover every allergen medically, you know. So, Dick hadn't bothered. We didn't think we needed to. Dickie kept away from everything he thought to be problematic." Eloise paused for a moment as if remembering something. Whether it was a fond memory or not wasn't obvious by her expression.

"They tested his sera fluid or something, but they will need his prior medical history to make an exact diagnosis about the allergen. If they can make one at all. Without a detailed allergy history, they can only determine that the anaphylaxis was fatal." Eloise shook her head slowly. "The EpiPen failed. I've read where they fail more than thirty percent of the time." She glanced briefly at Amy. "If only I had both pens with me..."

Amy frowned. Eloise only had one EpiPen in her pocket. Amy remembered watching her pull the device from her sweater and jam it into Dick's thigh. Yes, there had been two pens in the bathroom drawer. She remembered seeing the two protective cases side by side when she and Mona were looking for bees. She had been tempted to open one out of curiosity, but it was an intimidating looking device if you had never handled one. She hadn't even seen one before. She remembered it had a bright orange tip on the bottom, presumably the part where the needle ejected from the tube and then injected the solution. Thirty percent wasn't great odds. It was almost fifty-fifty.

"We are sorry for your loss," Genna said. She sounded genuine.

Eloise exhaled slowly. "Dickie was right. He really was allergic. All this time I doubted him. I didn't think …" Eloise buried her face in her mug.

"At least it wasn't that knock to the head," Genna added.

Eloise looked surprised. "Wasn't that strange? Poor Doris. I had no idea she had it in her."

"I don't think that was Doris," Amy said. "I believe it was one of the others. I think someone else put the mallet in her hands to pass the blame."

"Who would do such a thing?"

"That's what we're trying to find out," Amy answered. "We were thinking you might have an idea. We were wondering if Dick shared things with you in confidence. You know, the way husband and wife share things."

Eloise looked at Amy with hard gray eyes.

"He said I was rebellious and unyielding. Remember? You said that to me in the library."

Eloise sighed. "I shouldn't have told you that. I was surprised to find you were the opposite, that's all."

What was the opposite? Obedient and weak? Submissive and dense? Loyal and kindhearted felt a lot better. She thought of herself as being tenacious. Stubborn. Curious. That fit. But of course, Dick wouldn't see her with those qualities. He would see her as someone he couldn't manipulate, someone who didn't kowtow to his underhanded turbulence.

"He spoke about all of us, didn't he?"

Eloise nodded. "Oh, he had his opinions, all right."

"I bet he told you all about Doris and the mentor program."

Eloise dropped her eyes. "He was very young and ambitious in those days. He told her it was an honest mistake. She wouldn't accept his apology and it cost her the job."

"You're defending him?" Genna blurted.

"Well, I don't…"

"It's okay," Amy said, with a sidewise glance at Genna. "You only know what you were told. You only heard his side of the story. "

"I guess that's true. I only know the Doris that Dick told me about."

"And did he tell you why he objected to Gayle being president of the chamber?"

"Oh, goodness. What didn't he object to? He said things I can't repeat. But mostly he was against it because Rebecca Williams wanted it so much. He knew Rebecca would twist Reginald around her finger until she got what she wanted. "

"What was his issue with Rebecca Williams?"

"Why, she's divisive and vindictive!" Her tone rose again. "She was ungrateful for all the favors Dick did for her. He said she would never be a success if not for him. And frankly, I think he may have been right!"

Amy saw her chance. "Because of what she did to Caroline Gadling?"

There was a three beat pause. Amy could feel the blood thumping in her neck.

"Who?"

Amy shook her head. "Eloise, you know who Caroline Gadling was. We all know who she was. Rebecca brought her here for a reason. We want to know if you knew why."

Amy could see Eloise's jaw tensing. She was silent for a long time, her eyes focused somewhere near her feet.

"She was going to ruin everything," she said without looking up. "She was going to wreck his reputation." Eloise looked at Amy. "She was going to ruin our family. She was going to shatter everything we had worked so hard to build. She had to be stopped!"

Rian cleared her throat. "She had to be stopped?"

Eloise met Rian's eye. "Dickie told me all about her. He said she was overly flirtatious at work. He warned her that it was completely unacceptable in the workplace, and it had to stop, but she wouldn't leave him alone. He even threatened to fire her! She was just low rent and dimwitted," Eloise spat with apparent venom. "She didn't have enough sense to know when to leave well enough alone. And worse, she had the nerve to show up here! She came all the way to Ireland!  Dickie accused her of stealing from the bank, and then she claimed she would drag him down with her and laugh about it. She had to be stopped!"

"*Nach a Mool,*" Amy muttered. Had Eloise already shared this with Garda O'Shannon? Or were they hearing this firsthand?

"She got what was coming to her," Eloise said quietly, as if spent by the admission. "She shouldn't have done that. She should never have said the things she said."

# CHAPTER THIRTY NINE

They returned to the pub with their empty mugs and Amy felt she had run a mile. Maybe two. Crime puzzling was exhausting. At least, emotionally. Two flights of stairs was enough to draw a quick breath, but hearing the emotion that set murder in motion almost took her breath away. Dick saw Caroline as a threat to everything he was. Everything he pretended he was. Humans were so flawed by their deceptions. No one saw reality when they looked in the mirror. They saw the flaws no one else saw. She knew that firsthand.

There was still no sign of Zelda and Doris and Rebecca.

"Wouldn't they call with a message if they were in trouble?" Amy asked.

Genna looked at her sternly. "If they were in trouble, I doubt they could make a call."

"That makes me feel so much better," Amy retorted. "Thanks for nothing."

"Maybe they decided to stay overnight," Rian chipped in. "We know how that happens."

"Then they would definitely call the hotel if that were the case. I've checked with the front desk multiple times."

"It sounds as if this killer croquet has wrapped up on its own," Rian added. "I'm sure Eloise told the Garda that Dick killed Caroline and why. If not, she will. She wouldn't hold out on that. There'd be no reason for her to do so, now."

"At least I feel a little better about Rebecca kidnapping Zelda and Doris. I may have let my imagination get away from me."

"Oh, yeah," Genna said. "Your imagination is pretty far out there. Like on Mars. Or Neptune."

It was not long before they heard a car drive up. In the dusky dark of a sun that didn't quite set this time of year, Amy could see the familiar writing on the side of the car. Garda. Her heart thumped. Garda O'Shannon got out of the car and opened the rear door. Zelda, Doris, and Rebecca climbed out.

"What in the world?" Amy exclaimed as they climbed the stairs to the hotel, and she took in their appearance. To say they were bedraggled was an understatement. Their clothes were dirty and full of leaves and twigs and something that smelled questionable. Doris had scratches on her arms and Rebecca looked more unkempt than she had probably ever been. She smoothed her hair with a thin hand. Zelda held her packages to her chest, dark lines of mascara tears tracked down her cheeks.

"It was awful," Zelda wailed.

"What happened?"

Zelda glanced at Rebecca. "It was an accident. We came around a curve and there was a car in our lane!"

"You were in their lane," Garda O'Shannon said sternly. "We drive on the left."

Zelda glanced up at O'Shannon and narrowed her eyes.

"But you are okay?"

"More or less," Rebecca said. "No broken bones. Doris got the worst of it. She tumbled into a ditch when she exited the car."

"We got a late start home," Zelda explained. "Rebecca said she didn't see well at dusk and asked would I drive."

Amy heard Genna groan behind her. Zelda was one position ahead of Genna in the bad driver competition among the four friends.

"If that guy hadn't stopped, we'd still be lying on the side of the road," Zelda bellowed. "We'd be bear food or sheep food or whatever comes out at night to hunt."

"I keep telling you that sheep don't eat anything but grass," Doris said, clearly over their shopping adventure. "We were more in danger of getting hit by another car than anything!"

"I had the car towed," O'Shannon said. "Setting them on the road didn't seem the right thing to do. And here we are." He glanced at Amy. "Yet again."

"I need a shower," Doris said.

"Likewise," Rebecca said.

"I will need to take a report," O'Shannon said. "I'd prefer to do that before you disburse. If it's all the same to you."

He led them to the pub, and they settled around the table. Amy and Genna and Rian followed them and Garda O'Shannon didn't object. They listened as the three of them in turn told the chronicle of a shopping trip to a quaint little village and then how they ended up crashed on the side of the road. No doubt O'Shannon already knew most of it, but now he had pen and paper in front of him.

"One of my packages went into the ditch," Zelda complained. "I can't tell which one. I hope it wasn't the jewelry bag. I had Christmas lined out for the next two years!"

"You're lucky that's all that's lost," the Garda said. "You could have collided head on had the other driver not been alert."

Zelda didn't respond. When the three had answered his questions, he closed his notebook and nodded. "You are free to go. You can deal with the rental firm tomorrow."

When the three left the room, Amy looked at Garda O'Shannon. "Was it that bad?"

"It could have been worse. They could have been driving the ocean side. And there's no recovering from that."

"I'm so relieved," Amy admitted. "I was thinking Rebecca had kidnapped them."

His cheeks turned to dimples. "Kidnapped, you say? For whatever reason? Ransom for a few bags of souvenir and yoke?"

Amy frowned. "What's a yoke?"

"Oh, you know, just about anything that's so unimportant you can't remember the name of it. A yoke. A whatchamacallit. A thingamajig. But kidnapping? Isn't that by a stretch on the imagination?"

"Amy's been on Neptune," Genna added. "Her thinking is a little out there, if you know what I mean."

Amy ignored her. "We talked to Tom the photographer. We've seen the photos. He was convinced we were in danger and then Doris and Zelda disappeared. Why wouldn't we think the worse?"

"The worst is women loose in town with a credit card and driving on the wrong side of the road. There's the danger. But why would you put her on such a list if I may ask?"

"Well," Amy said. And before she could check herself, she shared her theory about Rebecca baiting Dick and Caroline, interrupted only when Rian and Genna had something to add. They shared all their versions — the one where Rebecca kills the maid and hides her in the staff elevator, and then kills Dick to finish the job. The one where Rebecca had them both killed — because maybe Nosey Parker was hired to get rid of the dirty laundry. And, although unbeknownst to them, Zelda and Doris might have been witnesses to the crime somehow. So, they had to be dealt with. Kidnapping seemed the most obvious. But now we know Dick did it. And they went through the same scenarios with Dick in the hot seat.

"The scene was staged sometime after her death," Garda O'Shannon admitted when they were finally quiet. "Your friend's observation about her shoes was certainly helpful. Too helpful, we thought at first. But there seemed no rhyme, no reason for her involvement. We could find no other connections between Zelda Carlisle and the deceased. Plus, the coroner confirmed that the taphonomic alterations were well in place by the time she was found. That confirms an earlier death."

"You don't like our theory of her being kept in the elevator? Or even in the Nosey Parker's room?"

He shook his head. "There is no evidence to support either theory."

"That proves it then. Dick killed Caroline like Eloise said," Amy declared. "Dick killed the maid and then got his moral come-uppance."

He looked surprised. "I don't discredit Mrs. Collins. She believes what her husband told her. But we still have no direct evidence to support that, and she can provide none." Garda O'Shannon drew back and folded his hands. "O'Dea told me you were a crafty lot with wild, brainy ideas, but I didn't know the extent," he said finally. Amy stared at him. To her ears it sounded like *weld and brownie ideeds*. "But I have warned you against your ways and wiles and meddlin'. And yet you persist. If there is danger in store for you, what have you to gain?"

"It's not in our nature to be idle targets," Genna said with a huff.

"Then let me put a couple of things straight to you now," he said, eyeing Genna with hard eyes. "This is no idle game. It is no small matter, a homicide. The young lady was kilt, not with the ice pick as you are so bent to believe. Put there to deceive us, it was. As you, yourself were deceived. It was shrewd and it was callous. And what's more, it was planned." He paused for effect. "Planned," he repeatedly slowly, his eyes still dark. "And we have not yet found the true weapon."

Amy was urgent. "What are we looking for? What kind of a weapon? Something that looks like an ice pick but isn't?"

"Did I not just say you were not to meddle? Did I not just say that?"

Amy frowned. He was making himself clear.

"Now, I will tell you, this," he began again, "the croquet mallet had no impact upon Mr. Collins death. He was struck with the mallet, yes, but it was only enough to knock him off balance. It appears he was hit with a shard of glass as the container shattered and thus the bleeding on his head. Neither of those circumstances was fatal. His death has been ruled asphyxiation due to anaphylaxis. He had an allergic reaction. Perhaps he had more than one."

"I knew it," Rian said. "Someone really was trying to kill him."

"He seemed to think so when we spoke last. At first I didn't believe him, but then, well, then matters took a different turn, now didn't they? And that is why I insist that you are not safe with your meddlin'. You will not interfere any further. That, or I will lock you up in Cork Bridewell and you will hope they don't toss the key!"

Rian didn't hesitate. "Then why are you telling us all this other stuff?"

"To make it as clear as ever I can — if you are not careful, the curiosity will kill the cat. You, are the cat."

"Mona said the same thing," Amy told them when the O'Shannon had left them to themselves. "She said curiosity killed the cat. It's an Irish expression."

"What does that have to do with anything?" Genna muttered. "And none of it fits your spidey-dream anyway. I'm beginning to think your dreams aren't working long distance any better than our cell phones. I can't even call home to check the weather."

Rian laughed. "It's sunny and hot in Arkansas, Genna. Trust me. It's sunny and hot."

# CHAPTER FORTY

They didn't see Rebecca the next day. Nor did that seem surprising. Reginald Williams overheard them all but accuse his wife of the crime. Actually, they *had* accused her. Now Amy didn't want to face either of the Williams' over coffee.

Rebecca was involved in setting up the chaos that ensued, and no doubt she had plenty of guilt over that. Amy felt satisfied, if satisfied was the right word. The front desk admitted the Williams couple had not checked out. Probably no one was checking out until the weapon was found.

And that was a problem. Amy doubted the police would ever find it. It was probably in the mud at the bottom of the lake. The only reason they found the wallet was because it floated to the top where James and Gayle had found it.

Garda O'Shannon said the ice pick was planted at the scene. So, what looked like an ice pick but wasn't? Surely there were many things that fit that description within the confines of a hotel. But all were falling short of probable. A garden tool? Not handy enough. A kitchen knife? It wasn't that kind of a blow. A relic from the chapel? Don't even go there. Nothing seemed to fit. The riddle had been churning through her head without an answer. No answer yet, anyway. She wasn't done pondering.

She was curious why Gayle was spying on Dick and Caroline that night, although the opportunity to ask had yet to present itself. It would soon. Rian had made a golf date with Gayle and James for the afternoon, and Amy had decided she would tag along. The front desk had called Eloise to ask if Rian could use the golf clubs left behind. Rian could have asked Eloise herself, of course, but she felt more comfortable with it coming from the clerk. Rian wouldn't be able to wear the gloves, since they'd been destroyed when they were cut off Dick's balloon sized hands, but she claimed she didn't wear gloves anyway. By the look on her face, she didn't think anyone should wear gloves to golf.

Zelda was upstairs unpacking her goodies from the shopping trip. And, as Zelda always did, cooing over her newfound treasures like Smaug the dragon from Middle-earth. Genna had booked the entire day at the hotel spa and was planning head to toe opulence. That left Doris, and Amy had a few things she needed to get straight in her mind about Doris.

Her knock was answered immediately.

"Oh, thank goodness, it's you," Doris said. "I'm as jumpy as a cat in a room full of rocking chairs."

Grandmother Ollie used to say that. "What's going on?"

"I can't get this croquet thing out of my mind."

"I don't know that any of us can, but it will fade over time."

Doris pushed at the bridge of her glasses. "I'm not talking about that. I'm talking about my croquet mallet. The one I was holding when the lights came on."

Intrigued, Amy's brows lifted.

"I've been going over and over in my head what color mallet everybody had. It has to do with the order in which they played, but I'm getting a little mixed up. I felt very disoriented in the dark. Nothing looked normal to me."

Amy nodded. Nothing was supposed to. That was the point.

"Not only that, but the colors were altered so they would glow. I know that Gayle and I played the yellow and we were last. You and Rebecca played on the orange. I'm pretty sure Rian and Genna drew the pink, but I'm having difficulty remembering who was the green and who was on the white. I want to say that Dick and Mr. Williams were on the white ball. And that leaves James and Eloise on the green."

"What color was the mallet put in your hands?"

"Green. I am one-hundred percent sure. Fluorescent green. I've been thinking about it for hours."

Amy counted on her fingers. "We had twelve players. Who are we missing?"

"Zelda and Mona," Doris said. "There were six balls and six mallets in play. We were doubled up, but I don't think Mona had a chance to play."

"Mona," Amy breathed. "Do you think she hit Dick in the head and then passed the mallet to you? Is that what you are saying?"

"I don't know what I'm saying. Not really. There could have been an extra mallet there. I don't know. But if anyone knew if there was, that would be Mona."

"Who do you think was on the green ball?"

"James and Eloise are the two in my mind. They went right after you. That would make them green."

"So, either one of them could have whacked Dick in the head and then shoved that mallet into your hands."

Doris nodded. "We didn't play after that. Remember? Dick yelled and then he dropped to the floor and then Eloise dropped with him."

"And then Mona turned on the lights."

Doris nodded. "That's when Mona turned on the lights."

They stood in silence again and Doris crossed the floor to the table. She plugged in the electric kettle and dropped tea bags into two cups. "Handy device they have here," she said. "It boils water in seconds. I'd like to have one for my desk at work. You want sugar?"

Amy shook her head and accepted the hot cup.

"Doris," she started, disbursing the steam with her breath, "do you think Eloise was the one who hit Dick with her mallet? Could she have just bubbled over with anger at how badly he behaved and whacked him good and solid?"

"I wouldn't blame her!"

They looked at each other for a moment and then sipped their tea.

"Do you have any idea what happens if you inject someone with an EpiPen and they're not having an allergic reaction?"

Doris shook her head. "I guess it would depend on a few things. Say if you had a weak heart."

"What is an EpiPen anyway?"

"Pure adrenaline," Doris answered. "Epinephrine. That's why they call it an EpiPen."

"Have you ever used one?"

"No, but my kid sister had a bologna allergy. That's what they called it, anyway. My mom kept an EpiPen in the medicine cabinet. We never had to use it. It's probably still there, although it would be very out of date. It's not like we threw anything away in our house. We were told not to play with it because it's one and done. Once you use it, it's trash. The orange injector part at the bottom covers the needle after it's been released, so you can't stick yourself twice."

Amy was silent for a moment. Her brain was tracking along like a high speed train.

"If you were *not* having an allergic reaction and you did *not* have bad heart and you got zapped with a dose of adrenaline, what would happen? Would you just get the shakes? Go all sweaty? Would you faint or what?"

"Something like that, I would guess."

"Could it kill you?"

"Probably not. Amy, where are you going with this?"

"Dick really did have an allergic reaction to something he ingested, just like Eloise said. Like Garda O'Shannon said. Asphyxiation due to anaphylaxis."

"Oh. Okay, but …"

"What if whoever hit him meant to kill him but just didn't hit him hard enough? That could have been Mona, but what motive did she have? It could have been Eloise, but then why bother with the adrenaline injection? And it could have been James. His wife stood to gain from Dick's death. And who knows what Gayle had against Caroline. Maybe she thought Caroline stood in the way of her new job at the chamber. Maybe Gayle thought Caroline was feeding Dick bad information about her. Maybe she was playing a game of pickleball from both sides of the court."

"What does that mean?" Doris looked confused.

"It means that maybe Gayle Brand isn't as innocent a player as we thought she was. Maybe she was playing Dick against Caroline and Caroline against Dick."

Doris wrinkled her brow. "And what about the allergy?"

Amy frowned as she looked at Doris and held her gaze. "That's where I'm getting stuck. It seems coincidental, but what if one person aimed at his head, and yet another put something in his drink? What if that someone had been trying to kill him? What if they'd been torturing him with little things like peanuts in his gloves. Or bees in a locked room."

Doris gasped and choked on her tea. Her face purpled and she sputtered. "Are you accusing me? Is that why you're here? I only put dead bees in his room! I just wanted to make him sweat. I only wanted to scare him enough to bring him down a notch. The bees were already dead! I promise you. And I never put anything in his gloves or anybody else's for that matter!"

Amy felt the relief all the way to her toes. "Oh, I can't tell you how happy I am to hear that, Doris. Because I don't think Dick killed Caroline. But I do think he knew who did."

"What?"

"Oh, it could have been any one of the seventy-odd guests at the hotel that day. It could even be one of the employees. It could have been a case of mistaken identity, seeing how Caroline was dressed as a maid.

"But, I've been thinking all along that Rebecca Williams was responsible. I thought maybe Tom the Nosey Parker was here to do her dirty work. Rebecca said she wanted to catch them in some fraud scheme and save the bank from ruin."

"Yeah," Doris said. "That's why they have that FDIC law about taking consecutive time off."

"But Eloise believed Dick killed Caroline to stop her from ruining his life. That's what he told her. She believed him. So, who was *he* protecting? Where was the maid really killed? And why did he plant the ice pick as the weapon?"

"It was planted?"

"Yep. According to Garda O'Shannon it was. He says they are still looking for the weapon and I think we are looking for two murder weapons. One that looks like an ice pick and one that looks like bologna."

Doris laughed in spite of herself. "You don't really mean bologna, bologna."

"No. But something as deadly to someone with allergies. And I'm not sure we will ever know, because they can't pinpoint the specific allergen and they can't find the weapon."

"You mean it's an unsolvable murder?" Doris' eyes were wide behind her butterscotch glasses.

Amy nodded. "I think this person may get away with murder. Not because the police aren't doing their job — because they certainly are. Garda O'Shannon is as good as they come, I'd say. It's just one of those things. One of those odds. A long shot horse that wins. A risk that pays off."

# CHAPTER FORTY ONE

Amy entered the silence of the library eager to see what the worldwide net of knowledge and gossip might uncover about the Arkansas gang. The curtains were closed, and the room looked darker than it had the other day. A familiar figure was seated at the desk.

Mona turned. "Good day, Miss Sparks. I mean, Amy."

"Hi, Mona."

"What are you up to, today?" She was the pleasant, open person who had been directing them through their activities. The frustrated and fearful concern was gone.

"I wanted to see if I could use the computer. I thought I would check in on my shop. See how things are going. Maybe look at my email."

"Of course," Mona answered, straightening the surface of the desk. "That's what this computer is here for. Although we hope our guests leave their jobs at home and enjoy what Ireland has to offer."

"What are you doing today?" Amy asked lightly.

"I have a new group checking in come the fortnight and I'm looking to see what activities I should plan for them," Mona answered. "There won't be croquet, I can tell you that. Our GM has put croquet on a long hold. No rebuttal allowed."

"You need a computer for that?"

"I like to do a little research on who's coming. That way I can match the activities with their personalities. What do you know about this corn hole fad in America? Is it all the rage it appears to be?"

"Wait. You mean you research your guests? You Google us before we arrive?"

Mona shook her head. "Well, it's not at all like that. Not as you frame it, so. But yes, I like to know who's in the group and what they may be interested in. That way I can schedule things they will enjoy and avoid things they may not."

"So, you Googled us?"

Mona raised a brow. It was clear she didn't want to answer. "Nothing invasive. We don't do criminal checks or anything. I just like to know a little something. Like what you do for fun. What you do for a living. Why you've come as a group. As you all did."

"What is the point of your get-to-know-you croquet, then?"

Mona pulled away from the desk. "Well, it's not for me at all. It's all about you getting to know each other better. But I admit, it's a brilliant way for me to see the group dynamics. I see how the group works together. Who leads and who follows. Who is cautious and who is direct. The adventurous and the timid. Who hides behind their polite manners and who doesn't. It's good to know these things when you manage a group of strangers."

Amy sat down with a thump.

"Oh dear. I shouldn't have been so outspoken. Now you think I spy on our guests with a guilty eye."

If the shoe fits. "I imagine you shared your *findings* with Garda O'Shannon?"

"Well, he did ask for a brief report."

"Anything juicy?"

Mona nodded. "Ah, I see what you are after. I know he warned you to stay out of his business. He said as much to me about it. You best mind the Gardai. They are not all as kind and tender as our dear O'Shannon."

Mona closed her laptop and vacated the seat at the desk. She moved the mouse on the guest computer and the screen opened to the search bar.

"Have a grand day, Amy," Mona said, her laptop tucked under her arm. "And do mind the Gardai," she added before she bustled out the door.

Amy stared at the screen. Mona knew who they were before they even arrived. She knew all about their jobs, their businesses, their social life. She probably even stalked their social media accounts.

If only she could tap into Mona's search history she might learn what Mona shared with the Gardai. But Mona used her laptop and wrangling that was a futile effort.

What did it matter, anyway? What's done was done, to quote Rebecca.

Amy had come into the room with a mental list of things she wanted to search. A look at her emails topped that list and she took a few moments to respond to those who needed to hear from her. The report from Tiddlywinks was good. Business was profitable. No problems at home. A picture of Victor snuggled up and purring proved he also was doing fine. That traitor cat. She left the spam in place and logged out of her email platform.

Now, on to other matters.

Richard Collins was a common name on the Internet. Scrolling the pages of obits with his namesake, articles and Wikipedia entries that obviously belonged to someone else, she finally landed on an article in a small town paper published in the late 1980s. The article touted a young graduate from a small college in Oklahoma, who had won a debate championship sponsored by the local chamber of commerce. It was all the rabbit hole she needed.

When she finally clicked out of the navigation pages, she knew everything she wanted to know and then some about Dick Collins and his second wife, Eloise. She saw inside their home which was featured in a photo spread in a local magazine. He was described as a man building wealth and stature in his community, and she was an aspiring artist who was content to support her husband's every need. The walls of their home showed weavings, tapestries, and artistic endeavors of all things fiber arts. In one photo, she stood next to an expensive looking vase of knitting needles of every color and size — an art project of its own — and the look on her face said she was proud and humble and content. In the photo of them together, Dick was not wearing purple, but his hair was as short and nubby as ever. Eloise looked much younger nestled against his shoulder, her hands held in front. He held his jaw like a man with a mission to thrive.

Amy thought of the magazine spread Genna orchestrated for the shops at the Cardboard Cottage. The exposure had a been a coup that launched their visibility as a destination tourist shop. Their little corner in Bluff Springs was showcased in several glossy pages as the next best thing since microwave ovens. And yet, the Cardboard Cottage was really nothing more than a shopping stop in a fun little tourist town. Funny how easy it was to create a splash larger than the real thing. Looks could be deceiving. Genna's story set the scene that made the splash. The camera had captured the best views, but it didn't catch what was going on behind the camera. Somehow she felt that way now. What did the picture of Dick and Eloise really say about their lives? What did any picture say of the people captured in the frame?

She opened another search. Rebecca Williams had won more awards than Amy thought possible. The short of it was -- Rebecca sold real estate. Big real estate. And she was good at it. In every photo that popped up, she was pristine perfect. She was fashionably styled, a winning gaze lighting up her pretty face, and the hand-holding handshake that said she was always your friend. There were so many stories about her success and charitable deeds, that Amy knew she'd be searching for days to find the crumb of a sullied deed. No one was this perfect, and yet it sure looked that way on the surface.

She scrolled some more, and that's when she saw his name. Amy clicked the link.

Bingo.

The article was an old one and it was brief. The account was the tail end of on an ongoing story about a possible conflict of interest involving a commercial brokerage firm and a financial institution. The latter was run by none other than Richard Collins. Amy did her best to follow the complicated story that had already been old news by the time this piece was published. It involved a piece of property offered to a city to build a new civic center. She didn't recognize the name of the town, but she did recognize the names involved. Reginald Williams was the commercial broker. The story suggested that he accepted monies from the seller while advising the city on the purchase. Funding was to go through Richard Collins' bank. Gayle Brand was listed as the city's director of finance.

Amy paused. Is this the history that brought them together?

She read on. The story ended because the city changed its plans for the civic center. None of the parties involved were charged with malfeasance of any kind. If there was something off, it was tabled. Or raked under the table, as the writer suggested. Dick Collins was quoted as saying, "It was a bureaucratic misunderstanding and probably all for the best."

All for the best. How ironic. Hadn't he said the same thing to Doris?

Reginald Williams had since changed career directions — maybe he had to, and so did Gayle. But the two of them were still connected. Amy wouldn't say they were connected at the hip, but they were still doing business together. Gayle was expecting to take Reginald's job when he retired. Was there more to that story than this? Did Gayle have some hold over Reginald? And Dick Collins, too? Maybe that was why he was against her rising in ranks at the chamber. What did Dick have to lose if she became president? Or gain if she didn't?

Caroline Gadling didn't come up anywhere in the search. Not unless she was born in the 1800s. There were no old pictures. No new pictures. No gossip. She didn't have a social media page under her name and the absence seemed odd in and of itself. Who was this Caroline? Amy scrolled on. Suddenly, she recognized her in the image feed. She was wearing the same fur as when she exited the chapel that first night. In the picture, Caroline was all Marilyn Monroe smile and cleavage – an image remarkably similar to a much younger, thinner, less busty Eloise. She was stepping into a helicopter, the pilot already on board. It was Caroline and Dick out for a ride in his purple helicopter. What had Eloise called it? A Welch's grape.

Maybe Zelda was right. Caroline the spy. The one who had stolen someone's passport and taken over their life. Maybe she had targeted Dick Collins and his bank. Maybe she was intent on becoming the next Mrs. Dick.

Was it possible? Yes. Probable? Not now.

So how did he get a pilot license if he was color deficient, as Eloise claimed?

It didn't take long to answer the query. There were many ways to get around it. He couldn't be a commercial or military pilot. And he probably couldn't fly at night. So, was he bluffing about his penchant for purple? Was it a joke? Was it just an excuse to parade around in his bank logo and colors? One of those idiosyncrasies that a person latches onto and can't let go? Didn't we all have some of that? Eloise was the one who kept Dick's closet organized so he wouldn't go to the office in mismatched socks. Was this the one little fragment of control Eloise had over him? Was that her thin thread of power in their marriage?

Amy closed the navigation windows.

*EpiPen,* she typed into the search bar.

She clicked the video option. YouTube popped up with page after page of "how to."

She clicked the first one and waited for it to load. Rian was right. The computer was a little slow, but eventually the video lit up the screen.

She watched and then watched it again. It was all she needed to know.

# CHAPTER FORTY TWO

There wasn't room for the four of them and their gear in one golf cart, so Rian put Dick's golf bag in the seat with Gayle and James and she and Amy walked the path to the green. It would take them longer to get there, but the view was part of the joy. The green of the mountains rose around them in every direction, and she was reminded of her walk to the chapel. That had been a special moment. She was hoping this walk would prove the same.

She and Rian walked for a while in silence.

It was the first day in several that the sun was out, and the sky was blue. It wasn't hot, but it was bright and warm. The air smelled like sunshine and something in heavy bloom. It didn't feel all that different from the Ozarks and she felt the pang of homesickness. The mountains were green, there, too. There would be wild honeysuckle blooming. The grapes in Rian's vineyard would be getting fat, maybe a few already turning a glorious shade of red. The rivers would be low, but the waterfalls hidden in the hills would be running, or trickling, or dripping over a bluff. In the winter, the water would freeze into icicles, some as thick as an elephant leg and some as delicate as a straw. Did the same thing happen here? Probably. There was certainly enough water to freeze into icicles.

It was easy to see why the transplanted natives of Ireland learned to love their new mountain homes in the Ozarks. She thought of Tarbert Bridewell and Elva Gráinne with her necklace and crest. Where had Elva and her newborn gone? Was it possible they had settled in America? Was Elva McKinney, the guide at Tarbert Bridewell somehow her kin? And did she want to dig for those roots? Could Grandmother Ollie really be part of that long-ago lineage of seers and healers who lived in the mountain caves of Ireland? It seemed too far-fetched to be true, and yet, Rian had found her roots. Out of all the O'Days in all the world, Rian had found her clan in County Clare.

Amy smiled at the thought. Arkansas was as good a place as any to set down roots and take up fiddling. Although, there were not as many sheep. Zelda was right about that. Ireland had way more sheep.

"I think she's going to get away with it," Amy said, finally breaking the silence. "They're not going to find the weapon that killed Caroline, and they can't prove Dick's allergy attack was premeditated. And you know what? I'm not sure how I feel about it."

Rian turned to face her. "Who are you talking about?"

"I'm talking about Eloise."

Rian stopped mid-step.

"She killed Caroline because she was going to ruin her family. And I broke Sam Ford's rule. I framed the question, but I predicted the answer. I wasn't listening and I heard what I wanted to hear.

"Eloise never said Dick killed Caroline. She told us the truth. She told us that Caroline wouldn't leave him alone. That she was stealing from the bank and planned on taking its president down with her. There was history in that triangle.

"Eloise called Caroline low rent and dimwitted. Isn't that how you would describe your husband's lover? She already knew about their tango. What wife wouldn't? I don't even think she cared, but that's not what tipped the scales. It was Richard who tipped the scales. Richard, her son. She was afraid that her son would be harmed by what was happening.

"Think about it. Bank fraud with the president of the bank is noisy news. Eloise saw public humiliation ahead of them. She saw her perfect little world crumbling. She saw Richard's college fund flowing out the door. Every penny spent to prove that Dick was innocent of his fraud. And Dick wasn't innocent. She knew it. And she knew if she didn't act, Richard *would be* harmed. She had to do it. She told us that. She said Caroline had to be stopped."

"Hail Mary," Rian said and the two resumed walking.

"I found part of an empty peanut bag in the trash in her bathroom. I smelled peanut dust in his gloves. Remember that picture Tom showed us? Doris and Eloise were passing each other in the lobby. Doris had a bouquet of flowers and a glass full of dead bees. Eloise had a pair of gloves. I'd say those were Dick's golf gloves. I think Eloise spent several days trying to see which allergy would bring him down for good."

"Arum berries!" Rian exclaimed. "Eloise picked Arum berries in the woods. She said they were for dyeing fibers, but they can be toxic. *Arum maculatum*. They call them Lords and Ladies because it's an aphrodisiac if you live."

"That's great irony for a cheating husband. And see, your degree in botany did you some good after all."

"My almost degree in botany. You know I never graduated. Arum," Rian repeated. "The taste is supposed to be dreadful."

"I'd say that's why Eloise hid the taste in a gin and tonic. She bartended at the blacklight croquet. Remember?"

Rian nodded again. "She must have tried all kinds of things on him because Dick had a rough few days while we were hunting the Irish. He said someone was trying to kill him and no one believed him. He never thought it might be his wife.

"Now that I think about it, I ran into Eloise walking in the woods by herself several times. I didn't think anything of it because

I like to walk in the woods, too. She was looking for plants he might react to. She had to be. There's a mushroom patch by the juniper grove. There's got to be poisonous liberty caps somewhere nearby. And Juniper berries are poisonous, too, and that's what gin is flavored with. She had access to so many things. Probably all kinds of poisons in the garden shed."

"She wasn't after poison," Amy countered. "She was after something he was allergic to that couldn't be traced. Something he couldn't taste and refuse to eat. Eloise was torturing him in a macabre, passive aggressive way. He knew what happened to Caroline. He knew who did it. And he had to do something to throw the Gardai off their trail. And that's when he picked up the ice pick. He didn't want anyone to know he was connected to Caroline, but then, the cat got out of the bag. And Eloise was afraid he would tell the police what she had done. Especially when he changed rooms. She wasn't happy about that. She knew he would sell her out sooner or later. And she knew that sooner or later, she would find some allergen that would drop him dead.

"And that brings me to the EpiPen," Amy added. "Eloise knew there was a chance it could fail but she didn't want to take a chance."

"The EpiPen," Rian repeated. "It didn't work."

"No, it didn't. And that's because it had already been ejected. The needle was hidden from view in the tip and safely in her pocket. She pretended to administer the drug, but it had already been released. He never got a dose of adrenaline."

"And no one would ever know," Rian added.

"I talked to Doris, too. That's how I knew the bees were dead. She put them in his room out of spite, but she never expected him to get hurt. And she didn't hit him with the mallet, either. We decided that was either James or Mona."

"Mona! Why would Mona want to hit him?"

"Why would any one of us want to hit him?"

"I get your point. You think it could be James who hit him?"

"I think we are about to find out," Amy said, as they reached the ridge at the green. James and Gayle were waiting at the tee. Gayle waved and Amy waved back.

"Let's go fishing for answers," Amy said.

"Yeah," Rian agreed. "Let's go fish."

"You ready?" James asked, when the pair arrived at the tee.

"Not quite," Rian said. "We have a few questions we need to ask first."

James repositioned his Razorback hat on his head. "Questions about golf? I thought you knew how to play."

"Questions about why you two have motive for murder," Amy said, regretting the outburst immediately.

Gayle looked startled. "Murder!"

"You knew who Caroline Gadling was, and you knew she was here. You lied to us. Maybe you lied to the police, too." Amy shifted her weight. "You knew they met in the chapel that night. The photographer caught you hiding in the shadows. Why were you following them?"

Gayle leaned the shaft of her club against her leg, and Amy remembered that same stance in the croquet game on their first outing. Gayle was wearing sunglasses beneath her hat, and Amy couldn't see her expression clearly. Gayle turned to James before turning to Amy.

"I get heartburn and can't sleep," she answered finally. "I went downstairs to see if I could find something to settle my stomach. I was looking for club soda or Alka Seltzer, or a packet of Tums. Anything that might help."

James nodded. "That's true. She gets heartburn when she's anxious. This trip has certainly been that."

"Why were you anxious that night?" Amy asked.

"You mean that's not obvious? I want to be named president of the chamber when Mr. Williams retires. In case you haven't noticed, I'm a woman of color with a bigoted, misogynistic barrier standing in my way. And this wasn't the first time he caused me major problems."

"You're talking about Dick Collins."

Gayle nodded.

"And now you don't have anyone standing in the way," Rian added.

Gayle exhaled. "You're right. Now I don't."

"Why were you following him?"

"It was just one of those weird things. I was in the pub looking for something to take for my heartburn when I saw the maid go out the door. Dick followed her. Eloise was not far behind. I didn't know what was happening, but I thought… well, maybe this was a sign." Gayle exhaled loudly. "Oh, I know that sounds horrible. It sounds like I was looking for leverage. I wasn't.

"Eloise came back quickly, and I had to hide in the shadows so she wouldn't see me. Dick didn't see me, either. And I didn't know who Caroline was!"

"That's true," James interjected. "We didn't know who she was then."

"How *did* you find out?"

"When we found the wallet."

"And not before that?" Rian asked. "Why should we believe you?"

"It doesn't matter if you do or don't," James said heatedly. "It doesn't change a thing."

"No, it doesn't," Rian conceded. "But it's hard to believe you didn't recognize her."

"I told you," Gayle said. "I had never met her. I only spoke with her by phone and email. I really didn't know what she looked like. I even asked the front desk if the maids stay on the premises after hours. They do not."

Gayle paused and then continued. "I planned to ask Eloise about it when we were watching the wedding, but I didn't know her well enough to ask a question like that outright. She was fretful that day. Is that the right word?" Gayle glanced at James. "I could tell Eloise was battling something behind that composed and stony facade. Frankly, I was relieved when she excused herself and left me to watch the wedding on my own. It was a beautiful thing to watch. But then…"

"I know all about the civic center," Amy interrupted. She sensed Gayle tense. "You, Reginald, and Dick had history and I have to wonder if it was shady enough to kill."

Gayle's grip tightened on the club. Amy turned to James. "Why did you hit Dick with the croquet mallet?"

His reaction was visceral. He jerked as if punched in the gut. Gayle reached out and put her hand on his arm, pulling herself closer to him as they stood side by side. Two against two. Amy felt Rian close the gap between them.

"What an insufferable ass," he said bitterly. "I tried to get him to understand why Gayle was the best choice for the job. I wanted him to know why it was important to us. He wasn't just stubborn, he was malicious. You heard what he said about Gayle. You heard him! Every word was a red-hot poker in my brain. I couldn't get it out my head. It kept ringing and ringing in that nasty, condescending tone of his. I just ….I don't even really remember, I just …"

"You whacked him and shoved your mallet in Doris' hands, so she'd be blamed."

James hung his head. "I know it was beyond cowardly. It was a knee jerk reaction."

Rian took a step closer toward Amy, closing what little gap there was already. "Did you mean to kill him?"

James was silent. A lone gull flew overhead. Its shadow darkened the green grass beneath their feet momentarily.

"No," he said finally. "I just swung out of anger. I didn't even realize I hit him. I was aiming for that jar." He drew quiet and then looked at Gayle. "I wasn't trying to kill him, but I can't say I cared one way or the other. And that's something for me and my Maker to face."

And the Garda. Amy felt his suffering in that moment. He would relive that swing for a long time, she knew. Another one-hit. Not quite out of the ballpark and not a home run.

Amy wanted to tell him that Doris was okay. That she had her own struggle with Dick Collins and had struck out against him, too. If it hadn't been for the bees, dead or not, Dick wouldn't have fallen down the stairs. She wanted to tell them about Eloise, but that wasn't her story to tell. Instead, she let the silence close in on them.

"Well," Rian said, as she pulled Dick's golf bag from the cart. "No sense in wasting a perfectly gorgeous day in Ireland, now is there? We might as well play a few holes, at least."

Rian unzipped the bag and tugged at one of the golf clubs. Something was giving resistance and she tugged harder. The club pulled free along with something else. What came to the surface was a sock. A man's knee length sock. Khaki colored. The neck was twisted into a knot. Rian glanced at Amy, unknotted the sock and peeked in.

"Will you look at that," Rian said, grinning like a fox who'd fooled the hunter.

Amy peered over her arm. "What is it?"

The heavy silver caps ends of two thick knitting needles poked through the neck of the sock.

"Don't touch it!" Amy cried. "You've just found the murder weapon. And now I know who Dick was protecting!"

Rian held the sock at arm's length. "Who was Dick protecting?"

"Himself. He didn't want anyone to know what Eloise had done. He didn't want anyone to know Eloise stabbed Caroline in the back with her knitting needles. The ice pick, the scene in the hall – that wasn't Dick looking after Eloise. That was Dick defending himself. He thought he could get away with all of it if no one recognized Caroline. If everyone thought she was just some maid in the hall. This sock was his insurance. His evidence against Eloise. If he needed it, all he had to do was turn it over to the police. He became an accomplice when he moved the body and planted the ice pick, but only that. An accomplice to murder. And that's when Eloise knew that Dickie Collins had to go.

# CHAPTER FORTY THREE

Eloise was taken into custody and Amy enjoyed watching Garda O'Shannon eat a little crow.

"The evidence was right in front of us," he said solemnly. "No one looked in the club bag. I was convinced the weapon was at the bottom of the lake."

"So did we," Amy agreed. "And yet the clue was in front of us the whole time. Eloise was obsessed with the characters in the *A Tale of Two Cities*. She thought of herself as Madame Defarge knitting her way through her murderous rage. Did she admit to what happened?"

Garda O'Shannon nodded.

"And you're not going to tell me, are you?"

The Garda shook his head, but his dimples creased his cheeks. 'You think you've earned it with your meddlin' ways, don't you now? You think you're smarter than the Gardai Síochána, you would say?"

"No, I wouldn't say that, but I am pretty good at meddling."

"To put a finer point on it," he agreed. "Another bloke is deceased and you're four for four. This isn't a good look for ya. Don't you know you'll never catch a good fella that a way." He reached out and pressed her shoulder lightly.

Amy bit her lip to still the laughter from breaking through. The husband always dies. That was no laughing matter. But Garda O'Shannon's idea that she should catch a man was.

"You'll not say you heard it from me," he said finally. "What you're about to overhear because you be listening in and shouldn't be."

He scanned the room. No one was paying them any attention.

"Eloise Collins said she was knitting when the maid knocked on the door of her room. Came in all smug and vainglorious, Mrs. Collins said. Had the nerve to go boasting about their affair happening right under her nose. And wasn't she about to become the new Mrs. Collins.

"The real Mrs. Collins said she didn't give a rat's tail about the affair. Said no one was going to divorce any one and lose half of everything Dick had worked so hard to have. Dick wouldn't stand for that. He wouldn't.

"Mrs. Collins claimed the woman wagged her finger right in her face." Garda O'Shannon's voice rose an octave as if mimicking the conversation from her point of view.

"*'You can't stand that I have both of your men wrapped around my little finger, can you? If Dick and I don't work out, there's always Dick Junior.'*"

"Oh, no, not Dick Junior," Amy said, remembering Eloise's reaction. They had been on the croquet court that first day when Gayle had called him Dick Junior. Eloise had nearly come unglued. "That was the wrong thing for Caroline to say."

"I guess so. You can picture the rest. If you must."

"So that really was Eloise and Dick arguing in the picture Tom took. They must have been arguing about what to do with the body."

"Mrs. Collins cleaned the spot on the rug while Mr. Collins was out tossing the maids room and her identification. And then Mrs. Collins had to clean his sleeve when he dragged his cuff through the blood rolling Caroline out in the hall. We found a partial smear of blood in Ms. Gadling's room, and we were quite perplexed as to how it got there. He must have tracked it in when he ransacked her room. The hotel maid complained the spot on that rug was wet for days, but we didn't test for blood. Didn't consider it until you spoke to Mona. Clear as day to us now. You asked Mona if blood was visible under a blacklight. Why was that?"

"Because the bottom of Dick's shoes were glowing in the dark. I thought he stepped in blood. It was soap from the rug."

He nodded. "Laundry soap. I should have caught that, I should."

"And that's why Eloise had to buy knitting needles in the wool shop," Amy exclaimed. "I thought she was being persnickety about which pair to buy, but it was something else. She was struggling. Or plotting. That scarf! The mollusk brine in the purple scarf. Dick had seafood allergies. She may have started plotting to kill him right then and there. She was hoping the brine in the scarf would cause an allergic reaction!"

O'Shannon frowned. "You have a mind for murder," he said. "I don't know if that's a good thing. I don't."

Amy ignored him. "Is that what did it? The seafood brine in the purple scarf? Did the coroner discover what the allergen was?"

"It's in the works, still. It will take a bit of testing to determine that on the nose, and they're backlogged for months. But I don't think it matters, much. She's admitted to the one murder and it's sure enough to put her behind bars. I told you before, our job is to find the culprit and bring her to justice. This I have done. Although I won't say I couldn't have done it without you." He paused and then laughed lightly. "I can't believe you two thought she was a spy eating too much banana puddin'. I got a cackle out of that, I did. We all got a cackle out of that." He chuckled again under his breath. "You'll be leaving soon?"

Amy nodded. "We're packing up, moving on. It's been a bucket list adventure but I'm ready to go home."

"Next time, leave your meddlin' behind, will ya? Next time, don't be messing with the Gardai."

"Next time," Amy agreed and turned to go. She didn't look back, but she had to fight the urge. She really would miss seeing Mr. Dimples.

Gayle didn't seem put out when the four of them opted for a private tour of the Ring of Kerry. Genna finally had taken over their tour agenda, which she had been aching to do the whole time. The rest of them — Doris, Gayle, James, Reginald and Rebecca — would take the tour coach the chamber had originally booked. They would see each other at the airport in a few days.

The four friends would travel the 100-mile trek and scenic drive around the Iveragh Peninsula at the southwestern tip of Ireland. They would travel at their own pace. Or at least Genna's pace. Stop when they wanted to stop. Eat when they were hungry and drink when thirst arose. They would drive through rugged landscapes and visit every seaside village that looked interesting. They'd take in the Cliffs of Kerry, walk a fairy trail through the woods, and go for a frigid swim in the Atlantic near Derrynane. They would shop, visit an ancient circle of stones, and then hit one last castle ruin before returning to Dublin and their last night on the town.

And that's what they did.

"Anybody up for a game of I Spy the Irish Guy?" Zelda asked. "I already packed my dominoes, so that's out." They were seated in the hotel pub, the last round, last draft Guinness before they caught a cab to the airport. "Winner gets a grab at my new ice trophy. The one I got from winning get-to-know-you croquet. Gayle said she didn't want it," Zelda added. "I can't tell if it's a Puffin or a Shar Pei. The nose looks all wrinkly. Kind of reminds me of Mary Poppins' umbrella. You know, the one that talks. I guess it must be a Puffin."

"Worse game, ever," Genna said. "Croquet."

"Just because you lost terribly," Zelda said. "You hate to lose."

"Are you saying we should retire our Tiddlywinks Trophy and bedazzle this bird?" Amy asked, her eyes wide with disbelief.

"Why not," Zelda said. "A Puffin trophy. Sounds like fun to me."

Rian chuckled. "I'm up for that. I'm feeling lucky. I found my roots and we helped solve a crime in Ireland."

"Well, even the dimwitted make a smart move now and again," Genna said, with a nudge of her elbow.

"Don't be calling anyone dimwitted on *this* side of the table," Zelda countered. "If you will remember I called it. I told you the hubs had a girlfriend on the side and the wife discovered she's not really the maid. The maid wound up dead and then the husbank wasbund wound up dead. And everybody else lives happily ever after. I said that, do you remember?"

"Even a blind squirrel gets a nut now again," Genna replied.

"And what does a cocky squirrel get," Zelda spat, her eyes narrowed at Genna.

"Battered and fried," Rian said, laughing. "Onion rings on the side."

Zelda looked at Genna and then they both burst into laughter that ended with Genna sputtering into her glass.

"Amy, you never told us what happened at the Kenmare Stone Circle on the Ring of Kerry," Genna said when she had recovered. "When that rabbit ran out from behind the stone, I thought you were going to lose it. You looked like you saw a ghost."

"I did see a ghost," Amy said. "Well, I thought I saw my grandmother's ghost. I wanted to go to her and put my arms around her. The feeling was so strong it made me ache."

"That's a little creepy," Genna said.

"It scared me at first," Amy continued, "because she looked so real, and I knew she wasn't. And then I saw something wink in the sunlight. I thought it was the diamond in her necklace. But it was just a penny. Harp's side up."

"Oh, for good luck. You picked it up, right?" Zelda asked.

"No, believe it or not, I didn't."

"I don't believe, it," Genna said. "You never pass up a penny heads side up."

"I knew the fae were watching me," Amy said and laughed. "And that's when I knew."

"Knew what?" Zelda asked quietly.

"Knew what it meant. *Death leaves a heartache no one can heal. Love leaves a memory no one can steal.* I don't know that I can explain it very well, but I know what it means."

Rian nodded. "I get it. When I was standing in front of that cross at Dysert O'Dea, it was as if I had been zapped to another time. Like it was me, but it wasn't me."

Genna frowned. "I don't get it. Did this have something to do with your snippet?"

"It had everything to do with it," Amy answered. "I believe some bonds are so strong they can't be pulled a part. Not by time. Not by death. Love is one of those bonds. And I believe motherhood tops the list. A mother's love for her child is deep. Deep enough to defend to the death if need be.

"But you never really know until it gets tested," Amy continued. "That's the-- *they will try* part. They will try to break the bonds, but they can't because that kind of love is forever. We have that, the four of us. I believe we do."

The conversation lulled and Amy let her thoughts rest on the realization that she had learned something valuable about herself. No, she still didn't understand her dreams, or why they came to her. But the burden was lessening in some thin way, like Limerick lace curtains in a window. This must have been how Grandmother

Ollie had learned to live with her predictive dreams. How she learned to make peace with them. She would learn to do this, too. She would allow herself to do what she could. She would accept what she couldn't.

The crest of Gráinne and her seer clan might be part of her origin and roots. It could also be nothing more than Irish lore and pure flannel. But what she had learned was that it didn't matter, because the bond, whatever that was, would never be broken. Love and intuition were powerful things. And if she let them speak to her, they would.

"I believe travels changes a person," Rian said quietly. "If you listen. You leave home as one person and return home as another."

"Too deep for me," Genna said. "I'm the same person now that I was two weeks ago."

"True enough," Zelda said. "And that's why we got you this." She reached into her bag and then held up a tee shirt, beaming at Genna. "We bought this just for you."

Genna huffed and then smiled. Rugged ocean cliffs were pictured on the front. *Cliffs of Moher Coastal Walk* was stenciled around the top edge. *Doolin to Hags Head* was written on the bottom.

"Been there, got the tee shirt," Zelda said and laughed. "We won't tell if you don't."

"Hags Head," Genna said. "I guess cocktails are on me."

"Yeah, this bar tab's on you" Amy said and raised her pint. "May fair and faithful friends be yours, wherever you may roam."

**THE END**

# Acknowledgements

A trip to Ireland is something you never forget, and I am delighted to dedicate this book to my travel buddy and BFF, Doris. We spent many wet, windy days chasing sheep and the Running Man. I will treasure those memories always. What's next when we win the lottery?

Special thanks to retired archaeologist and author Risteárd Ua Cróinín of Dysert O'Dea, Co. Clare, for sharing his book, *"Ua Déaghaidh, The Story Of A Rebel Clan"(Ballinakella Press, Whitegate, County Clare, Ireland),* and for not taking offense about the Dick in this story, named long before we met by email. Rian couldn't have found her roots without you. Although I took wide literary license in the Tarbert Bridewell scenes in the story, they were inspired by Linda's generously shared experiences and emails. Thanks for the ideas.

A book doesn't publish without a team of enthusiastic talent and die-hard supporters. A humble thank you and big hugs to Susan, Michelle, Mary, Elise, Paula, Ger, and June for all the time and heart you give. Big love to cover designer, Bailey McGinn, for being the magic wand in the Jane Elzey brand. And thanks to all the VIP Members who keep encouraging me to pick up the pen and start on the next story. Which, by the way, is already in the works. *Ouija and Haints in the Silent City* is set in the Bluff Springs Cemetery, where the Arkansas 4 uncover evidence of a cold case murder from the early 1920s. Even back then, #TheHusbandAlwaysDies. Look for Book 5, *Ouija and Haints* in Spring 2025 (Scorpius Carta Press).

*Killer Croquet* is the third husband bumped off (in the literary sense) from the VIP Killer Club, where members have the privilege of naming a husband (boyfriend, boss, etc.) for an upcoming book in the series. If you are looking for a gift for a friend who has everything– including a bad ex– consider gifting them the Killer Club for her/his own VIP literary game of Clue. Ponder the possibilities. There's a waiting list... so get in the queue! For details visit CardboardCottageMystery.com/VIP-Club. Join the VIP Club at JaneElzey.com

## About the Author

Jane Elzey is a mischief-maker, story-teller, and bender of the facts. A retired career journalist, she now writes modern not-so-cozy mysteries without much regard for the truth. Born and raised on Florida's sandy beaches, Jane now lives in the Ozark Mountains of Arkansas, with her fur family and a neighborhood of deer, racoon, opossum, and an occasional but very fat groundhog. An insatiable world traveler, Jane turns her bucket list travels into backdrop settings for her books, sharing destinations with armchair readers on the hunt for whodunnit. Jane loves to play board games, is always up for a bottle of wine or a Scotch served neat, a trip down river in a kayak, friends, good food and a good laugh.

Jane Elzey writes about four mature women who play to win… while the husbands die trying. The husband always dies. *Killer Croquet on the Emerald Isle* is book four in the Cardboard Cottage Mystery series. To schedule an author signing, book club event, or to join Jane Elzey's VIP Club of Very Important Players, visit JaneElzey.com.